The Eye of the Virgin

7/24

Books by Frederick Ramsay

The Ike Schwartz Mysteries

Artscape
Secrets
Buffalo Mountain
Stranger Room
Choker
The Eye of the Virgin

Other Novels

Impulse
Judas
Predators

The Eye of
the Virgin

Frederick Ramsay

Poisoned Pen Press

Library of Congress Catalog Card Number: 2009924200
ISBN: 9781590587614   Large Print

Poisoned Pen Press
6962 E. First Ave. Ste. 103
Scottsdale, AZ 85251
www.poisonedpenpress.com
info@poisonedpenpress.com
Printed in the United States of America

Monty Montee

Monty Montee was the first voice I heard from The Poisoned Pen Press. His gentle encouragement and wise guidance ushered me into the world of mystery story writing, a world I might otherwise never have known.

We will miss you, Monty.

Acknowledgments

For some few, I suspect, writing is a job, a source of income, a necessary facet of career advancement, or perhaps just a means of quiet communication in an otherwise noisy world. For others, and I number myself among them, writing is a joy, a passion, a thing as necessary to life as breathing. Perhaps this overstates the case, but it captures the sense of it, I think. Therefore, I must thank all the people who make it possible for me to do this thing. That would include at least, Barbara Peters, editor, critic, savant of the mystery story genre; Robert Rosenwald, who runs The Poisoned Pen Press as if he were polishing diamonds and who allows all the authors in the stable to scribble away without a care in the world (well, almost without a care).

Thanks, too, to the gang behind the scenes at the press, Jessica, Nan, Marilyn, Geetha, Elizabeth, and in particular, Annette, who helped me sort out the snarl in which my characters through no fault of their own, found themselves. Also, a grateful nod in the direction of our cover artists who gild our lilies. Thanks also to Glenda Sibley, Nelson Bennett, and Connie Collins, my "comma police" who, at some risk to their eyesight and sanity, attempt to regularize my creative use of punctuation and grammar.

Finally, to Susan, who has put up with this enterprise, this distracter from the everyday, this mistress of mine, with never a jealous moment.

Chapter One

Nail polish remover.

The eye-watering reek of the acetone-based solvent assailed Louis Dakis the moment he opened his door. No matter how often you work with it, you never quite get used to the odor. It did not concern him, not at first, anyway. He'd been painting a medium-sized Christ Pantocrator and was working in acrylics instead of egg tempera. One needed uninterrupted time, even leisure, to paint with the latter, a luxury he no longer enjoyed. This afternoon, running late, and as usual, he'd dashed out the door for his class after he'd rinsed his brushes in distilled water and then soaked the older ones in the solvent to break up the accumulated pigment at their base. Commercial nail polish remover was cheaper than straight acetone, and easier for him to acquire out here in the sticks. He couldn't remember if he'd put away the rag he used to wipe them. Must have forgotten. Even so, the odor seemed pretty strong.

He leaned the icon, *Eleousa, The Virgin of Tenderness*, the topic of his lecture that day, which he'd been carrying under his arm, against the door jamb and stepped into the foyer. There was only the one small reading lamp alight in the room's corner next to a battered leather upholstered chair. Even so, its feeble light was sufficient to cause the glass shards littered across the carpet under his front window to glitter and attract his notice. Thin curtains fluttered in a brisk March evening breeze. Cold air pooled across the floor, and even though he'd just come in from the outside, he shivered.

Several competing thoughts vied for his attention. He nudged the door closed and shook his head, trying to arrange them in some coherent fashion, not necessarily in order of their importance. An open window should have meant lower intensity for the odor. Perhaps the wind had caused the polish remover bottle to tip over and spill its contents. But he was sure he'd capped it, hadn't he? A broken window pane…Had someone broken a pane and then opened the window, broken into the house, spilled the bottle? Windows did not break spontaneously, did they? He brushed the knuckle of his index finger across his mustache and dislodged a bit of something. The trouble with facial hair he thought, not for the first time, is that you never knew what bit of your most recent meal might still linger in it. A frown settled on his forehead.

A noise at the back of the cottage, toward the kitchen, brought a halt to this checklist and confirmed at least part of the last entry. Might became had—someone *had* come in and was still there.

"Who's that?"

He realized after he'd spoken that he'd made a mistake, perhaps a serious one. A reasonable man would have backed out and called the police. All the security courses he'd taken while working in the nation's capital had emphasized that point: do not confront criminals or, indeed, even a potential lawbreaker whatever the circumstance might be. He or she could be armed, could be desperate. As this admonition percolated up from the lower reaches of his conscious, he thought he heard the back door open, slam shut, and footsteps clomp across the back porch and then go silent in the grass of his back yard. The house was on the edge of Callend University's campus close to a copse of cedars and forsythia and well away from its nearest neighbor.

He stood frozen in place. His heart rate jumped as adrenaline coursed through his circulatory system. Caution said *call the police*. Curiosity said *go look*. Curiosity won.

By the time he reached the back of the house

and leaned over the sink to peer through the leaded glass of a kitchen window, there was nothing left for him to see. Perhaps a shadow had moved out near the cherry tree. He couldn't be sure. It might have been the wind, which had picked up in the last hour. He flipped on the porch light. The feeble light pushed back the darkness no more than twenty feet or so, but past the tree at least. If there had been someone out there, he was gone now. The wind whipped the tree's lower branches as if to taunt him. Whoever had entered his house had melted into the night. All he could make out beyond the dim pool of light from the porch were silhouettes of evergreens, black against a gray sky, and lighter gray splotches of forsythia blooms, bright yellow in daylight, and the long, very dense and dark hedge that bordered the northern edge of the yard. A movement over there. Was it possible that the shadow that caught the corner of his eye, near the back of that hedge might have been his intruder? He couldn't be sure. Anyway, it had melted away almost the instant he'd swung his gaze toward it. He must be seeing things. Whether real or not, he could not say. Perhaps if he stepped outside he could see better.

He reached for the door knob but stopped his hand in midair. Fingerprints, there might be finger-prints. This would not be the first time he'd called the police about a break-in, and in the process, he'd learned his lessons about crime scenes. And he did not want to confront anyone, armed or otherwise. Been there, done that, got the eight stitches in his scalp. He pulled out his cell phone and punched in 9-1-1 and then went to close the spilled bottle of nail polish remover which had rolled into the hallway, and to wipe up its contents and contemplate the mess it had made of the varnish on the hardwood floor.

The man sitting on the ugly plastic chair was unremarkable in appearance, youngish, maybe late thirties or early forties. Shaggy black hair and dressed in jeans, tattered white button-down shirt, and a bomber jacket, both of which seemed a size too large. He could have been Middle Eastern, or not, Mediterranean, certainly. He had been seated for several hours in the corner on the row of chairs toward the rear of the waiting area. No one could recall how long or even when he had come in.

URGENT-C, the urgent care facility on Picketsville's Main Street, did not offer the drama-filled weekends associated with big-city hospital emergency rooms; no *ER* here, no frenetic arrival of ambulances, drop-dead gorgeous nurses in scrubs and high heels, just the usual small town occasional semi-emergencies. But once in a while it did become crowded. A nearby automobile accident could create some excitement until the injured could be moved to Lexington and its hospital. On this particular Friday it had become unusually busy due, in part, to a sudden rash of intestinal influenza cases, which seemed to affect small children in particular.

"Under six, after six," Jerry Stempak, the center's director, said when he surveyed the bawling kids and looked at his watch.

Added to this mini-epidemic was the fact that in the past several years the town's senior medical practitioners, it seemed, had retired to condos at Hilton Head or Palm Beach to be replaced with for-profit clinics irreverently dubbed docs-in-a-box and staffed by young health-care professionals who preferred to keep strict office hours and not work outside them—either the hours or their clinics. As a consequence, the urgent care facility would begin to fill after five in the evening and would see patients off and on until midnight. This evening it had begun to fill around six-thirty with the sick children. Shortly after seven, a troop of Boy Scouts who had all shared a meal consisting of tuna surprise and egg salad, both prepared by their bachelor assistant Scoutmaster earlier in the day, arrived to augment the smaller children. All the scouts needed to be dosed with Compazine and fluids. They created a considerable distracting hubbub as vomiting children competed with wailing tykes for the staff's attention. Soon the waiting and examining rooms filled to overflowing with sick children, anxious parents, keening, unpleasant odors, and harried caregivers.

No one had noticed when or how the man had entered. The nursing staff and the physician's assistant on duty assumed he must either have been a parent of one of the scouts or flu victims, or have a minor complaint that the triage nurse had deemed non-urgent. By eleven-thirty the crowd had thinned sufficiently to allow one of the nurses to approach him.

"Sir, can I help you?"

He didn't respond. He sat slouched in the chair with his head lolled to one side, chin on his chest. She could not see his eyes. She only noticed that he sat awkwardly on the chair's electric blue plastic seat. She glanced back at the reception desk.

Laurie Kratz looked up, shrugged, and shook her head. "He didn't register. I thought he must be…" She shrugged again waved her hand over the desk, and returned to the paperwork stacked in untidy piles in front of her.

The nurse turned back to the man. "Sir? Are you all right? Sir?"

Assuming he'd fallen asleep, she shook his shoulder gently. His head lolled to the other side. He slid off the chair and crumpled onto the floor at her feet. Startled, she stepped back and stared at the form on the floor, which seemed to be stuck in a sitting position, albeit he now lay on his side. She knelt, found no trace of a pulse and felt the cold skin under her fingers.

"I need a cart over here." She flailed her arms at the entry clerk. "Get Elaine out here."

Elaine Franks, the physician's assistant on duty, bustled out and knelt beside the nurse. She needed only to feel the body to realize a cart with resuscitation equipment and defib kit would be useless. The man was very dead and had been for some time. Nevertheless, her training kicked in, and she opened his jacket in order to use her stethoscope. She yanked his shirt up, popping buttons and tearing the material. That's when she saw the entry wound under his armpit. She rocked back on her heels and shook her head.

"Cancel the cart. Call 9-1-1, stat."

Chapter Two

"What have we got?" Ike Schwartz, Sheriff of Picketsville, at least until the election in November, followed a gust of damp March wind into the sheriff's department and glanced at his watch. He pushed the door shut. Eight-thirty, not too late, all things being considered. He filled his coffee cup at the credenza behind the booking desk, added creamer and sweetener. He turned his gaze on his dispatcher, Essie Sutherlin, recently married to Billy and more recently with child, as the Bible would delicately put it.

"Looks like we caught us a B and E and a homicide, Ike. Not too shabby for a Friday night in March." Essie sat enthroned behind her desk, regally pregnant, and glowing as only first time expectant women can. "Must be the Ides of March, huh? Wasn't that when that old emperor, Jules somebody, bought it from his buddies?"

Ike grinned and nodded, and gestured toward

her obvious bump. "Not quite, the ides will be the fifteenth, middle of the month, the fifteenth day of March, May, July, or October; otherwise the thirteenth day of the other months, but only in the ancient Roman calendar, which was different than the one we use now, of course."

"I knew that." Essie said, eyes wide and ingenuous.

"Naturally. Picketsville High is known for its classics curriculum, Anyway, you're close enough and it was Julius Caesar—like the salad—who, as you say, bought it. How's junior behaving today?"

The progress of Essie's impending motherhood had displaced the usual office gossip. The jury was still out on whether that qualified as an improvement. A little bit of chat about massive hormonal shifts and morning sickness went a long way. But then, a preoccupation with deer hunting and NASCAR standings did, too, so he'd go along with prenatal physiology for a while and hope the work at hand would engender some new conversational opportunities. And for that reason, he welcomed the news of a homicide.

"He's growing, Ike. The doc says I might have me a bruiser. Ma, that's Billy's momma, says all her boys was big so she's guessing this one will top out at eight or nine pounds, too. Scary, ain't it?"

"I reckon it must be and by God would be

if I were the one carting around the future of the Sutherlin clan. But, as it happens, it is not an area about which I have much in the way of working knowledge. Who took the calls?"

"Which one?"

"Either. Start with the homicide."

"Frank caught the homicide and Billy the breaking and entering. Their write-ups are on your desk. Today is a shift change so they will both be back in an hour or so."

Ike headed to his office and the reports. He had difficulty making out Billy Sutherlin's scrawl and set that report aside against the time he'd get the details in person. Frank Sutherlin, Billy's older brother, had a neater, almost feminine, hand, if there was such a thing. In this era of correct, that is to say, mind-numbing conventional thinking, he wasn't sure. He read the report and scratched his head. This one would be a poser, no doubt about it. He fetched another cup of coffee, put his feet up on his desk, and stared unseeing through the glass windows that separated his office from the rest of the area.

A body deposited in the urgent care center. Why would anybody go to all that trouble? Why not dump him in the woods like everybody else? Something screwy here.

◇◇◇

Frank and Billy Sutherlin did not, as a rule, pull the same shifts. Ike initiated that policy after his first year as sheriff and after a viewing of *Saving Private Ryan*. It was probably an overreaction and didn't work in practicality, but he liked the concept. Major crime was not a big concern for Picketsville, but the chance that there might be a situation that could go south in a big way always hovered in the back of his mind. There's been one near miss the previous summer. He did not want to face Dorothy Sutherlin and have to tell her another one of her sons was dead, much less two. She'd lost one of the twins already in Iraq and except for her youngest, all were in professions that put them in harm's way. But this weekend, Amos Pettigrew, who preferred night work, called in sick, and Billy, eager to pile up compensatory time against the day his child would be born, volunteered to take the shift. Now, both brothers sat across from Ike blowing on their coffee and looking bleary-eyed. Since the time they had entered the office, the ambient aroma had shifted from that of burnt coffee to something closer to that of wet leaves. A modest improvement he thought.

"So, Frank, we'll start with you. I read your report. I have the details. Just give me the sense of it."

Frank Sutherlin screwed up his face in concentration. "Hard to figure, Ike. We'll have to wait for the ME's report, but the guy on the scene last night…By the way we were lucky to find someone as quick as we did to come out from the ME's office, or one of us would have had to camp out all night with the stiff—sorry, the victim. Anyway, the guy from the ME's office said our shooting victim looked like he'd been shot with a small caliber weapon under the arm. I wrote that up but either it was a light load or it hit bone because we couldn't find an exit wound. He guessed the bullet might have severed that big blood vessel in the chest."

"There are two, if I remember my freshman biology right. One is the vena cava, or some such, and the other is the aorta."

"Yeah, that last one I think he said, and then the guy bled out. Best guess, that would be the cause of death, doc says. It looked like whoever he was had been shot someplace else and then the person who shot him changed his shirt and put an oversized jacket on him before he was dumped in the clinic."

"Nobody saw him brought in?"

"Apparently not. We quizzed all the staff and everyone we could locate, but nobody could remember seeing him come in or even noticed him after he got there. The staff was run ragged by a bunch of sick scouts and a mini-flu epidemic. Most of the people I talked to assumed he was a parent of one of the patients. But, like I said, there's a bunch of people we couldn't question last night."

"Will you have any trouble finding out who all was there?"

"No. We have the names from the admission forms. Addresses too. We should be able to interview them all pretty quick."

"It brings up the question, though, doesn't it?"

"How so?"

"Why would anyone go to all that trouble? Why not leave him in an alley or a parking lot?"

"It's a poser for sure."

Billy sipped his coffee and made a face. "Maybe whoever did it hoped that the hospital could do something, like, after the fact. You know, an accident, shooter feels guilty and brings him in but is afraid to stick around. Sort of like a denial thing."

"It's a stretch but, okay, maybe. We'll have to wait for the ME's final report. Either way we have a homicide. You wrote there was no identification on the vic. Was there anything to tell us who he was or why he was here? I gather he's not local."

"Nothing, Ike, no wallet, no cards, no receipts, nothing. Nobody knew him, you know. Out-of-town person, it seems."

"We have any finger prints?"

"They should be coming over this afternoon.

I'll have Samantha run them through her fancy computer program thing—AFIS."

Frank had not yet been able to call Samantha Ryder by her nickname, Sam, although everyone else did and she'd asked him to more than once. Her main contribution to the Sheriff's office was her computer skills. She made the television versions seen on *CSI* in its many permutations seem inept. Most of that stemmed from her ability to hack into nearly any program she wished to. Ike made a point of not asking how she did it or whether she was siphoning off information he'd otherwise have to pay for with a license fee. Picketsville did not have a large budget devoted to technology. Not in the sheriff's office, not anywhere. Depending on the availability of federal subsidies, small towns were either annoying in their sophistication or they were in the electronic Stone Age, computer-wise. Except for Sam and her machinery tucked away in the back corner, Picketsville was Early Pleistocene.

"Let's hope. I am, for one, not that eager to have a John Doe on my hands. Okay. We'll have to wait. Okay Billy, your turn.

Chapter Three

"Straight up and down breaking and entering, Ike. This guy…" Billy consulted his notes. "Louis Dakis, came back from doing an evening class up at the college—"

"University now."

"Tell me the difference. One day it's Callend College for women. A week later it's Callend University. What happened in a week?"

"Not weeks, months. Callend was, for a hundred years or so a college. It started as a ladies' finishing school, very popular back in the day in this part of the world. Then, it evolved into a liberal arts college, but still only for women, and then last summer it merged with Carter Union, a business college, added a business school offering advanced degrees, and became coed. Because it has a school of liberal arts, a school of business, and now a separate school of fine arts, it qualifies as a university, which is usually defined as a collection of schools or colleges gathered in one place. Not always, however. Being called a university doesn't mean what it used to."

"Yeah, whatever, college, university, school for rich kids is what that place is. Anyway, Dakis says he comes back to his house and finds somebody busted a window and climbed in and ransacked a bunch of holy pictures he had stacked up in the dining room."

"Holy pictures? What kind of holy pictures are we talking about here?"

"Like in them foreign churches. You know, lots of pictures of Jesus with his fingers crossed, Mary and the baby Jesus all pretty like only she looks like she's wearing a football helmet, and other people, saints, I guess the kind of pictures that they hang up in them churches. Not like normal ones like you see in somebody's front room, *Jesus Knocks at the Door,* and like that, but stiff and a little, you know, hard-looking. Like they know what you're thinking. Can't think why anybody would want a picture like that."

"Icons?"

"What? Yeah, now that you mention it, that's what he called them. But they didn't look nothing like them little things on the computer screen so I didn't pay much attention. But yeah, that's what he said they were."

"Any follow-up?"

"Crime scene techs came and dusted. Dakis took a quick inventory and said nothing was missing. Looked like somebody had knocked over a big bottle of nail polish remover. I asked him what he used it for because I didn't see no sign of a woman in the place. He said he cleaned his brushes with it sometimes. Me, I'd a thought he'd be better off with turp or gasoline but he said no, the kind of paint he used to paint up them pictures, them icons, only dissolved in acetone, which, he said, is found in nail polish remover. He used water first and the remover only if the paint had dried before he could wash them. New to me."

"You said he taught at the university?"

"That's what he said. I didn't recognize him, so I guess he wasn't one of the regulars up there at the college."

"I'll call the school and find out. He might be adjunct. Since the economy's gone south, they, like many places, are making do with part-time people where they don't have to fund the fringe package, pay tenured professor salaries, and so on. He's one of them, I'm guessing. Any luck on the prints?"

"Tech said the guy who broke in must have been wearing gloves. All he could find were Dakis' prints and smudges on the door knob and some of the pictures. Dakis had a duck fit when he saw the tech dusting them. He said they were, like, valuable and they should be careful not to disturb the surface. I tell you what, Ike, some of them pictures was so old and chipped, and dirty, you would never have known if they messed with the surface or not. Who'd want to buy an old beat-up picture like that, anyway? I mean, they weren't even painted on cloth like a real picture. I swear it looked like somebody went out to the barn and got him couple of old boards and slap-dashed a picture of a saint or something on it, then decided it weren't much to look at after all and tossed it on the compost pile."

Ike resisted the temptation to lecture Billy on iconography in general and the collectability of ancient icons in particular. "No accounting for taste, Billy."

"You can say that again. Ma was telling me about one of them college professors that had a collection of dinner plates. Some all chipped and cracked. She said she, that's the professor, a lady, kept them in a locked china cabinet. And Mrs. Pettigrew, that's Amos' granny, has a passel of cat statues that Amos says is insured for a bunch of money. Me, I'd take the money."

"Right. Okay, you two take it easy today and try to stay awake. I don't expect much will happen around here until later tonight and the Saturday night partying begins up at Callend and/or down at Eddie Knox's Roadhouse, but still…Put a watch on Dakis' house. Whoever was in there didn't take anything, so maybe he was spooked before he found what he was looking for and left. If so, he might try again."

"Say, Ike, maybe we could get us some adjunct deputies. You know, cheap help. Ain't you got a slot open?"

"No, but I'd be happy to turn yours into one if you think it's that good an idea."

"Reckon I'll get on my rounds. Oh, wait, there is one thing I forgot to mention."

Ike waited as Billy scratched his head and pursed his lips. "It's probably nothing but, you know the place smelled like nail polish remover and like I said, that has acetone in it, right?"

"If I remember my practical chemistry correctly, it does. And that is important how?"

"I noticed this guy had a couple of bottles of peroxide in the bathroom too. I seem to recall that bomb makers used them two ingredients with some kind of acid to make explosives. That's all."

"I'll check it out. I don't think that is where this is going, however…but you never know. You're sure about the peroxide?"

"Billy rolled his eyes toward Essie and her Dolly Parton locks. "Oh yeah, I know all about that stuff."

Ike dismissed them with a grin. What had Dolly Parton said? "You have to spend some real money to look this cheap." When they'd cleared the office he lifted the phone from its cradle and dialed the university. He raised the president's office. Agnes Ewalt, Ruth Harris' secretary, answered.

Agnes Ewalt sat at her desk outside Ruth Harris' office like Horatio at the bridge, screening her boss' visitors and phone calls with a diligence bordering on compulsion. She was a stereotypical spinster who had spent the previous year trying to keep Ruth, as president of the then college, now university, and Ike apart. She seemed to feel it her duty to maintain what she assumed to be a respectable and necessary distance between town and gown. And the town's sheriff, in her estimation, was the quintessential townie who needed to be kept at bay. She had failed in that, but her efforts had exacted a cost in the general area of aggravation. Since the fall, however, she had moved not quite one hundred and eighty degrees in her estimation of Ike, and now provided aid and comfort to her boss and the man Agnes insisted on calling her *boyfriend* against the as yet still hostile faculty.

"Sheriff, she has a visitor. I'm afraid I can't disturb her short of an emergency. She did leave a message for you though."

"That's okay, Agnes. I can ask you the question I had for her. But what was the message?"

"Tonight, dash, dash, A-frame, question mark."

"Got it. Tell her yes, and leave me a voice message telling me what she wants for dinner. Okay? Now, what can you tell me about a man named Louis Dakis?"

"He's an adjunct faculty member. I know that. I think he joined this quarter, sort of at the last minute. The chairman of the Art Department had an FTE line in his budget open up and he knew his friend Mr. Dakis needed a place temporarily, so he brought him down."

"FTE means full time equivalent, I assume. Down from where, exactly?"

"FTE—correct. Down from Washington, D.C., I think. He is something of an expert in his field, whatever it is, and the department thinks they have pulled off a coup. I don't know. But anyway, that's the story."

"He's an iconographer. Is that right?"

"You know, Sheriff, that sounds about right. Hold on a sec." The line went silent and Ike thought he could hear paper rustling. "Here it is, in the supplemental catalogue. 'Iconography 101'— you were right—'a course which will explore the history of the icon, or holy images, as practiced in the East and the recent resurgence of interest in them in the West.' There's an optional lab offered, too. Let's see, students will be taught the basics of icon making and will paint one for themselves. There's a note attached in Dr. Harris' handwriting that says the optional lab filled in two hours after the course was announced. My, my, imagine that."

"Thank you, Agnes. You wouldn't happen to have Dakis' phone number and schedule handy, too, would you?"

"Phone number, yes. Schedule, no. But I'll look it up and have Dr. Harris give it to you this evening."

"Perfect. Thank you." Ike took down the phone number and hung up. Question: why would someone break into an iconographer's house, ransack the inventory, and leave empty-handed? Whoever it was had something else in mind other than to steal icons, but what? Perhaps Dakis came home too soon and he or she had to duck out before loading up. Maybe. Or the person was searching for a particular image and didn't find it. He would need to talk to Dakis.

Chapter Four

Ruth Harris and Ike Schwartz were, as they would say in grocery store check-out line magazines, an item. When they first met, it had not been their intent to become gossip fodder, and either would have said the likelihood of that happening approached zero, indeed, might even move into negative numbers. But circumstance and the magic that comes when two people have a good deal more in common than either will admit held them together, and their relationship, however spiky, had taken an erratic but always positive course over the previous fifteen months. They were, however, approaching a major decision point in their relationship: to move on to the next logical step, which meant contemplating marriage, or backing down to remain permanently uncommitted. Each had vacillated on that point at one time or another.

Unfortunately, their respective positions rarely coincided. If, and when they did, there might be some significant forward progress. But that had not happened yet. It was not as if they were kids, nor were there any compelling reasons to advance. But Ike believed relationships either grew or they died. Ruth thought he was an incurable romantic, and besides, she had a university to run.

Ruth stepped onto the deck of Ike's A-frame and stood, arms folded taking in the view down the mountainside toward the valley a thousand feet beneath her. "You never get used to this, do you? It's spectacular no matter what time of day or what the season."

"I suppose you might after a while. Eventually everything pales. Familiarity, they say, breeds contempt." Ike stretched his legs out and waved his arm toward the trees. "Ready for a drink?"

"Always. So, do you think I will eventually pale, become a familiar object of contempt?"

"Not likely. You are uniquely unique."

"That's a terrible redundancy. And not true. Maybe I should go blonde, get a makeover?"

"No need. I will never tire of you, I don't think, but now that you mention it, blonde…that would be something else. Do you remember the scene in *I, the Jury,* something about whether the bleach stung? I can't remember exactly, but it's a thought."

"I have no idea what you're talking about. We have tonight and Sunday and then it's back to the grind, so let's move along. Where's my drink?"

"Oh, I remember now. The girl says to Mike Hammer when he asked if the peroxide stung, 'no, but the ammonia did.' I think that's right. My memory isn't what it used to be."

"I see. Just as well, if you're going to clutter it up with Mickey Spillane. So, you win the trivia prize today. My drink?"

Ike dropped ice cubes into two glasses, mixed a gin and tonic for himself, poured her a small scotch and water, and handed it over. She sat, her gaze still fixed on the panorama that spread out before her, a view that captured the mountainside and, far in the distance, the traffic on Route 11.

"In the old days, before hair color came in two gazillion shades, ammonia was used to help the peroxide along. I think. It smells to high heaven. I don't know if it would sting though," she said.

"You just reclaimed the prize. It would sting if you realized the reference Mickey Spillane had in mind."

"I don't think I want to and don't care anyway. You never told me about this house. I always assumed it belonged to your family, this and the farm. But the last time I talked to your dad he said it didn't. He said it was your escape hatch, or something."

"It was and is. After what happened to Eloise and I left my previous employer—"

"You mean after you wife was killed and you stormed out of the CIA."

"That's what I said."

"Not quite, but go on."

"Okay, after that I wanted to be left alone. A friend of mine, a guy I went to high school with, started building this but he had run out of money. I relieved him of his debt, you could say. I finished it and thought I would live up here and write a book. You know, when you're angry about something or somebody, or in my case, an institution, you think you'll write a big exposé and get even. Something like *Killing Hope*."

"But you didn't."

"No, I bought a computer, printer, and a ream of paper, but in the end I let it go. I don't have it in me to stay angry very long nor do I have much in the way of writerly talent. Then there is the problem of keeping faith with the facts on the one hand and not letting my anger color what I wrote. And about that time my mother was diagnosed with cancer, so I moved back to the farm and hung around town a bit. The sheriff's office, I discovered, was an open sore on the community, and since my father had been after me to follow him into politics, I ran for sheriff. It wasn't the career he had in mind for me, but there you are."

"And you had to move into town?"

"Not so much a 'have to,' but, as you can appreciate, the hours are bad and I didn't want to cause a lot of ruckus coming and going so, yeah, I took that little apartment near the college."

"So, how is your dad?"

"When my mother died, he spiraled down into a real funk. Understandable, of course, but it had me worried. Now he seems pretty chipper. He's been running over to Richmond a lot lately. I guess he's been catching up with his old political pals. You know, sitting around and swapping lies about the good old days, before the Party became politically correct."

"You're not going start again, are you? I don't want to hear your political correctness rant today."

"Nope, beyond pointing out to you, who, after all, represents that line of country as well as anyone I know, that political correctness is neither."

"Excuse me?"

"It is neither political nor correct, just posturing."

"You won't get me tonight, Schwartz. I did not come out here to have you ruin the view with your prehistoric maunderings."

"Maunderings? Wow, That's impressive. I'm impressed."

"Shut up. What's for dinner?"

"I have imported some very nice tuna salad with pistachios in it, no less, Fresh tomatoes, or nearly so, as fresh as the super market can supply anyway, and a choice of either a baked potato or canned whatever is in the larder."

"Potato, please, a small one. Since I began hanging around with you I have gained one whole dress size. You'd better watch it or this particular view will change a whole lot more than blond."

"*Zaftig*, Rubenesque—"

"Enough. What's going on in the sheriff's office?"

"A breaking and entering, but you know that—your faculty guy, and an odd murder. At least I think it's a murder."

"How odd?"

Ike filled her in on the corpse in the clinic. "It's sort of weird, if you follow."

"That's my boy, solver of weirdnesses."

"Right. So, how're your folks?"

"I told you my mother left my dad. She's gone off a little, I think."

"Off?"

"You know she was my father's second wife. The first one I never met. My father would only say that she was 'difficult.' I'm not sure I know what that meant. Anyway, he married one of his students. She is much younger than he."

"I remember her vaguely. Always in the background when we would visit the dean's house. It was a big deal then."

"For you, maybe, but not for me and certainly not for her. I guess she missed not having a youth of her own, and the age difference got to her. Anyway, my father contracted Alzheimer's. Is that right? Do you contract, or does it creep up on you?" Ruth raised one eyebrow and lowered the other. Ike called it her Popeye look. "She spent the next six years taking care of him, until she couldn't anymore. He's in a constant care facility and doesn't know who she is."

"It happens, I guess."

"It's worse. My father, demented and all, met a woman who looks remarkably like his first wife, and he thinks they are married. He yells at my mother to go away when she visits. So she stopped going. She decamped and has kept herself occupied since then with personal improvements."

"She's gone back to school?"

"No. That would be fine. She's been busy reinventing herself, recreating her image. Physically."

"I don't follow."

"She exploded."

"Exploded? Sorry, you lost me."

"She's changed. You know what popcorn looks like before you pop it? It's all those little seedy things and not very interesting to look at. Then you heat them up and they explode, pop, pop, pop… they're different. She was a corn kernel and then she popped."

"Popped?"

"Kablooie. I guess she figured since my father didn't recognize her as she was, there was no reason to for her to stay that way. She's had plastic surgery, nip, tuck, and, um…enhancements."

"Enhancements? You mean—"

"Exactly. She was never very big up top. Now she's, good Lord, buxom. What do you say to a woman who's had a boob job? And especially if she's your mother?"

"I would remain silent."

"Coward."

"As the saw has it, discretion is the better part of valor. Let's eat. We can discuss physical attributes later—not your mother's—yours."

"Dream on."

"Yes, that would be part of it."

"She wants to come and live with me."

"Is that good news or bad?"

"I don't know. I mean, with her enhancements and new persona, what will she do in a small college town?"

"Become a cougar and chase undergraduate students."

"Oh, please. Don't even think it. It's bad enough with you mooning around the campus."

"I never moon, at least not in the sense you

mean…or in any other sense either, come to think of it."

"I could introduce her to your dad."

"That would be exciting. That could make you my sister. The implications of that are scatological not to mention incestuous."

"You have become a very dirty old man."

"Thank you. I thought you'd never notice. Besides, if your mother felt left out with your father because of the difference in their ages, how would it work with mine who is, at least, five years older than yours?"

"That's the happy thought for the day. Let's eat."

The sun had set when they returned to the deck with their coffee. Ruth slid into Ike's lap and sighed.

"Don't start any smart-ass talk, okay? The view is too beautiful and I'm relaxed. Let's sit, be quiet, and admire the view, or what's left of it."

"Done."

"So how was your day, week, whatever?"

"We are not sitting quietly when you ask me that."

"As a taxpayer, I'm interested in the local sheriff and how he combats crime in my neighborhood."

"Okay. You know about Dakis and the

break-in. We also had the weird homicide at the urgent care clinic that's a puzzle."

"Someone was killed at the clinic?"

"Left for dead, more accurately. Why would anyone want to shoot somebody and then carry him to the clinic, prop him up in a chair, and leave?"

"Maybe they cared for him in a way. You know, he was family or something. They couldn't just dump him. They wanted him found intact, I suppose."

"I guess. It's still a puzzle."

Chapter Five

Lorraine tried Franco's number a third time. Still no answer. Now she began to worry. She'd expected him back from his trip the night before, but he didn't show and he hadn't called either. She could dismiss the fact he hadn't picked up earlier, still enroute, bad connections, too few bars. And so, now, maybe he'd gone out to get his morning coffee or he was in the shower. By nine-thirty she had exhausted her list of excuses. She called the store. Not there either. Why had he left town at all? He'd been vague about the trip and as much as she did not want to think it of him, she had an uneasy feeling that he might have lied to her. Business in New York, he'd said, meetings with buyers for certain parts of the collection. She'd asked who the buyers were, which pieces, and that's when he became vague. He didn't know that many buyers in the first place and she doubted he knew any in New York. That didn't mean there were none, of course. New York housed millions of people and some of them were wealthy enough to indulge in pricy art collections. But where could he be?

He said he'd take Amtrak's Vermonter up and probably come back on it Sunday. This was Monday. Where was he? There had been only one phone call and then nothing except those damned text messages since. When had he started texting? Lorraine could manage one in a pinch but she couldn't see the point. A telephone was designed so that people could speak to one another. Then— texting, and another important human interaction shifted from a communal activity to solipsism. Why don't people talk any more?

She tried his cell phone once more.

"Hello?"

A voice. She didn't recognize it. A woman's voice—a very young woman's voice.

"Franco?"

She heard giggling and someone, a different voice, said. "Hang up, stupid. They can, like, trace those things."

"No Franco here."

"Who…?"

"Bye," the first voice said and the line went dead.

"Hello, hello?" She held the phone in her outstretched hand and stared at it as if to force it to connect properly.

"If you want to make a call, please hang up…" the disembodied voice of the phone company chanted. She did.

Should she call the police? What would she say? "My fiancé said he went to New York last Monday. He has not returned, and somebody, I don't know who, answered his cell phone." That would get her nowhere. If it had not been for the voice answering the phone, she'd have simply worried, then become angry, and let Franco have it when he finally turned up. But who answered the phone? She dialed again and got Franco's voice mail. She left a message. Why, she didn't know, but she did. She hung up and picked up her keys and purse.

Mondays she usually opened the shop late. Weekends were her busy times and Mondays, in the collectables business, as in the restaurant business, were slow. With reduced inventory and a bad economy, she had fewer customers, but she needed sales. Mrs. Strickland had called and wanted to meet early. So, she would open early.

The fact that Louis had taken the good pieces when he left galled her. The market for icons was iffy at best. People either wanted reproductions or cheap prints which they could buy online, or they wanted fine examples which she could supply. People would occasionally commission Louis to create one especially for them, but not many and not lately. The expensive icons, their bread and butter, she and her husband—ex-husband, now—imported from Europe, Russia chiefly, but also from Israel and Egypt. Louis had the eye for the better pieces. He was, after all, the iconographer and knew the field. Her strength had always been sales and promotion. But Louis was gone. Teaching...was that right? Doing something down in Virginia somewhere and he'd taken the good pieces with him. Franco was supposed to help her get at least some of them back this week, but he wasn't answering his phone. Where was he?

It took her twenty minutes to get to Eastern Vision, the store she and her husband—ex-husband—started five years before. They'd built up a very nice business and things looked good until Italy. Franco Sacci had swept her off her feet. Trite but true, and like the heroine of a bad romance novel, she returned to the states, declared her intention to divorce Louis, and within a week Franco was installed in her home and bed and Louis was dealing with attorneys and...well, he'd be all right eventually. He had talent and contacts. Life's a bitch, get over it, Louis.

Father Franklin from the National Cathedral and Mrs. Lenora Strickland, Lorraine's appointment and a presumptive buyer of an expensive Archangel Michael, were waiting for her as she paid off her cab and stepped onto the curb. Mrs. Strickland pointedly looked at her watch.

"I'm so sorry to have kept you waiting. There's been a…" A what? A crisis? No. "A mix-up with a shipment," she lied and fumbled at the lock. Once inside she started toward the back and the light switches, but froze in her tracks as she surveyed the chaos in the shop. All of the icons, at least it seemed like all of them, lay scattered across the floor, on counters, in untidy piles, and in complete disarray.

"Holy cow," Mrs. Strickland muttered and backed out the door.

"I should say so," Father Franklin said and jerked his cell phone from his overcoat. "I'll call the police." He lifted his phone and flipped it open, stating the obvious. "It appears you've had a break in." He punched in the numbers and spoke to the 9-1-1 operator.

"But this is impossible. I have an alarm system. It would have gone off. It was a silent alarm. The police should have been here already. I don't understand."

She picked her way to the back of the store, turned on the lights and inspected the alarm. It read DISARMED.

"I'm sure I set it Sunday afternoon when I locked up. I always do that last thing before I leave." Had she forgotten?

Mrs. Strickland took one more look at the mess and waved goodbye. She disappeared around the corner.

"Shall I fetch her back?" Father Franklin asked.

"No, yes, I don't know. What do you think?"

"You have her address. If the police want a statement from her, you can give it to them. I think she's a little publicity shy lately, since…she's been struggling, if I read the gossip in *The Post* aright. Can I help you, Lorraine? It appears you have some cleaning up to do."

"No, I think we should leave it as is until the police do their thing." Break-ins and robberies were part of the urban landscape nowadays. She'd been down this road before.

Chapter Six

Ike pulled his unmarked cruiser up to the front steps of Callend University's main building. Ruth checked her watch and muttered something that sounded like "damn," but Ike couldn't be sure. Ruth rarely swore.

"Damn, I'm late. Look what you've done, Schwartz."

Apparently this was not a no-swear day. "Tell Agnes you overslept."

"What we were doing cannot under any stretch of the imagination, be described as sleeping."

"Then you can tell her we were having hot steamy sex and lost track of the time. The world stood still, so to speak."

"In the first place neither the world nor even the small part of the Shenandoah Valley you occupy stood still or even hesitated, if you must know, and Agnes doesn't need to be told. She'll have figured it out on her own."

The Eye of the Virgin 41

"It didn't move? I'm hurt."

"Men! Okay, I have to get out of here. Call me later. I'll run through the files and check out Louis Dakis for you. But, I think he's okay." She squinted at Ike. "What? You're stewing about the earth's stability?"

"When are you going to move that ring from your right ring finger to your left?"

In the fall, Ike had been caught up in an auction and purchased a large diamond ring. He'd presented it to Ruth. She took it, but apparently was not quite ready to accept the symbolism inherent in it.

Ruth swiveled her head to gaze out the passenger side window and bit her lip. "I don't know, Ike. It's…It's a big step and I need space to work through it. We are different people and live in different worlds…I…It's a beautiful ring and you shouldn't have…I don't know."

"I'll call you this afternoon." Ike reached across her lap and opened the door. She kissed him quickly and slipped out. "Mayday."

"What? Is that a call for help? You need the Coast Guard?"

"Yes and no, I guess. What I meant was the first of May. We will reprise this discussion then."

"Mayday? A month and a half? Okay, it's a deal…maybe."

"No maybe."

Ike put the car in gear and drove off. He would be late as well. But, like Ruth, he was the boss and could set his own hours.

The overly heavy breakfast Ike had prepared for the two of them that morning—the immediate cause of their lateness, in fact—meant he would miss his morning ritual at the Crossroads Diner. No significant nutritional loss there but he did rely on the small-town telegraph—gossip—to keep him abreast of the local news. He'd have to rely on Essie this morning instead. She'd been good for that in the past but now, as the bearer of future Sutherlins, her chat tended to revolve more around local population statistics than hard news. She could tell you which of Picketsville's matrons were expecting, the likely birth weight, sex, due date, and any potential complications expected. It was not the heady stuff he sought. He'd make a point to have breakfast at the Crossroads tomorrow.

He pushed into the office and realized immediately that the coffee had burned. That meant it must be close to, or after, ten. Frank Sutherlin waved him over.

"You have something, Frank?"

"I might and I might not. Samantha ran the prints of the dead guy at the clinic and got a hit."

"She ID'd the vic?"

"Not exactly. She got blocked and a notice to check with Homeland Security. Apparently he was on their watch list."

"Oh, crap. I don't want another international hoo-hah. What did the HS people say?"

"They want you to contact them personally. I guess us peons aren't important enough for them to share information with us."

"Consider yourself lucky. Interfacing with the egos at the national level can lead to temporomandibular joint problems, chronic headaches, and unusually large dental bills. You have a number for me?"

"Temporoman…that's like jaw busting, right?" Frank slid a sheet of paper across his desk. It had a number and a name. "They want you to ask for this guy. I guess it's a guy. They said Francis. But I guess it could have been Frances, like with an E."

"Got it." Ike pointed at Essie Sutherlin. "When she's done charting the hormone levels around town, ask Earth Mother over there to brew us up a fresh pot of coffee."

Ike retreated to his office, the glass enclosed room that gave him no privacy whatsoever, and picked up the phone. The call went through and a voice, a woman's voice, answered. Frances?

"This is Sheriff Schwartz in Picketsville,

Virginia. I was told I needed to talk to you people about a set of prints we lifted from a murder victim."

"You're kidding, right? Picketsville? No way. Who is this?"

"You heard it right the first time, ma'am. Can you help me or not?"

Ike heard the woman speak to someone else, apparently also in the room. She had not completely covered the mouthpiece, it seemed. "Do you believe this? Some cracker is on the line and says he's from Picketsville, Virginia. What is this…a rerun of 'Green Acres?' What? Who? Oh." There was a pause and a man's voice came on the line.

"Sorry about that, Sheriff. She's new to the agency."

"It's not my place to say, but if I were you, she'd also be the newest recipient of a boot to the rear. But it's your game."

"Yes, it is. Good help is hard to find and booting a federal employee, figuratively or otherwise, is next to impossible. Okay, so you found a set of prints that we need to chat about."

"This Francis I'm speaking to?"

"Yes. Francis Drake. Don't even say it."

"Wasn't planning to. No, we didn't find a set of prints. We found a set of fingers. The prints were lifted from them, a man who had the bad luck to turn up dead in an emergency clinic. What can you tell me about him?"

"Sorry, not on the phone. We have assigned this case to the FBI. They will contact you personally and fill you in. I can only tell you what I told your people, the man was on the watch list."

"Oh, goody, the FBI. That's all I need to make my week complete."

"Yes. Okay, an agent will contact you shortly. That's all I am prepared to say at this point in time."

Ike hung up. Point in time? What in hell was a *point in time*? When did time get points? A moment in time he could understand, but a point? Governmental double speak. And soon, an FBI agent on his turf.

"Essie, where in the Billy Blue blazes is that fresh coffee?" Ike's breakfast had started talking to him.

Chapter Seven

Louis Dakis knew he had a soft berth. He only taught three one hour classes—Monday, Wednesday, and Friday mornings at ten forty-five, and two three-hour labs in the evenings on Wednesdays and Fridays. The labs consisted of instructing students in the craft of iconography, and each would, if they could harness their predilection for creativity, produce a passable icon. So far, only one student had grasped the central tenet of iconography: it should not be thought of as an outlet to make a statement, create a new format, or experiment with spiritual symbolism, but rather to execute a faithful copy of an older example of the same subject. By placing a stopper on the students' need to splash paint, he had already driven two students from the class.

At any rate, the university considered his schedule as full time and he drew a salary commensurate with that estimate. He didn't make as much as he might have if he were an appointed faculty member with tenure and seniority rather than a hire, but it was enough. When combined with the low rent he paid for his faculty housing, he was pretty well set. Unfortunately, it would not last. He only had a contract for a single quarter. What he would do in June when it ended was another matter. He had been wracking his brain for a proposal to put in front of the Art Department's chairman. He doubted he could sell him another round of Iconography 101—Iconography 102? It was the sort of course a college might offer only once every four years. Perhaps he could bone up on egg tempera painting. Not a popular medium since Andrew Wyeth passed, but trends come and go and any art department worth its salt would be interested in providing the broadest technical base to its students. He hoped.

His phone rang. He glanced at his watch. Who would be calling him at four-thirty in the afternoon? He glanced at the caller ID, gritted his teeth, and picked up.

"Louis, what were you thinking? How dare you."

"Lorraine? Is that you? Nice of you to call. How dare I what?"

"You know very well, what. Breaking into the shop Sunday night, that's what? Like, you don't have enough of my stock, you're back to collect more?"

"Our stock, Sweetie, at least until the papers are signed. I have no idea what you're going on about. You say someone broke into the shop?"

"Don't play stupid with me, buster. The place was tossed. I almost lost a sale to Mrs. Strickland. Hell, I bet I did lose it, so thanks a lot. What were you up to anyway?"

"Whoa. When did this happen?"

"I told you, Sunday…or Saturday night or maybe Monday early…the police can't be sure."

"Police. You called the police? And you, what? Told them that I might have been the one to… Lorraine, you didn't."

"Who else could it have been? You came in once already and grabbed off all the good stuff, so why not you? I mean who else?"

"The store is in metro D.C. Robberies are two a penny there. Anyone could have. However, you may recall when I took the stock, I still worked there, and I did it in broad daylight. I hope you also told them that you changed the locks and the security system password right after that and only you and…who? Who else has the new keys and password? Not me. You remember telling me that you'd done it? Your exact words were—"

"I remember what I said. Okay, you don't have a key."

"Or the new password. So, you will concede

it probably wasn't me." Louis waited. "Lorraine?"

"It wasn't you, I guess."

"You guess? You know. And who, pray tell, *did* you entrust the keys and password to? Not the Italian Stallion?"

"Franco has a key."

"And?"

"Okay, he has a key and the password and he could get in. But there would be no reason for him to break in. All he had to do was come by and look at anything he wanted."

"Did you ask him about it?"

"No, not yet. Why would I? Besides I can't seem to get in touch with him. He's missing. I mean…rats, he went to New York last Friday and he hasn't come back. He won't answer his phone and…I don't know."

"So Franco Sacci is missing and the store was burglarized. Coincidence? Or was it? Burglarized, I mean."

"I don't know if it counts as a burglary. Nothing is missing, I don't think."

"Was it a break-in? Busted locks, windows, whatever?"

"No."

"Not a burglary then. That's interesting. You had a break-in last Saturday, Sunday, Monday, and nothing's missing. I had one Friday night."

"You what? Someone broke into your…house, apartment, where do you live, Louis?"

"Little house on the edge of Callend University's campus. I have a short term teaching gig. It's very nice. It's in Picketsville, Virginia. Very academic and all that."

"Lucky you. Did your thief take anything?"

"No, I came back early from my evening class and caught him or her. Whoever it was beat it out the back door before I could get a look. So, no nothing missing here either. And your robbery? Nothing missing. That is odd, wouldn't you say?"

"I guess so. That's the funny thing. Icons were scattered all over the place. None of the other paintings or statuary was touched. I ran through the inventory and everything is here, except for The Virgin of Tenderness that we bought in Egypt. You know the nice variant of the Virgin of Vladimir, the one where the figures have been reversed out so that Mary looks to her left instead of to her right, that one."

"The one I took. I found it in the catalogue you sent if you remember. I have it here."

"I know you do, but it's still on my inventory and it's supposed to be here."

"Lorraine—"

"No, I'm serious. A guy came in Thursday looking for one. He didn't like any I had. I said…I mentioned you had it, but I could lay my hands on it. He said he'd be back. I want that icon, Louis. I need the sale."

"Lorraine, we've been over this a hundred times. You want a settlement, talk to the attorneys. It was your decision to force a divorce. You and your grease ball Italian lover. So, if you want to divide the goods, talk to the lawyers. I have what I think is mine by right. That's it."

"I will, you can bet on that. As soon as Franco gets his ass back here, you'll be hearing from a whole lot of people." The line went dead.

Something about a woman scorned. No, that's not right. I am the one being scorned, she's the scorner. I am the scornee. A man scorned—doesn't have the same *gravitas*.

Louis returned to the desk where he had set up his small easel and studied the tracing of an archangel. Until he added color to the robes and a symbol in its hand, it could be any of the four better-known archangels. But this was one he hoped to sell, so it would be either a Michael or a Gabriel. Not much demand for Raphael or Ariel, and none at all for the rest of the archangelic crowd: Azrael, Jeremiel, Jophiel, Metatron, Raguel, Raziel, Sandalphon, Uriel, Zadkiel, Chamuel. Leave it to the Persians to clutter up the heavens with an excess of beatific personae.

No, the buyers of this sort of artwork wanted the familiar, the tried and true, Gabe and Mike. He'd work on this icon for an hour or so and then head out for something to eat. The faculty recommended a restaurant called Frank's. It had once been *Chez François* and had failed in that incarnation, so the owner changed the menu from phony French cuisine to plain fare and reopened as Frank's. There was also the possibility of eating at that diner at the crossroad downtown, but he guessed that would be a better bet for breakfast. Of course diners served breakfast all day.

He'd decide later.

Chapter Eight

Ike held the scrap of paper out toward the fading sunlight and peered at the number he'd scrawled on it earlier. He turned and glanced at the number on the wall beside the door frame. This was the place. He climbed the porch's steps. He didn't see a door bell so he knocked. There was no answer. He stepped back, leaned to his right, and checked the driveway. A car sat toward the rear of the house. Somebody should be home. He raised his hand to knock again when the door swung open.

"Yes?"

"You must be Louis Dakis. I am Sheriff Ike Schwartz. I thought I'd drop by to ask you a few questions. May I come in?"

"I told the other cop everything I know on Friday night, but sure, come in."

Ike stepped through the door and glanced around. No odor of acetone, only the faint residue of after-shave. Dakis gestured toward a chair and sat down as well.

"You had some questions?"

"Yes. More importantly, I wanted to get a feel for the house and the break-in. You say someone broke a window and entered through it?"

"I think so. It's an assumption. As you can see, I've taped a piece of cardboard over the broken pane. The university's maintenance crew said they'd be out tomorrow to fix the window. But if you want me to, I can remove it so you can see that the window pane had been shattered. When I returned from my class the window sash had been pushed up, that is the window was open and I am sure I closed it before I left earlier, and someone was in the house. *Ergo*, the assumption."

Ergo, my patoot. "You never saw the person, I take it."

"Never saw him, no."

"And, as far as you can tell, nothing was taken?"

"Nope."

"Could I see the items that were disturbed?"

Dakis led Ike into the study area where the easel was set up. An array of icons leaned against the wall, each separated at its edge from its neighbor by a thin slip of cardboard. Ike eyed the material on the easel and leaned closer to have a better look.

"An archangel? Which?"

Dakis seemed taken aback. "You recognized the image in the tracing?"

"Lucky guess. I spent some time in Saint Petersburg—Russia, not Florida—back when I was otherwise employed and had some time on my hands. You've been to the Church of Spilled Blood, I assume?"

"Once, yes. I didn't want to leave. I could have spent a week in that place. Those magnificent icons, inside and out. Amazing...now, this one will be a Michael, I think. I will work on him but be prepared to switch to Gabriel if I receive a commission before I'm finished."

"Is that likely? I would think you'd want the commission first."

"I would, but right now, I'm in an inconvenient place for that. My wife and I used to own a shop in Washington and we sold these items." He waved his hand in the semicircle at the icons leaning against the wall. "I could paint any angel and we could sell it. But she is soon to be my ex-wife and so I only get a commission if she feels like handing one off to me. I'm guessing she's in the market for another iconographer, and when she finds him those opportunities will go away, too. But either way, archangels sell. Hell, even professing agnostics and nonbelievers love angels. Never could figure that one out—a heaven filled with angels but no God. Still, a sale is a sale. If I don't find a buyer locally, I'll put it on a web site I'm building. We'll see."

Ike shook his head. "There are many iconographers available? I would have thought they were pretty rare."

"Compared to watercolorists, oil painters, potters, sculptors, and so on, we are, but not as rare as we once were. Twenty years ago it seems the only iconographers were attached to Orthodox communities of one sort or another. Now, there has been a resurgence in the craft, at least here on the East Coast, and there are hundreds of us. Not all good, but all available."

"What would one of these cost, if I may ask?"

"Are you in the market?"

"Not likely. Put it down to curiosity on the one hand and professional interest on the other. I want to know if they are worth stealing."

"A small icon done in acrylics I sell for two to five dollars a square inch. That would be with minimum gold leaf. Larger, more complicated ones with elaborate borders will go for six to ten dollars per, and very complex multi-scene icons up from there."

Ike nodded. "So, they are worth stealing?"

"Yes and no. It's a little like owning a classic car. Irrespective of what it's worth on paper, you still need a buyer. It's one thing to have a valuable piece, you understand, quite another to sell it. The expensive works are sought by collectors. There aren't that many of them, to be honest, and then you have to know who they are and how to reach them. The cheaper renderings you can place in religious bookstores, on line, and so on, but a thief would have to know the who, the what, and the where. An ordinary break-and-enter thief would not, I suspect."

"You've had thefts attempted before?"

"Yes, several. Usually, a thief will go for the cash register. Rarely will he or she take a picture. If the thief is a high end burglar, however, he may go for one of these but will more often than not target a specific piece or pieces. One which I assume means he has a client and an assignment, so to speak."

"And you said nothing was taken Friday night?"

"Nothing."

"Were all the icons here?"

"Yes. Sorry, no. I had one with me at the time. I took one to my class to show them what competent gilding can do to an icon. The one I took was very old, yet the gold shone like new. It's the nature of gold. It never tarnishes. So, all but the one were here."

"I see. Is there anything else you can tell me? Maybe something that slipped your mind Saturday?"

"Now that you mention it, there is something.

Not something that I forgot, but something that happened more recently."

Ike slipped a notebook from his pocket, disengaged the pen attached to its side, and one eyebrow lifted, looked at Dakis.

"I had a call from my ex. It seems the store was broken into Sunday or maybe early Monday night, as well."

"Where is the store?"

"Washington, D.C., near DuPont Circle. I don't know if you know the city, but—"

"I know it."

"It seems she had a break-in, too."

"Let me guess: nothing was taken."

"Right. Icons scattered all over the place but nothing missing, except..."

"Except what?"

"It seems that I have one of the icons that is still on her inventory, so she thought maybe—"

"That you took it?"

"No, she knew I had it, but it may appear on the police report as missing. That might be embarrassing for me. Oh! Is that why you're here? My wife tipped the Metro police and they called you to come and check me out?"

"No. No one has contacted me from Washington. Perhaps they will, but not yet. It's a good thing you told me about the icon in advance. Save me a trip."

Ike stepped over to the stacks of icons and gently lifted them apart, studying the images. "There's something I never understood. None of the icons I have seen has that little white dot in the eyes. I don't know what it's called. Do you know what I mean?"

"A reflecting highlight. I call them reflectives for my students. The tradition is they are left out because the image represented is supposed to be the source of the light, not reflect light. All symbolic, of course. But, to tell the truth, when the gold has been applied in the nimbus it does seem to be a source of light."

Ike continued to sift through the icons. He noticed that Dakis seemed nervous when he did. He guessed if their positions were reversed, he'd feel the same way. Buford T. Justice rummaging through anything expensive would give anyone pause.

"Which of these is the one you had with you Friday night?"

Dakis eased an icon from the stack and laid it on the desk.

"This one?" Ike picked the icon up and studied it. "And this was supposed to be in the store in D.C.?"

"Yes. Please be careful. She said someone was in the store asking about it."

"Was there, indeed?" Ike tilted the icon so that he held it horizontally and sighted along its length. "Mr. Dakis, I will need to take this icon into custody—as evidence."

"You can't. What evidence? Evidence of what? It wasn't even here during the robbery."

"Yes, I know. That is why I need it. Unless I miss my guess, you will be visited again. The thieves, if that is what they were, did not find what they were looking for. The only common denominator between your failed robbery and your wife's is this icon. Someone wants this particular piece. I don't know why, but I aim to find out. You can be sure he will be back for it. In the meantime, I think it best if he doesn't find it. I will give you a receipt." Ike pursed his lips and stared at the icon. "By the way, how long would it take you to reproduce this?"

"Are you buying?"

"I have a buyer in mind. But it would be a rush job."

"Rushing is not what we do."

"But if you could be persuaded to?"

"Two days, but I wouldn't be responsible for the outcome."

"Do it."

"You want me to...It will not be very good as a collectable."

"As long as it looks like this one in the dark, old and expensive."

"In the dark? It will."

"Then, do it."

Chapter Nine

Ike placed the icon on the back seat of his unmarked police pursuit Ford Crown Victoria. A reluctant Dakis had relinquished it to his care and then only after swathing it in double layers of bubble wrap. If Ike had indeed seen what he thought he'd seen on its varnished surface, he'd need to call the CIA. He did not want to do that. Every time he found himself involved with his former employer, things seemed to come apart. But there was that worrisome thing on the icon's surface. Who employed outdated spycraft these days? He'd call Charlie and ask. Charlie owed him a favor for ruining Ike's last, and only, vacation. Charlie could send someone down to have a look. Charlie Garland was not on his speed dial, but he knew the number.

"Garland. Is that you, Ike?"

"You know it is. You must have industrial strength caller ID which can crack my blocked number, and I suspect you've picked up the GPS signal as well. You know who and where I am."

"Not on a personal call. This is a personal call, isn't it? I thought you said you were never going to call me again. Washed your hands and all that, or am I misremembering?"

"I didn't say that. I said I hoped I never had to call you again, and no, this is not personal, I'm afraid."

"What's up?"

"I need you to send a tech down here and look at a painting. Make it someone who's been around a while and will recognize out-of-date spycraft."

"Do you want to tell me what this is about?"

"I have a murder. You may have a problem."

"That's it?"

"It will have to do. Your man, or woman, will fill you in, if and when."

"I'll call you. Can't get anybody down there before Wednesday or Thursday."

"Try to make it sooner, Charlie. We have a civilian, at least I think he's a civilian, at risk here. Why don't you come yourself? I'll buy you lunch, show you the mountains. Too soon for much in the way of flowers, but the forsythia is out. You've never been here."

"I'll see. Wait for my call."

Ike had snapped the phone closed when it buzzed.

"Ike? Is that you?" Abe Schwartz shouted. He used the phone as if no important technological advances had occurred since the demise of manual dials and operators saying "number please." *The voice with a smile.*

"It's me, Pop. What's up?"

"Up? Nothing's up, Ike. But I was thinking if you ain't ate yet I was wondering if you were free for dinner."

"No, I haven't eaten. I was on my way to do that. Why?"

"Why? Because I asked you is why."

"I mean, what's the occasion? You almost never ask me to eat out with you. No offense, but we don't break bread except on rare weekends and holidays, and then out at the farm. I ask you but..." Ike left the remainder of the sentence unsaid.

"This is different. I want you to meet someone."

"This isn't one of your moves to get me into politics again, is it?"

"No. No sirree. This here is different, way different."

"How is it way different?"

"Ike you have become very suspicious. It don't become you. If I say it ain't politics, it ain't. So, can you come?"

"Okay. I know I will kick myself later, but I'll come. Where and when?"

"I'm figuring seven this evening—that's an hour from now, so's you'll have time to make yourself presentable and all. Put on a coat and tie. And, say, how's about you ask your lady to join us."

"My lady? You mean Ruth. I can ask but, on short notice the chances of her being free are pretty slim. Why Ruth?"

"I'm thinking another woman might make it easier. You call her and try. Either way, I'll see you at Frank's at seven this evening." Abe hung up. Ike stared at the phone in his hand.

Another woman?

He speed-dialed Ruth at her office. No answer. He tried her home number. She picked up on the third ring.

"Hello, Blocked Number, what can I do for you?"

"I had a call from Abe. He wants me to join him for dinner, and he asked if you could come too. Have you eaten yet?"

"No, as a matter of fact, I haven't. I was about to heat up a can of soup and make myself a grilled cheese. Why does he want me to join him?"

"He didn't say. But he did drop that having 'another woman' might help. What does that mean?"

"My, my, it looks like Abe has got himself a girlfriend. He wants me there to kick you under the table if you misbehave."

"Girlfriend? Abe is on the wrong side of seventy. If he has company, it sure won't be a girl. And shame on you for using a diminutive. What happened to your determined-at-any-cost-to-rein-in-sexism spirit?"

"Like you care. It's a figure of speech that is appropriate and fitting for geriatric couples."

"You think Abe has a friend?"

"My guess? Yes. Is that a problem for you? It is for some men. They get all mushy about their parents having a life outside of the one they've cast them in. That your problem, Bunky?"

"What? No. He wants you there to shield me from saying something stupid?"

"He knows I can make you behave. He thinks I can make you jump through hoops. I can, too."

"When have you ever made me do something merely on your whim?"

"Plenty of times, Sweetheart."

"Name one,"

"What was the first thing I asked you to do Saturday night after the lights were turned down low?"

Ike started the car and put it into gear. The evening had turned cool and he hit the switches to raise the windows. "That doesn't qualify."

"No? Explain to me why it doesn't."

"It happens that I am very fond of plum sauce."

"I would say under the circumstances, *very fond* doesn't cover it. You—"

"Can you come or not? I need to get back to my cave, change into something normal, and meet Abe at seven."

"Where is this confrontation supposed to take place?"

"Frank's. I can pick you up about ten 'til."

"I'll come. I wouldn't miss this for a million dollars. I'll drive myself, though. I have things I must do tonight before the faculty senate meeting tomorrow morning. If I get in the car with you I may never get home."

"Nonsense. I'll take you straight home— unless you're packing plum sauce. Then I will not be responsible for my actions."

"There, you see? I can make you jump through hoops."

"You are an evil woman, and you will pay for this. The day will come when you run out of M&Ms, and I will be there with a quart of chocolate sauce. Then we will see who has power over whom. Ha."

"I'll meet you at Frank's. And don't wear the purple tie with the ducks on it. It makes you look dopey."

"I'll wear the one with the plum sauce stains on it."

"That's not where I remember the stains were. See ya."

Ike closed his phone and concentrated on his driving. Abe with a lady friend. How did he feel about that? His mother had died over a year ago. Abe had not taken it very well, even though the disease that took her had been drawn out. It still took a while to get used to the silence. Why shouldn't Abe have a girlfriend, or two or even three? He liked the larger number better, he decided. Less chance of a permanent attachment.

Another woman.

Chapter Ten

A cool Monday evening, breezy and who knew, perhaps a hint of snow, certainly possible in the Shenandoah Valley in early March, rare, but possible. The custom was light at Frank's. If Ike trusted his olfactory senses correctly, tonight's special would be roast beef. It was the only dish Frank's served that had been edible in the restaurant's previous manifestation as *Chez François*. Ike spotted Abe at a corner table. Alone. Something not right with this picture. He'd expected Abe to be seated with an elderly matron. He'd scoured his brain to turn up likely candidates. He couldn't quite bring himself to say "lovers," and even "girlfriends" stuck in his throat. He walked to the table, pulled up a chair, and sat. Abe was deep in conversation with the mayor and his wife at an adjoining table. Ike acknowledged the mayor and waited.

"I'm here, Pop, and Ruth is on her way. Where is the person I'm supposed to meet? You weren't stood up. Were you?" Ike almost hoped it was true.

"Stood up? No sirree. In the little girl's room is where, powdering her nose. Be out directly. I was telling the mayor here he ought to think about finding something for you to do after your term as sheriff is up."

Ike sighed, an intentionally audible one. "Pop, you promised me no politics. I'm leaving."

"Sit still for a minute, Ike. Land sakes, I'm just saying."

"I could run for reelection, you know. And besides, the mayor has candidates for office ready to pounce at a moment's notice. He doesn't need my name added to the list."

"Law enforcement is a waste of your God-given talents, and that's the truth. Ain't that right?" He turned to the mayor for support. He, in turn, smiled and shrugged. Ike took the gesture as polite but noncommittal. "Ah, here she is." Abe stood and turned toward the rear of the restaurant. Ike stood as well and looked in the same direction.

"Aunt Dolly," he said.

"My, there you are, Ike. It's been dog's years. How are you keeping yourself? My, and you remembered my nickname. Bless you."

"How could I forget?"

Dolly Frankenfeld had been his mother's best friend in the years Abe served in various elective offices in the state. The Schwartzes kept a house in Richmond and spent weekends on the farm in the valley. Dolly became Ike's adopted auntie when her inability to have children of her own had been confirmed.

"See, there she is." Abe gushed. Like a school boy, Ike thought. "Ain't she something?"

"You're looking fine, Aunt Dolly."

"Tush, I bet you say that to all the ladies."

"In the past, I confess. Not often lately."

"Ike has himself a lady, too." Abe winked.

"So I hear. Are we going to meet her?"

"She's on her way. So, how did you and…" Ike wasn't at all sure how to proceed. *Hook up* seemed a little too modern, and he didn't like its implications. *Meet* was a given.

"You want to know what I'm doing here in this restaurant on a Monday night instead of back home in Richmond watching TV?"

"I was up to a meeting in the governor's office a while back," Abe interrupted, "and there was this dinner afterwards. I told you all about that meeting, but you probably forgot. Anyway, Dolly was there and we got to reminiscing and such and one thing led to another…"

Ike noticed Dolly blushed at *one thing led to another.* Oh, my God.

"You know, my Murray died about the same

time as your mother, Ike. Your father invited me down for the weekend. You know, in all the years I knew you all, I never got to the valley to visit. So, now here I am."

Dolly sat straight and very ladylike, hands folded in her lap, ankles crossed. She had been taught that as a child and had been sitting on chairs, benches, sofas, and settees like that for over sixty years. All she needed was a hat with a little veil and white gloves, and it could be 1959. Ike struggled to find words to fill the silence that descended around the table like a heavy fog. Abe was oblivious to it and sat with adoring, puppy eyes fixed on Dolly.

As Ike steeled himself to raise the topic of the weather, always a safe conversational filler and diversion, a gambit to kill time, Ruth arrived. The two men stood. Ruth was introduced to Dolly and the three sat.

"Ike never told me he had an aunt."

"She's not—"

"I'm not—" They both began and stopped.

"Ike, you first. We'll check your version with Aunt Dolly after."

"Dolly, Mrs. Frankenfeld, is…was my mother's friend…best friend…for years when we stayed in Richmond. She is an honorary aunt, you could say."

Dolly nodded her head. "It's so nice to meet you, Miz Harris; oops, Doctor Harris. I understand there might be a little announcement coming from you and Ike pretty soon."

Ruth screwed up her face in a puzzled frown, the Popeye look. "Announcement? I'm not sure what that would be."

"Oh, I understood you and Ike were very close. That sort of announcement."

"Oh that, yes, ah…" Ruth shifted her frown from puzzlement to concentration. "Okay, so, I am not pregnant. Is that what you had in mind?"

"Oh, no, I mean of course you aren't, why would you be? I mean…mercy."

Ike tapped Ruth's ankle under the table with his shoe and muttered "Behave!" out of the corner of his mouth.

Ruth smiled. Pure innocence. Ike groaned. He recognized the look. He'd seen it hundreds of times. Ruth was on a roll.

"And you, Dolly, do you and Abe have an announcement to share, too?" Ike kicked her harder. "Ow!"

"An announcement, why. . ." Dolly's blush started at the neckline of her dress and advanced like the red tide up to and past her hair line. "No, I don't think so. Do we, Abe?" Abe had a coughing fit.

"No, sir. I mean…no. So, how have you been, Ruth? Busy up at the college, I reckon." Abe looked at his son, who fixed on Ruth a look that qualified as one that could kill or at least maim.

"Wine," Ike said. "Frank has a very nice wine selection, residual from his days as the proprietor of a French restaurant. Red or white? A nice *pinot noir* perhaps."

"Champagne," Ruth said. She turned to face the three others. "I'm sorry, I have not been behaving. Please forgive me. It's Ike's fault." Ike's eyebrows shot up and he started to protest but Ruth sailed on. "It's just that I enjoy pushing his buttons. And he, mine, as a matter of fact. But, he's been so patient with me and I've been so vague these past months, he was beginning to think it was hopeless, you see?"

They didn't.

"Okay, then, here we go. And Ike, please don't kick my shins anymore. I bruise easily. Of course you knew that already, because when…but that's something we can discuss another day."

Ruth paused and held up her right hand. The diamond ring caught the candlelight and sent bright sparks of light dancing across the ceiling.

"You see this obscene rock? Ike gave that to me last fall. He spent his children's inheritance on it. Fortunately, he has no children, as I have now affirmed, but you get the point. Are you with me?"

Dolly's face had a sly grin. Abe looked confused and Ike stared blankly at Ruth. He, better than anyone, knew what she was capable of, and he hoped she wouldn't go off. He had a fleeting vision of one of those joke cigars with a powder charge in it that would explode when lit. Kablam.

"You do, don't you, Dolly? Wow, okay, here we go."

Ruth slipped the ring from her right ring finger and held it out toward Ike. He shook his head. She grinned and slipped it on her left ring finger. "Is that the announcement you were asking about?"

"Hallelujah," Abe barked. "Champagne it is. The best."

Chapter Eleven

"Turn on the engine and let's get some heat in here. It's cold. Did Ike tell you why we're staking out this place?" Billy Sutherlin slapped his arms against his chest and puffed.

Sam Ryder shifted in the seat and peered into the night. "Sissy. It's March. Where I come from this is like summer. Why didn't you wear your jacket if you're cold?"

"It's in the wash."

"You don't wash a down jacket, Billy."

"Yeah, I found that out the hard way. Essie gave me hell. Listen, laundry ain't something I was raised up to be doing."

Sam smiled and shook her head. Men. "Ike said to me we were to keep an eye on the place, and should park so we can see around back as well. Something to do with the break-in you wrote up Saturday."

The moon, though not yet full, provided enough light to allow the two deputies to see without night vision goggles, which was a good thing, as the several federal programs aimed at upgrading law enforcement agencies across the country had missed Picketsville. The sheriff's department had to manage without the goggles and a number of other bits of technology they could have used, now deemed standard in larger, more affluent jurisdictions.

"You Yankees are used to the snow and ice. That's why you can sit there so smug. What else, besides that, reindeer, and permanent frost bite, do you have up there in Minnesota?"

"In the summertime we have mosquitoes big enough to take your cat."

"Heard that. Did Ike think the bad guy would be back for another go?"

"That was my take. Something to do with him, or her, or them not finding what they came for the first time. You see anything up front?"

"Nope. Why would they come back this soon? Seems sorta risky to me."

"You know Ike."

"So, what do you hear from your boy Karl?"

"He's been assigned to a tactical unit, so I don't always know where he is. It's not something I like, I can tell you."

"I reckon you wish he'd taken Ike's offer last spring and stayed on here as a deputy? He was good,

I'll give him that, but I reckon his heart was set on going back and being a G-man."

"Nobody says G-man anymore, Billy. FBI Special Agent is the correct term. Yeah, he said he needed to know." Sam sat still and put the binoculars to her eyes again. "It was so good those months when he was here all the time and, you know, it was, like, peaceful."

"Except, of course, when them jackass LeBruns come near to killing me and Essie. But you're right, I do know. Since us two been married and having our own place, it's like a different life. And we all owe Karl a bunch. Saved my cookies, that's for sure."

"Is that something moving down the road there?" Sam pointed to a spot a few yards to the east.

Billy scanned the road. "It's only a dog, big German shepherd. If someone is sneaking around here tonight, they'll have us and the dog to deal with. I know that mutt. He's a mean son-of-a-bitch."

"I guess you can say that about a dog, can't you?"

Billy looked confused and then brightened. "Oh, yeah, it being a dog, you mean. So, what will you and Karl do? You can't be every other weekend forever."

"No, that is wearying, not to mention frustrating. I don't know. One of us is going to have to sacrifice. I love my job, he loves his. Mine keeps me here, his keeps him there, wherever there is, and they don't work together."

"How's that?"

"He's FBI. They move about a lot. If I were to go with him, I can't stay here. The chances are slim to none I could hook on to the Bureau, and even if I did, there's no way we could be sure to be assigned to the same place."

"I figure you'd be a helluva FBI with your computer skills and all."

"At Quantico or up in the Hoover Building maybe, but not in Cleveland or Phoenix. I mean he could be sent anywhere. Right now he's been assigned to a tactical unit in Washington, but next year? Next week? Who knows?"

"So, one of you has to let it go and be a stay-at-home or have a moveable career. That don't make for easy choices." Billy thought for a while. "If you was to get married, what about kids?"

"There's that, too. Not only would I have to step aside, you know to have a child, but there's the race thing. People are pretty open now about mixed marriages, but there are always those who, you know, can't get with the program."

Billy nodded and sipped from his cup. "Coffee's gone cold. Is there any hot left in the thermos?" He handed the cup to Sam. She shook the bottle.

"Nope. Empty. We should have planned this

better. So how're you getting on being a father?"

"Scary is what that is, but pretty exciting, too. I'm going to take a stroll around the other side of the house there and check that hedge. You hold down the fort here."

"Men are so lucky."

"No dessert for me, duty calls." Ruth folded her napkin and stood. Ike rose with her.

"I'll see you to your car."

Abe rose as well. "Aw, don't go. You all stay a while. My goodness this is a big night." Dolly smiled and sipped the last of her champagne.

"I can't, Abe and there's no need to escort me, Ike. Stay and visit with your dad and Dolly."

Ike turned to the two of them. "I'll come right back, only be a minute." He took Ruth's elbow and walked her to the door.

"Are you being gallant or do you have some other, possibly lecherous, purpose in mind? I do have to work. I told you when you asked—"

"I need a minute. Indulge me."

"I guess if it's just a minute, I'm safe enough."

When they reached her car Ike turned her to face him. "I'm delighted, no, ecstatic. But I am also confused. This morning you said you couldn't make the move…the ring and all, and now, what?

Less than twelve hours later, and it's a done deal. What did I miss?"

"You didn't miss anything. I'm the one who's been missing things. I mean, I kept putting you off. For months, in fact. It's my personality, I guess. What am I, type A? I don't know. I never trust over-simplifications, particularly when they presume to define people, but at dinner while I was zinging Dolly…I'm sorry about that, by the way…"

"You should be, but I have to tell you, I thought it was wonderfully funny, and the expression on Aunt Dolly's face was priceless."

"Yes, still, it was a little mean. Anyway, I saw the way those two old people looked at each other and I realized how wrong I had been. They were so, what is the word? Adoring, I guess, and I realized that I was stuck eight inches from having something wonderful."

"Come again?"

"You know, those hokey inspirational speakers do it all the time. Point to their head, 'Victory ain't here.' Point to their heart, 'It's here, eight inches away.' I think they're off a few inches, but you get the idea."

"And this relates to you, to us, how?"

"I spend my days on task. A time and a place for everything, priorities, due dates, deadlines, think it through, measure twice, cut once, all the clichés of the hyperorganized. And watching those two old coots, I realized that relationships are not rational, itemizable, or quantifiable. In short, love ain't cerebral." She paused and gave Ike a wan smile. "So, how are we going to make this public? Or are we?"

"By morning everybody in town will know. Even if I were to muzzle Abe, which is not likely by the way, the town grapevine will have had it within an hour after you said it, and tomorrow I will be expected to buy breakfast for the crowd at the Crossroads Diner."

"Maybe you should have breakfast with me instead."

"You mean it?"

"I do. Now, I have to go. Give me an engagement kiss and go back and let you dad show you off to his lady friend."

"We need to talk about this. How do we—"

"I know, where do we live, how do we mesh? Another day, Ike. Let's take it a day at a time. This much alone will take some getting used to."

"Right. Okay, give me an hour. No, make that an hour and a half. I have a stop to make. Will that be enough time for you to get your work done?"

"It's enough to get it started. Park on the visitor's lot. I'll leave the kitchen door unlocked and tell Claude the night watchman not to shoot you."

"Thanks for that. You're sure?"

"It's the new me, impulse over reason. So, yes."

Chapter Twelve

Billy and Sam had taken turns walking the perimeter of the quarter acre of Callend's campus that Dakis' house occupied when Ike raised them on the radio. He asked for a status report. He said that if he had reckoned correctly, Dakis should have another visitor or visitors soon. How soon, he could not say, but soon.

"Nothing much happening here, Ike."

"Okay, another thing—this is important. I know you and Sam are on second shift, but I need you in the office for an hour or so tomorrow first thing in the morning. We have someone from the Bureau coming to ID the dead guy from the clinic. I'll need you, Sam, to run some of your fancy software."

"Won't he be bringing a complete file?"

"Based on the way the Bureau has interfaced with us in the past, Karl Hedrick notwithstanding, my opinion is no, he won't. I'll need you to poke around in cyberspace, I think. And Billy, we may have somebody from the CIA dropping in also, and I want you to listen in on what he has to say. Our little B and E has taken on a whole new look."

"I'll be there, for sure. What kind of new look?"

"You'll see tomorrow. I'm going off-duty as of now but my cell phone will be on in case anything happens out there tonight. Amos and Buck will relieve you in about two hours. Tell them where I can be reached."

"Roger that."

Sam looked at Billy. "What was that all about?"

"You know Ike. Seems like he's a step or two ahead of the game most of the time. How do you suppose he does that?"

"I think it must come from all those years when he was an agent."

"They call CIA spooks agents?"

"I don't know. Agent, operative, spook, spy, does it matter? He will tell you all that's behind him, but I'm not so sure. Anyway, I think he developed one of those paranoid minds that you have to have to survive in that business. He always looks at things different than you or I. He sees the significance in things that we miss and is suspicious of everything, at least when he's working. I don't know how he is otherwise. I hope different."

"Yeah, wouldn't you like to know how he is

with your old boss, Miz Harris? It's scary sometimes the way he does his thinking. You think he'll ever go back to the CIA?"

Sam shook her head. "I don't know what happened to push him out, and I know he'll help those people from time to time, but I get the feeling he'd as soon cover himself in molasses and roll around on a hill of fire ants as go back to Langley."

"Ouch."

"Stupid. You two are stupid." Jacob sounded furious. "If I didn't need you to finish this business you would be on your way home."

The two men, who for the moment called themselves Wentz and Brown, stared at one another. Wentz dug at the carpet with his toe and looked up. "He said it wasn't there and that it must be in Washington. How could we know he lied?"

"You killed him before you checked? Just because he said it was or wasn't here or there does not mean it was either."

"But he looked and said since it wasn't at the husband's, so it must be in Washington."

"And you killed him, then?"

"Not then, later. We had to have the password and the key to his store."

"Then you killed him."

"No, we didn't." The speaker looked at his partner for confirmation, "It was Avi. Avi Kolb killed him."

"Kolb? What was he doing there?"

"He said you wanted him with us, to be sure."

"Idiot! I never said anything of the sort. And you stood there and watched him eliminate any chance we have of recovering the thing?"

"It was an accident."

"Killing Zaki was an accident? How can it be an accident?"

"Avi put the gun in his side to threaten him when he tried to run. It went off. You said we should eliminate him when the job was done anyway. I think he must have known that because he started to run away."

"And so, Avi Kolb, who wasn't supposed to be there, shoots him."

"We were sure he was trying to escape."

These morons are lying, he thought. Why would Avi Kolb shoot anyone? As if to confirm his thoughts one said, "It's true, it was Avi Kolb." *The man protests too much. Leave it to these knuckleheads to screw up and blame the missing Kolb. Why am I always saddled with idiots?*

"Fools. Now the only source we had to absolutely identify the painting is dead and the police are looking for the men who killed him. It is only a matter of time before their Homeland Security people match up his fingerprints and will be down on us. We must get that picture before they realize what we're after."

"What are we after? Not only a holy picture. If that is all you want there are hundreds in that shop we went into Saturday."

"When this crew was put together, I thought it had first-raters. You two are like trainees. How did you ever—"

"Serak hired us, Jacob. He said to report to you and you would be in charge of the operation. He said he had the connection in the CIA and he wanted us especially. We are not…whatever you said. This is not the first job we've been on, okay?"

"Okay, okay, enough. First, this is not an *operation*. You were to find an icon and steal it and then disappear, that's all. Now, I must find Kolb. Who is he working for? Not us, it seems. As for you, remember it is not any picture, it is one picture in particular. It is called *The Virgin of Tenderness*. You have photographs. Look at them again and then go back to that place in Virginia and get it."

"What if the guy is there?"

"Get that picture. If that means taking care of him, then do it. We are running out of time. Do you understand?"

The two men looked at the floor. One of

them, Brown, shook his head. "It is a blasphemy even to touch it."

"Tell that to your Rabbi. I haven't time for religious scruples—theirs or yours. I have a job to do. And you two have seventy-two hours to get us that picture before the people who shipped it here tumble to the fact their man is out of the loop and they send someone or something else."

Ike parked on the visitor's lot and walked down the lighted pathway to the president's house. As promised, the kitchen door was unlocked. He stepped in, closed the door and threw the bolt. Ruth had her lap-top open in the small room off the main drawing room that served as her office away from the office.

"You made it," she said, not lifting her eyes from the screen.

"I did. Claude only fired three shots before I hit the porch. He needs target practice."

"Very funny. Fix us a drink and sit down somewhere and behave. I'll be a half hour or so at this."

Ike poured her a small Scotch and made himself a gin and tonic. He placed the Scotch on the desk beside her, stroked her hair, and walked to the door.

"I'll be in the upstairs sitting room if you need me. And I hope you do. Need me, I mean."

Ruth nodded, eyes still fixed on the laptop, and waved him away. On task, absorbed, working—focused.

Ike trudged up the stairs to the small room off the bedroom. It had a television, a small sofa, end tables, and side chairs grouped around a silver Bokhara. To one side, a fireplace broke a large set of book shelves into two sections. A fire had been laid. He stooped and lit a match to the kindling. The fire caught. Ike flopped onto the sofa, sipped his drink and savored the scent of burning wood. Apple, if he guessed right.

Forty-five minutes later Ruth found him asleep. She debated whether to wake him or not. She thought he'd be angry at her if she didn't. She poked him in the ribs. Ike recoiled from the sofa like a scalded cat. That was the cliché that came to mind at any rate.

"Wow, what's up with you?"

"I must have dozed off. Sorry."

"No problem. But what's up with the jumping at me?"

"Bad dream."

"You want to tell Momma?"

"I want Momma to induce a nice dream. Are you finished with your agenda?"

"Not quite. You're next."

Chapter Thirteen

Sam bounced into the office grinning like she'd been voted prom queen or perhaps cast to play Tigger in the school play. Ike hadn't seen a smile on her face like that in months.

"Hey, there, Deputy Ryder," Essie called from her post at the dispatch desk, "what's up? You look like you won the lottery."

"Better. I'm here to greet the FBI liaison officer assigned to the 'cide out at the clinic."

"All that's got you so bouncy? Lord, it must be the shade of J. Edgar himself that's coming."

"Again, better."

"Oh, my, let me guess. Mr. Tall, Dark, and Handsome, and I do mean dark, is coming to town. Hey, Ike, you hear that? Ryder's Mr. Wonderful is going to be in town. I don't reckon we'll get much work out of her today."

Sam leaned on the door frame of Ike's office. "Karl called me this morning. He's here for as long as it takes to get us up to speed. You think you could make that a couple of years?"

"That would be nice. How about we try to stretch a couple of days anyway. When did Karl say he'd arrive?"

Sam turned her wrist over and looked at her watch. "He'll be here in an hour, unless there are problems on the Sixty-six or the Eighty-one."

"Not likely this time of year,. So, see if you can manufacture a professional demeanor, turn on that battery of electronic machinery in your space, and start digging around. If I know you, you will find out who they're going to surprise us with before your boyfriend gets here."

"He'll be disappointed if I do."

"He'll be disappointed if you don't. By now he's told them we are a good deal better at what we do than they give us credit for and they, that would be his team leader and the rest of the Quantico crowd, don't believe him. They never do. The Bureau mavens always think the cops in the sticks are hopeless and hapless. We need to keep reminding them that more often than not, we make them look good, not the other way around."

"Not Karl."

"No, not Karl. So, give him something to report back."

Billy Sutherlin slouched in and sat heavily at the desk he shared with the other shifts.

"Did you get the dishes in the machine before you came in?" Essie's cornflower blue eyes locked on her husband like lasers. If she hadn't also been beaming when she said it, Ike thought there might be trouble brewing.

"Done that and put the clothes away, Darlin'. How you, Ike?"

"Up and at 'em. The CIA called. Won't be here 'til lunch time. If you want to head back home, it's alright with me."

Billy glanced at Essie out of the corner of his eye, turned to Ike and said, *sotto voce*, "No thanks. If I do I'll end up doing chores all morning and I'll tell you, I'm beat. Keep me here. Give me a job to do or something."

"How about running up the street to the Shop 'n' Save and bring back a box of mixed pastries—whatever you like."

"I'm on it."

"Oh, and when you get back, there's a package wrapped in the trunk of my car. Bring it in here and log it in as evidence for the robbery attempt you covered."

"Package?"

"It's an icon. Be careful with it. It's double-wrapped in plastic protective. No matter what, don't touch the surface."

"No touching the surface, right. Which first, evidence or eats?"

"Get the pastries. When Karl Hedrick arrives we'll have a party. Essie," Ike shouted across the room, "dig out those paper plates we have stowed away somewhere and the coffee mugs the county gave us and put them out. Oh, and make a fresh pot."

"How come it's always the woman has to do that?"

"Because it's your job. If you were a man, God forbid, it would still be your job. Back in your home, you're the boss—no offense, Billy—but here, the dispatcher, he or she, tends to coffee pot and related chores. Before you ask 'how come?' it's because I said so."

"Have to keep the boss happy." Essie started pulling open drawers. "Well, git on out of here and find us some sweet rolls, Billy."

"Yes, ma'am."

Ike pulled the two folders containing the details of the crimes in question toward him and flipped them open. He studied the photographs of the dead man. There was very little blood. The body had apparently been stripped and redressed, at least the shirt and jacket. The shooting had to have taken place elsewhere, probably close by. Why did the killers, he had to assume at least two, bring the body into the clinic? Did they think he might be still alive? He'd read about similar situations somewhere. One of a group of hunting buddies accidently shot. The others cleaned him up and dropped him off in an emergency room in the hope he hadn't expired. They were very drunk, so their idiocy held a certain alcoholic logic. Perhaps this was another case of drunken denial.

The second folder he found more interesting. Charlie Garland had decided to come himself, as it turned out. He would like this puzzle. Old time spying, real cloak and dagger stuff. Ike wondered what *cloak and dagger* had to do with intrigue. He liked words and origins of expressions. Where or when, he wondered, did cloaks and daggers become associated with intelligence gathering? He never owned either a cloak or a dagger in his day; didn't own a trench coat either, come to that.

"You sneaky so-and-so." Essie stood in his door, hands on hips, a pose that made her belly seem like she'd swallowed a good-sized watermelon. "You weren't going to say anything?"

Ike scratched his head. "About what?"

"I had a call from Ellen Capehart down at the Shop 'n' Save. You went and got yourself engaged to the lucky Miz Harris, is what."

"Oh, yes I intended to say something later.

Lot happening today. What do you mean, lucky?"

"In case you didn't know it, Ike, you have been the catch of the day, so to say. There'll be some busted hearts in Picketsville today for sure."

"Essie, you exaggerate. Nobody—"

"Sometimes, Ike, as smart as you are, you can be a real dope, with due respect, 'course. I know at least a dozen women would faint dead away if you so much as give them the time of day. And three of them is married."

Sam rounded the corner with a piece of paper in her hand. "Ike, I think I have the name. It's strange."

"Don't tell anyone. Put it in an envelope and seal it. After Karl gets here and tells us, we'll open it. It'll be like Karnack, and your answer was…tah dah."

Essie grabbed Sam's elbow. "Did you know Ike, here, is engaged?"

"Wow. To Dr. Harris?"

"Shoot, Sam, who else has he been seeing lately? Of course it's her. I'm calling Billy. If he's still at the bakery, I'll get him to buy us a big old sheet cake or something."

The door opened with a gust of wind and Karl Hedrick entered. "Cake? What's the occasion?"

Sam raced across the room and wrapped her arms around Karl's neck. "Ike's going to marry Dr. Harris."

Karl's eyebrows shot up. "That so?"

Ike wagged his hand vaguely at Karl. "Hey, Karl, how's the FBI treating you?"

"Fine, Ike. Congratulations. You the man. So you're going to…that's going to create some logistical problems for you, won't it? I mean where will you live?"

Ike shook his head and shrugged. "There'll be time to figure that out later. Questions you might have on your list someday, as well, I'm thinking. Sam, is that envelope sealed? Okay, Karl, tell us who our murder victim is."

Chapter Fourteen

"Farouk Zaki." Karl waited for a response. "What? No 'I told you so?' Sam, didn't you find anything?"

Sam's face fell. "That can't be right. Farouk…?"

"Zaki, yes, that's the guy's name."

Ike opened the envelope, removed the slip of paper on which Sam had written a name and handed it to Sam. "Read it."

"Franco Sacci, like the movie guy only without the H. I don't understand how that can be." She turned to Karl, "You made that up. You knew what we would do and you made up another name. Whoever heard of a guy named Farouk? Except the Egyptian guy who…he's from Egypt? "

"I didn't make it up, and yes, he's Egyptian, we think, and yes again, that's the name of the guy we're looking at. Before you ask, the name is a very common one in that part of the world. Check out the Internet, or is that too obvious? Of course, you will check it out," Karl sighed and rolled his eyes.

"Anyway, you picked off his alias. Now," he spun around and addressed Ike, "this has got to stop. It is a serious offense to hack into the FBI computers. It's not only difficult to do but it is a federal crime. Ike, Sam could be in big trouble if she were caught."

"I'm police, just like you," Sam snapped, but looked worried nonetheless.

"You're local and subject to federal statutes like any other citizen. If I were to return to the Big House and tell them you had discovered the name of the person I was sent to discuss with you, they would have a task force down here before you could say, 'there goes my pension.' You've got to stop this, Ike. Sam could be—"

"I hear you, Karl. Sam, stop it!"

Sam smiled. "Yes, sir, Ike, sir."

"Okay, that's that. Now tell us about Zaki or Sacci, or whoever he is."

Karl closed his eyes and shook his head. "I mean it, Ike. I know you're connected and can probably wiggle out of something like this, but Sam isn't and you need to consider that."

"Sam works for me, and as you know, or should remember, we are family. Nobody does anything here but everyone does it. You try to take down one of us, you take us all. Am I correct in assuming that your people up there in the rarified ether around the nation's capitol are thinking they might have a security problem and have murmured in your ear to put us in our place?"

"Something like that, if I understand what ether means."

"Here's a bit of advice for you to take back with you, when you go. If the wonks in Quantico have a system that a rube police department out in the sticks like ours can penetrate, they have a bigger problem than trying to frighten the aforementioned rubes. Tell them they need to upgrade their software and tighten their security, not threaten police and any others who can bust in. And as a favor to them, because we do want to help, we will keep trying to punch in until they've managed to put a finger in all the holes in their dike."

"I'm not sure I can do that."

"Then tell them to call me and I will tell them. Now, about Farouk…that's his real name?"

"Ike I'm…oh, never mind. Right, okay, Farouk Zaki, aka Franco Sacci. He's on the watch list but there is nothing heavy in his file."

"Then why is he on the list?"

"You know the watch list. It's about the same size as the Manhattan telephone directory, practically. Apparently his name came up in an interview at Guantánamo. A name on a list of names. But considering the source, the decision was made to keep tabs on him."

"He's in the country using an assumed name and there's nothing 'heavy' in his file? How does that work?"

"In the first place, there is no law in this country that requires you use your real or legal name. If there were, nine-tenths of Hollywood and 100 percent of the exotic dancers would be in the slammer. Secondly, he has a work visa issued to him in Italy by our consulate there. It's real."

"He's on a watch list using an alias and the consulate issued a visa so he can enter the country? What's wrong with this picture?"

"We are fair, if not terribly bright, when it comes to our borders. There was no reason to deny it. He was vouched for by a sponsor in this country who assured the authorities the work was real. What can I say?"

"What dingbat would sponsor a suspected terrorist to enter the country? Don't they vet the sponsors?"

"They do. They did. The person is an art dealer of some sort and has a solid reputation. The only note in the file that might raise an eyebrow is the consul thought the connection between Zaki and the dealer was more than professional. That's it."

"Okay, I give up. This didn't used to be the way we did things. So, what do we do with all this? The Bureau didn't send you all the way down here to tell us that. A phone call from Francis what's-his-name, Drake, would have sufficed."

"Right. The Bureau, believe it or not, shares your concerns about the seeming laxity in this matter. We want to know if this is merely an example of episodic incompetence, or if something more complicated is involved. And secondly and probably more importantly, what was this guy doing in your part of the world if he worked in D.C.?"

"What do you need from us?"

"For starters, how about some of those goodies Essie has arranged on the tray, coffee, and maybe a slice of cake. You can run me through the scene and the ME's report after that."

"You realize this may take several days to clear up. Us rural cops are a bit slow, you know. Sam here thinks she might need some extra tuition, like night school, you could say, to get up to speed."

"Slow study, that's me. I think I may need hands-on teaching to figure this out." Sam had the decency to blush.

"Hey," Essie shouted, "as the only married woman in the room, I think you should tone down this here smutty talk."

Sam threw a piece of sheet cake at her.

"We will be visited by a member of the CIA this afternoon, unofficially visited, just so you know. You might be interested in what he has to say."

"Why is that?"

"Because, unless I miss my guess, the business he will confirm for us may eventually fall into your, that is, the bureau's, lap at the end of the day. Now, Frank will fill you in on what we have learned about the Zaki person."

Chapter Fifteen

Charlie Garland arrived before lunch. Ike assumed he'd timed it so that he could mooch a free meal and told him so.

"There has to be some benefit for losing oneself in the hinterlands. Nice place you have here, Ike."

"Whether you get a free lunch depends entirely on whether or not you brought the things I asked for."

"Ah, as to that, I did." He patted his jacket pocket. "The lab guys wanted to know what I was up to and of course—"

"And, of course, you lied to them."

"Of course? Oh, come on, Ike…"

"Yes, *of course*. And I am sure they were okay with that. Public relations people have that as their stock in trade, I'm told."

"We do. I'm afraid it's the company we keep. Aren't you going to introduce me to your playmates?"

"Certainly." Ike went around the room. Charlie lifted one eyebrow when Karl and the FBI came up. Ike gave him a look and shook his head. Since it appeared he might overlook her, Essie raised her hand.

"And Essie Sutherlin, née Falco, our dispatcher and resident mom-to-be." Essie beamed. "Mr. Garland, did you know Ike is engaged?"

"What kind of spy do you think I am? Of course I did…are you, Ike? Wow. Congratulations. Sorry, I think 'best wishes' is the mannerly thing to say. It's a good thing. We need to talk."

"You're not a spy, Charlie, thank you, and no, we don't."

"Excuse me, Ike," Karl said, "but are we going to be enlightened in some fashion by the CIA's PR flak, who, it seems, is not a spy? What's up with that?"

"Looks can be deceiving, remember that when you go to bed tonight. Now, Charlie, it's time I introduced you to a real Picketsville institution. We are having lunch at the Crossroads Diner. It is across the street."

The staff groaned.

"Hey, it's a celebration in honor of me, and if you want to eat on the department's dime you will partake. Otherwise lunch is on your own."

"Lucky for me I can't leave my desk." Essie said and retrieved a brown paper bag from a drawer and unwrapped her lunch.

"Can they make a salad?" Sam asked.

"They can. I don't know if it is edible, however. It depends on how you feel about tomatoes that have no taste and ranch dressing that tastes very much like a ranch. My advice, Charlie, stick to the breakfast menu. Everyone does."

"Why do I not feel a great sense of gustatory anticipation?"

"You shouldn't complain. I've eaten at your house."

"I'm hurt."

"Call this the sheriff's revenge."

They returned an hour later, their serum cholesterol elevated by fifty or sixty points, and all of them close to succumbing to food coma.

"Coffee, Essie. A gallon or two or we will all collapse on the spot."

"Don't you want to know if any important messages came in while you were out?"

"No."

"The mayor called."

"I don't consider communications from the mayor important."

"I know. I took a message. He says congratulations and best wishes."

"Right. The mayor must have attended the

same finishing school as you, Charlie. Now, I want you to look at something and tell me what you see. Billy, bring in the piece of evidence I had you retrieve from my car." Billy carried in the icon and Ike carefully removed the bubble wrap. He handed it to Charlie.

"What do you see?"

"Been a while, but this is…what? *The Virgin of Vladimir?*"

"Close. It is reversed out. The guy that owns it called it The *Virgin of Tenderness.* Now, hold flat at eye level and let the light glance off the surface."

Charlie lifted the image and tilted it so that the daylight streaming in through the windows shone on its surface.

"What do you see now?"

"Well, well, look at that, will you? My goodness, so that's why you wanted the…I haven't seen this bit of spycraft in years."

"I think I speak for the group," Karl said. "We have sacrificed our bodies for you at the diner, and at the very least we deserve to be told what Mr. Garland sees before our arteries clog up completely or we all die of food poisoning."

Charlie removed a pair of tweezers from his coat pocket and picked at one of the icon's eyes. "There's just the one. That's interesting. You'd think if they went to all that trouble they'd have maxed this icon out."

"Hello? Please, what are you talking about?"

"A moment, Karl. Lift it off, Charlie."

Charlie picked some more and then held the tweezers aloft. *"Voilà."*

"What?" Billy and Karl leaned forward, Sam back. "A microdot?" she said.

"Precisely."

"What's a microdot doing on the picture?"

"Ah, that is the sixty-four-dollar question. What indeed, in this day and age of sophisticated encryption transmitted electronically, satellite communications, iridium phones, and even Twitter, for crying out loud, is an old fashioned microdot doing on an icon, and then, why would anyone put it there or want to?"

"We'll have to look at it to find out why. It could be old but useful, you know, left over from the bad old days. Who knows?"

"You have the replacement I asked for?"

Charlie slid an envelope from his blazer pocket and handed it to Ike who held it up to the light. "Right. But this one is bigger and thicker. Usually they are about the size of the period you'd find in a large print book. Curious, wouldn't you say?"

"I don't know. I guess, if you say so."

"Maybe it's just old. Are you going to replace it?"

"I'm hoping we have a day or two before the Bozos who tried to steal this icon come back for another go. I'm having a copy made and I will put your little microdot on it and embed this homing device in the back. Then, we're going to let them steal it. Since this comes under Homeland Security task-forcing—that is to say you two—who do I send the bill for the icon to, the Company or the Bureau?"

"Ah, this is domestic…outside our mandate. We can't touch it, Ike." Charlie swung his gaze to Karl.

"Hey, I'm not authorized to commit funds for—"

"Didn't you learn anything when you were with us on temporary duty? Mercy. What's the rule on spending money?"

Karl sighed. "It's easier to seek forgiveness than permission."

"You are training your people well, I can see," Charlie said. "So, the bill goes to the Hoover Building. They'll be thrilled. Now, there is one problem with your plan, Ike."

"That is? Wait, don't tell me. If they know, more or less, what's supposed to be on the chip, they'll figure out you're on to them and disappear. And you want them collared, right?"

"That, and as I look at this bit of low-tech spycraft, that it is not quite what you, I should say, we assumed it must be. I think I need to take this home and find you a better substitute."

"I'll have to find a way to keep the baddies away from Dakis' house. You okay with all this, Karl?"

Karl shrugged. Sam looked worried. Karl had been on the bureau's carpet once already. She didn't want him there again. "That's not fair. Karl could get in trouble, and what if they come before the new icon is ready?"

"Then they will steal the real one with the same provisos. I hate to damage the thing but, we do what we have to do. Karl will be fine. If we have this thing figured correctly, he may even get a commendation. Right, Karl?"

Karl did not look convinced.

Chapter Sixteen

The D.C. metro cop looked up from the slip of paper in his hand. "Where the hell is Picketsville, Virginia?"

"Where is what? Picketsville? You're kidding, right?"

"It's in the Shenandoah Valley, Lieutenant, why?"

"They have a trace on the guy's phone, the one who's missing from that art place, what's his name...Sacci? The report has the coordinates where the phone is, and it says the thing is there. So what is the big deal about the Shenandoah Valley?"

"Civil War, Sheridan's Burning, Robert E. Lee, Stonewall Jackson, Washington and Lee University, Virginia Military Institute, Virginia Tech—"

"Okay, okay, I get it, important place."

"—and Mary Matalin, not that I'd put her up there with the generals, but she can be pretty feisty. So, is the phone in use?"

"Off and on, not regular. It's shut down most of the time, but the chip is still powered up, so they could trace it. It's not moving around much."

"Call the local police and see if they can find it and the missing guy. I'd like to get this one off the board."

"I'm on it, Lieutenant. Who's Mary Matalin?"

Frank Sutherlin had not said a word all day except to comment on lunch at the diner. He didn't like it. It was his own fault, he'd been told. "Order breakfast," Ike had said, but he went for the pot roast and spent the first hour afterward trying to remove the strings of beef caught between his teeth. Finally, his sister-in-law, Essie, handed him a box of tooth picks, and he restored his mouth to some measure of normality.

"Do you suppose," he said dropping the last of his tooth picks in a nearby trash can, "that the two crimes are connected?"

"It would be a huge coincidence," Ike said. "Why do you ask, or why do you think they might be?" Ike trusted Frank's judgment. He was the most experienced of his deputies, although he had the shortest tenure, having only transferred in from the Highway Patrol some months before.

"Why? I don't know for sure, but they both

involve someone interested in art. They happened the same night, we think. Maybe the dead guy was the same one that tried to break into Dakis' house."

"And what? He didn't find what he was looking for, so someone killed him. It doesn't track, Frank."

"No, it doesn't, but I still...Oh well, don't mind me. I have a suspicious mind. I don't like coincidences."

"Oh, come on, deputy," Charlie said. "Multiple crimes happen all the time. We have break-ins and murders every night, it seems, in the D.C. area, and nobody thinks they're related."

"Yes, I know all about that. Cities have crime in multiples. But this is Picketsville, Virginia. We don't have that much crime to begin with, and murder is a big deal. Multiples? In Picketsville? I'm wondering, that's all."

"Point taken, but we can't connect them, Frank. I don't like coincidences either. But for now, we work them separately." Ike said, but Frank heard the doubt in his voice. "And speaking of coincidences, Dakis told me his wife had a break-in over the weekend, too. I'm guessing the icon is the point of similarity."

"That is interesting, I guess. Right. So, where do I begin?"

"I want you to go over every statement you took from the people in the urgent care center that night. Then take Amos and knock on doors. See if anybody remembers anything unusual. I mean anything. I don't see how it is possible to unload a corpse from a vehicle, haul it into a busy emergency room, and nobody notices anything. Also, get out to the local motels with pictures and see if any of the clerks remember seeing the guy, if he registered, and if so under what name." Ike swiveled around. "Billy, you do the same out at the college."

"Ike, I already done that. I got nothing."

"If you didn't find anything, you must have missed somebody. College types are nosey as hell. Somebody saw something. Maybe they didn't see the significance."

"What about me?" Sam said.

Ike looked first at her and then at Karl. "You're off duty until tomorrow. Then, I want you to scour cyberspace for anything you can find about Zaki/Sacci. Charlie here will tell you how to access Langley, and, as we all know by now, we already have the back door to the FBI."

"Right."

"I'll do no such thing." Charlie said and handed Sam a slip of paper and winked. "Ike is the only person I would trust with that information if I had it, which I don't."

"And add Louis Dakis to your search, him and his estranged wife, whoever she is. Find out what his story is, the works. Now, everybody, go—except you, Charlie. We need to talk."

Louis Dakis' phone rang. He put down the board on which he was tracing the image the sheriff had commissioned and picked up.

"Hello?"

"Louis, it's me, Anne Scott—Anne Scott Jacobs." Anne was Lorraine's oldest and best friend. She had two first names. That is, no one called her Anne. It was Annescott, her first and second name run together. Not hyphenated, not a southern Luella-Mae or Billy-Bob thing, just—Annescott. She had been that since grammar school. Her parents called her that, everyone did.

"Yes, hello. It's nice to hear from you, I guess. How did you find me?"

"Four-one-one, information, you know. Lorraine said you were in Virginia. Someone else, I can't remember who, thought it was down there, so I called around and found you."

"And now that you have, what can I do for you?"

"Oh, Louis, what happened to you two?"

"You mean me and Lorraine? Ask her."

"I did, she said something like 'not now.' I mean I was away on the West Coast for three

months and I come back and you two, my two
favorite people, are separated. What happened?"

"She didn't tell you? You don't know?"

"No, I…"

"She went to Italy to check out an estate, lots
of things we could sell, old stuff, collectibles. Then,
I received a presale catalogue on the Internet about
a piece, an icon, in Cairo that looked good. So I
sent her there and she met a guy…some hot-shot
Italian art dealer, she says. Long story short, she
came home with him and asked me to leave. She
wants a divorce and a settlement, and then she says
she will marry him. That's it." Louis felt his temper
slipping. He didn't want to air his problems with
Annescott. Not now, anyway. "You never met the
grease ball, Annescott?"

"Noooo…"

But it didn't sound like she hadn't, too much
hesitation.

Louis ignored the disclaimer "What do you
think of him, then?"

"I said I didn't…okay, I met him. I didn't like
him, if you must know. He didn't seem genuine.
You know I studied Italian in college and spent part
of my junior year in Rome. If he's Italian, I'm Aunt
Jemima. Oh, that's…You can't say things like that
anymore, can you? Okay, if he's Italian, I'm Paris
Hilton. There, that's better. We can disrespect one

of our own. At least until some militant group forms to defend the rights of the congenitally stupid and vacuum-brained."

"Then you know how I feel, and like you, I am confused and…Well, that's it."

"Would it be too much if I said something to you, you know, straight up?"

"I guess so. Shoot." Now what, he thought. More feminist crap about sharing?

"I did talk to Lorraine before. I mean when you were still together. She told me…"

"What, Annescott? She told you what?"

"Okay, you are a workaholic, Lois. You're never home, never anywhere except in your studio painting, or at the store, or going through the stock, or reading catalogs. Always something, but not her. She felt abandoned half the time. She told you that didn't she?"

She had done, many times. And he'd told her they had a business to run and that meant he had to work. He told her she might be better off giving him some credit for all the work he put in building it. But he did not repeat that to Annescott.

"She might have said something."

"There's one thing more."

"What else?" Louis clenched his teeth. His jaw began to throb.

"You know about her wish for…Her biological

clock was ticking away, Louis. She wanted to start a family and you kept putting her off even to the point of—"

He knew. He feared she'd "forget" the pill and have an accidental pregnancy, so he'd stopped their sex life for all practical purposes. Did Lorraine confide all this to Annescott? Women had no sense of confidentiality. They'd blab any and all to their friends. Men didn't do that. Not in his experience anyway.

"It was a difficult time," he said by way of apology.

"Would it help if I had a talk with her? You know, I'll say we had this chat, and you want her back, and like that."

"You could. You'd be lying, but you could."

"There's no hope then?"

"None that I can see."

"I'm sorry to have had to say all this and I hope, um, I'll talk to her again. You should too."

"Perhaps I will," he said and hung up. In a pig's eye I will.

Chapter Seventeen

Ike ushered Charlie into his office. It didn't provide much in the way of privacy. It more nearly resembled a fish bowl, a human aquarium, than a proper office, a box partitioned off from the main reception area with large casement windows instead of walls. Ike could see and be seen; could close his door but that was about the extent of his privacy. Still, he needed a moment with Charlie and it was better than nothing.

"Charlie, I need you to go with me up to Callend and brace Ruth."

"I would love to meet her, of course, but brace? Why does your fiancée need bracing?"

"She has never met you, and you know her only from what I've told you about her. There are some things I haven't mentioned." Ike tapped a pencil on his desk top. "She can be, shall we say, stubborn about the sort of things you do, that is, we did, or I used to do. She comes from the part of society that has this notion about an intrusive government and—"

"Ike, for Pete's sake. She leases us that old storage facility, your old 'bunker,' now museum, on her campus, the one where the art used to be stored. It is now our building and—"

"I know what it is now. She knows, too, sort of. But she doesn't like it and will not renew her lease, if and when."

"The lease is for twenty years and if she knew what we're up to down in the depths of her basement, she'd be grateful."

"And what is that? No, no, don't tell me. If I know, I'll owe you and I don't want to go there. Besides, I doubt if gratitude is what she'd feel."

"You already owe me."

"Wrong. I pulled your chestnuts out of the fire last fall. You and the director owe me big time, so don't even start."

"Okay, we owe you. Is that the problem that has you all snarky and mean spirited?"

"Not quite. We, that is, the FBI, possibly your people, and certainly mine as well, if I have this pegged right, are going to be all over her turf for a while. She will not be happy."

"Why will we, as you say, be all over her turf?"

"Someone wants that icon. They will come back to get it. If we make a substitute, when they find out, they will not be happy and then bad things could happen. If her people happen to be caught in the middle, she, in turn, will not be happy. The very fact we have brought this to her campus will not make her happy, understand?"

"Yes. I suppose so. What ever happened to trust in the essential righteousness of your cause?"

"You know better than to ask. Too many young men lying dead in ditches in far-off deserts and snow-covered mountains because we decided to respond to maniacs in hijacked airplanes and bring democracy to the unanointed."

Charlie heaved a sigh, a very stagey one "I will explain all to her, assure her it is a trivial pursuit, a trifle, a bagatelle, a—"

"You'll tell her the truth or she will, as the Brits used to say, have your guts for garters."

"They still say it and it is silly, no one wears garters anymore. Except at weddings and that is only for that awful bit of business between the bride and groom where he has to…Did I tell you about my sister's second wedding? Poor dear is in her forties and no longer lithe, you could say. Imagine this, she wore white—for her second. I don't know what has happened to the usage of proper sartorial symbolism. Where have we gone wrong? Anyway, the groom went diving for that garter, slipped, lurched forward as only the obese and alcoholically impaired can, and knocked her off the chair. Both of them ended up on the floor, he with his head under a mountain of tulle, and she grasping at air like a beached whale, unable to move. It was awful."

"That's fascinating. Now, back to the point of this chat, garters notwithstanding, you will have to turn on all your boyish charm to get around her, and the problem with that is, she doesn't respond well to charm and as you aren't a boy anymore anyway, you will need to be at your best."

"You're too kind. Ike, I've been doing this sort of thing for years. As Will Rogers said, 'I never met a woman I couldn't schmooze.'"

"He didn't say that, and you never came across a woman like Ruth. All I'm saying is, forewarned is forearmed."

"Not a problem, Ike. I will be charming, persuasive, and if that doesn't work I'll send one of our contractors down here to snuff her. Okay?"

"If the latter, my sympathies go to the contractor's widow."

The voice on the phone sounded like it came from the depths of an empty garbage can. This was not good.

"Where are you, Jacob? I cannot wait much

longer. Do you have the merchandise or not?" Why would Serak call it merchandise? It sounded like dialogue from a bad television show.

"We failed to find it in either place. Sacci looked in the man's house and reported it was not there. He said it must still be at the store in spite of what the woman told him earlier. He thought she might be getting suspicious. He is not reliable, as you know. So, we tried the store as well. No picture there either."

"And still, you trusted him to tell you the truth?"

"What other choice did I have? He is not a significant person, a delivery boy, a weakling, and he gave it up as soon as we threatened him."

"Okay, if it is not there, is it possible the man sold it?"

"I suppose he might have. Sacci didn't think so. He said the market for such things is slim enough in cities. In the country…?"

"Find out."

"Serak, with respect, I must ask you this, are you sure you gave us the right photograph? All of these holy pictures look alike to me."

"I have assurances that it is correct. By the way, where is Sacci? He must have made a mistake. Make him talk if you have to."

"That will be difficult. Sacci isn't volunteering any information anymore."

"Make him."

"As I said, that will be difficult. He's dead."

"Dead? What do you mean, dead?"

"There was a misunderstanding, it seems. He was in custody with the two idiots you hired for me and attempted to escape, they said. They reported that Avi Kolb shot him during the attempt. And that brings up my next question. Why did you send Kolb to us anyway?"

"Avi Kolb? I didn't send him. He's not one of us."

"He said you sent him, that he was contracted by you to do a thing with Sacci and the other two. He knew all about what we were doing and we assumed…"

"You didn't think to check back with me?"

"Why would I? He knew all about…You didn't send him?"

"I told you already, and no. This creates another problem for me. It means someone else knows about the merchandise…" there was that word again, "or something else more important." A silence followed. He waited. Silences made Jacob nervous. "This is not good. You cannot waste any more time. Go back to that man's house and get that icon."

"The police are there. It is a crime scene now. We will have to wait for a while, until they leave.

Then we break in and retrieve the picture if it is there. A day or two."

"As soon as you can. I will contact our friend in Washington. He will know what Kolb was up to." The line went dead. What was Kolb doing? What was going on here, and where were those two idiots they'd hired? He hated contract help. No matter how dedicated they seemed, the lack of professionalism could cost.

Chapter Eighteen

The Reverend Blake Fisher turned to his bride of less than four months and pointed toward the church's altar. "I would like to put icons up front, maybe on either side of the altar. What do you think?"

"Icons? Like in Greek Orthodox churches? Those kind of icons?"

"Yes. Only not so large, you know. I don't think I could manage a full iconostasis even if I wanted to, but something simple. I have that Jesus Pantocrator hanging in my office I bought in Jerusalem a few years ago. I'd put it on the Epistle side and a Virgin and Child on the Gospel side. Maybe on little stands."

"I don't know, Blake. This is the Shenandoah Valley, not mainline Philadelphia. High church trappings don't sell too well down here in the South."

"Come on, Mary, this has nothing to do with high or low church. It has to do with ambience and focus. We have the nation's flag up there, we have hymn boards bolted to the wall with the assigned hymns and Psalter, even though the same information is printed in the service bulletin and no one even looks at them any more. We have plaques commemorating the dozens of dead donors the church has had over the years. I want something to remind us where we are and what we're supposed to be about."

"But Greek icons?"

"Orthodox icons. Russian, Greek, Armenian, whatever. Why is it nobody has a problem with saints rendered in stained glass along the side windows, but a painted version of the same saint up front causes an uproar in Protestant churches?"

"It's about what we're used to, Blake."

"And that is the problem. We get used to things and they gray out in our conscious. We repeat things we no longer understand and then act silly when someone suggests we might want to change them, rearrange them, or whatever. For example, do you see that window in the back corner? Do you know which 'saint' is depicted there?"

"It's not one, is it? I thought it was a civil war thing."

"Precisely. A Civil War thing, The War of Northern Aggression thing, a symbol of a time that came and went. You can plainly see that window carries the image of, you should pardon the expression, our patron 'saint,' General Stonewall Jackson. I'm told the donor wanted an equestrian portrait, but the window wasn't big enough to include the horse. And the good general was a Presbyterian to boot."

"Now you're being silly. It's because when this church was built, loyalties and memories were still strong. And people are accustomed to stained glass. We only notice it if it's missing."

"And thereby you make my point. The benefit of having a congregation surrounded by the heavenly host is lost. If I intrude on their Protestant sensibilities with pictures, front and center, of two of the three central figures in the Christian story, perhaps they will focus on the purpose of their attendance for a change."

"You sound annoyed. What's happened? Something go wrong at the vestry meeting last night? You were late coming to bed." She blushed. Mary was famous for her blushes and the thought of bed, and the two of them in it together, was sufficient to produce one. He smiled.

"Did you know you snore?"

"I don't. How can you say that?"

He bent down and kissed her forehead. "It's a very sweet snore, more a whisper, a promise of things to come, or erotic dreams."

She smacked him on the shoulder. "Keep that up and you're in the guest room."

"Ouch."

"That didn't hurt"

"It might have. You don't know your own strength. Okay. Icons are out of the ordinary for us in the Valley, foreign even, so we can't impose them on the folks. Is that what you're saying?"

"Maybe, I don't know. I began this journey as a Methodist. We sometimes have problems with vestments and collars. But I asked you about the vestry meeting. Did something happen?"

"Some people are unhappy, I guess. It is the nature of churches in general. There are always people who don't like something you do, or something you don't do. If you change one bit of the routine, people get unhappy. If you don't change it and people are aware of new things in other churches, they are unhappy. People come and go. You know the axiom of the clergyman's life? Put new ones in as fast as the old ones leave."

"Now you're being cynical."

"Maybe, but there is truth in it. The fact is, if you are a clergyman or clergywoman and popularity is your goal, you will be perpetually disappointed or cease to be clergy. I know some of my colleagues work their congregations like they're contestants on *American Idol*…if you loved the sermon, call 888-GOTTALUVIT, or text YOUDAMAN."

"As I said, cynical. Come on, Blake, it's me you're talking to here…so where would you get the second icon?"

"You think I should?"

"I didn't say that. I wondered, if you decide to do it, where would you find one?"

"There is an iconographer up at the college, I mean the university. He's an adjunct faculty member. He came to church Sunday; do you remember?"

"The man with the sad eyes, moustache and longish hair?"

"Yes. His name is Dakis, and he paints the things. I talked to him, and he said he could do one for us. Not big, like I said, you know, about the same size as the Jesus. Placed correctly, they would force your eyes forward front and center toward the altar."

"Ah ha, you brought this up at your vestry meeting and were met with something less than an enthusiastic reception."

"I mentioned it."

"And they said?"

"Pretty much what you said, 'Never been done. Not a Protestant thing,' et cetera. You know, the first icons I ever saw close up were at Tabka in

Israel, where the miracle of the loaves and fishes is memorialized up in the Galilee. It's a Lutheran church, by the way. It was quite effective."

"But the vestry wasn't impressed. We're not Lutherans and we're not Greek. We don't need that stuff in our church. Right?"

"Almost. They weren't bubbling over, but they said they were not against it either."

"But what they didn't know, and what you didn't tell them, you already ordered the second icon."

Blake shuffled his feet. "Yes, sort of."

"Sort of? Did you or didn't you?"

"I did. I thought I'd try. If there is too much flak after a month or so, I'll take them down and hang them up in my office instead. So no permanent damage…"

Mary touched his arm and smiled. "Do you think it will help?"

He grinned back. "Probably not, but it will give me something to work with. Icons have a wonderful effect on people over time. I don't know what it is, but you cannot stare at one for any length of time and not be drawn out of yourself and into another place."

"Then you should do it. But no incense. It makes me sneeze."

"Right, no incense. Yet."

She bopped him on the shoulder again.

Louis Dakis placed a second gessoed board next to the first. He'd had few commissions in the last several months and now two in a row. One for the sheriff—God only knows what a Jewish sheriff—he guessed Schwartz was Jewish—wanted with an icon of the Virgin Mary, and a close copy at that. There was no accounting for taste. Some of the best icons were to be found in Israel, part of the post-World War II Russian Diaspora.

The Episcopal priest's interest he could understand. In fact, that was the reason he'd dropped in on the Episcopal Church with the bizarre name in the first place. What kind of church is named Stonewall Jackson Memorial? Icons were a fairly steady market for him among the clergy of the traditional denominations in and around the Washington area. Something about increasing interest in form over substance, perhaps. He supposed it represented the logical product of the labyrinthine thinking that characterized so many postmodern clerics.

It didn't matter to him. Money was money.

Chapter Nineteen

Meetings like this one could be dangerous, he reminded himself, especially when someone else controlled the set-up. He had a firm rule to never let that happen, and now he'd broken it big time. He felt on edge. The man who, at the moment, called himself Avi Kolb drove slowly through Rock Creek Park, looking for the pull-off he'd been told to take. He glided around one of the many curves that characterized the parkway and spotted the fire-blistered trash container emblazoned with "The King Lives." Elvis or Michael? Not that he cared. He pulled in and parked next to the can.

His training required that he wait a moment. Listening, watching. Nothing. He still didn't like it. But he had no reason to question his sources. It had sounded real enough, certainly worth a shot, and this needed follow-up. He stepped out and made a three-sixty surveil of the area. To his right, a small path left the parking area on its northern

verge and disappeared first into some shrubbery
and then into the trees. His instructions were to
walk in fifty yards, wait until he heard his horn
sound, and return. The information he needed
would be on the floor of his car.

He didn't like it. His preferred meeting places
that were in the open, in public, busy Metro sta-
tions, restaurants, and food courts. Sit on a bench,
pass the envelope, and leave. Nothing simpler.
Alone and isolated like this begged for trouble.
Maybe he should have taken a pass, set up the
meet somewhere else, sometime later, somewhere
he could manage. Have some backup, perhaps. Too
late to second-guess now.

He took a breath and spun slowly around a
second time. Still nothing. He walked away from
the unlocked car and picked his way down the path,
avoiding the brambles that clutched at his slacks.
They were new; a present from his fiancée, if that
was what she was. He wasn't sure if the word meant
anything anymore.

When he estimated he'd gone fifty yards, he
stopped, glanced at his watch, and thought to light
a cigarette. Then he remembered, he'd promised
Marti he would quit and as a token had thrown
away a half-full pack the night before. A gaudy
gesture but a serious mistake. It was times like these

when he needed a smoke. He puffed up his cheeks and listened.

Years before, he might have sneaked back to a point where he could watch the car and get a glimpse of his informant. He'd learned the hard way not to do that. Now, he waited, uncertain, glancing at his watch, and fidgeting, as only a reformed smoker with second thoughts would. When he heard the horn's bleat, he sighed, glanced once more at the lush stand of hardwoods around him, and made his way back. He would buy cigarettes on his way home. Quitting would be something he'd undertake later; maybe when he took some leave time, he would do it then. He was due for a time-out. He heard the unmistakable racket of an old VW Beetle with a bad muffler moving away, south. Who drove old VW Beetles anymore? Superannuated hippies, Mexicans? No one he knew. He climbed the embankment up onto the parking pad and walked to his car.

Once behind the wheel, he fished the plain manila envelope off the floor. He inspected the outside. No clue there. He fished around in the ash tray and found a bent, but still smokable cigarette butt. He rolled down the window next to him, lit the stub, fought the momentary guilt the smoke brought, and slit the bulky envelope open with his thumbnail. A blue jay squalled its rusty pump-handle call somewhere off in the woods. Another joined it.

He removed a loose batch of mismatched papers, most poorly reproduced, and scanned them, looking for the first clue as to whether or not he had wasted an hour of his time on a meaningless meet. The blue jays switched to a louder and simpler call racketing "jay, jay, jay" back and forth across the forest floor.

"Holy Mary, Mother of God!" he murmured as he reread the words he could make out, this time carefully. His Arabic was not what it should be, his Hebrew slightly better, French nonexistent. He flipped through the dozen or so pages and studied a series of blurred snapshots. This was supposed to be what he had been searching for, what he'd been tasked to find, and would have had if he hadn't gotten the impression that those two morons had tumbled to him. And then they had to go and shoot Zaki on top of that. No chance to get any closer then. Idiots. Had they retrieved the electronic bit of business on the damned picture, it might have opened a door or two, gotten him closer, and all this would have been unnecessary. He'd been so close and now this falls into his lap.

He stared out through the windscreen at the trees. Something was wrong with this set-up. Too easy. Somebody's razor—the easy answer is always the best one? Maybe, maybe not. He shuffled through the papers again. Something not right. Almost but…too easy. The blue jays screamed louder and closer. Their raucous, insistent calling resonated with his growing panic. No doubt about it now, he'd made a mistake. A rookie mistake. He'd sensed it the moment he'd opened the packet. He wanted it to be right. He wanted to end this assignment. So many false leads and now this. Too easy. Too eager. The thought of having closure finally, of shutting down the operation, of slamming the door, as his control had put it, had made him careless.

He tossed the cigarette stub out the window and scrabbled for the car keys. He dropped them, retrieved them, and stabbed at the ignition. On the third try, he got the key in the slot and started the engine. He stuffed the papers clumsily back into the envelope, shoved it aside, and reached for the gearshift.

He heard the gun being cocked, but didn't bother to turn to see who held it. He knew. He'd seen his picture among the several he'd scanned, standing in a group, assault rifles slung rakishly across their chests, grinning, and a Hummer burning in the background. It was a familiar face. A face he knew. It should have been a trusted face. He suddenly felt very sad and at the same time very betrayed.

The shot rang hollowly through the trees, the sound muffled by the shrubbery. The blue jays, their warnings unheeded, flew down the valley in a cacophony of "I told you so's."

Avi Kolb had been born Thomas Wainwright in Cedar Rapids, Iowa, thirty-five years before. He attended parochial school, lettered in football, basketball, and baseball in High School. His year book said he'd been voted "Most Likely to Succeed" and, oddly, "Best Kisser." His life ended before the first could be established, and he was a very private person, so there was no data on the second.

He toppled over on the seat and settled in the spreading stain his blood and brains made on the upholstery. The envelope was gently removed; the still warm .45 caliber pistol placed in his hand.

The park police found his body an hour later and reported an apparent suicide.

The jays had returned and were quiet.

"Excuse me, Ike, I have to take this. Charlie flipped open his cell phone and listened. It was a short message. He closed the phone without speaking. Ike watched him out of the corner of his eye. He wheeled the car through the gates that formed the entrance to Callend University, its newly gilded sign in place. He recognized the look on Charlie's face.

"Bad news," he said. It was not a question. Charlie nodded. Ike drove on. Asking would not be appropriate nor would it help. If Charlie had something to say, he would say it. Otherwise, Ike knew from past experience, that when a cold wind blew out of Langley, it was not a time for either jollification or idle curiosity. The CIA was full of secrets and private disasters. Maintaining one's ignorance of them he considered to be a blessing, a *mitzvah*.

"This place looks like a movie set, Ike."

Ike nodded. "There was some talk last year about shooting one here. Someone wanted to make a for-TV film or documentary, I never knew which, about the robbery we had back then."

"I remember. We recruited Harry Grafton after that. I take it they didn't. Make the movie, I mean."

"No. Apparently that's the way the industry works. Many more treatments than projects."

"Did you ever run across Tommy Wainwright back when you were with us?"

"No, can't say that I did. Should I have?"

"I guess not. After your time. Worked the Near East section—Israel. We pulled him in last year and then the director tasked him to…Homeland Security."

Ike waited. Charlie had hesitated a millisecond before he'd said Homeland Security. So, if not there, where? Did Ike care? No, by God, he didn't.

"Here we are. I can't wait to meet the fabulous Doctor Harris."

"What about Tommy Wainwright?"

"He's dead."

Chapter Twenty

Agnes, all agog, ushered Charlie and Ike into Ruth's office. She'd been told that Ike's friend was from the CIA. With visions of Matt Damon as Jason Bourne in mind, she'd met them in the lobby. She'd looked over Ike's shoulder expectantly and seeing no one else, swung her gaze back to Charlie. She hid her disappointment well, Ike thought. Charlie's presence was entirely and self-consciously forgettable. He worked at it.

"So, this is the Charles Garland who routinely corrupts our local sheriff. How do you do," Ruth said, and extended her hand.

"I corrupt no one. I am a man in whom you will find no guile."

"Quoting the Bible will not score points in this venue, Mr. Garland. You are a corrupter of my fiancée and a doer of dark deeds, not Nathaniel."

"I am but a humble PR flak who happens to work for the President of the United States."

"Hi, how are you, Ruth?" Ike said, and leaned forward to give her a kiss on the cheek. She stepped back and pointed a finger at the two men.

"Not so fast, Schwartz. Not until you explain why you have brought this figure from the Dark Side to me."

Ike collapsed into one of the crewel-covered side chairs that faced her desk. "Well—"

"I asked to meet you." Charlie interrupted. "But to be clear, I am in this delightful town at Ike's invitation. He needs me."

"Bull, Ike rarely needs anybody. Just ask me… that's not entirely true, though. Sometimes he requires my presence, and I his. But that's pretty much it."

"Nevertheless, he called; I came. *Veni, vidi, vici,* or words to that effect."

"Charlie is showing off his classical education. Once a Princeton man, always a Princeton man. Recite one of Shakespeare's sonnets for Ruth, Charlie. He knows sixteen of them by heart."

"They that have power to hurt and will do none…"

"That's ninety-four, very impressive. I ask again, why are you here, Willie?"

"The wench doth have wit."

"Careful, Charlie, you are mixing it up with a verbal black belt. You can't win."

"Ah, then. We…emphasis on the *we*…are here because the little break-in on one of your faculty cottages has escalated into something more than a break-in. It is now a subject that interests the government's intelligence community, you could say."

"I wasn't aware the government possessed intelligence—in community or otherwise."

"Um, I think we have gotten off on the wrong foot here, Ike. I propose we exit, and have Doctor Harris' delightful secretary, or is it administrative assistant? Whichever, she can usher us in again. We will forego the sonnets, et cetera, and get straight to the point."

"Skip it. Just tell me in standard English why are you here?"

"Let me try, Charlie," Ike said and waved him into the other chair, the twin of the one in which he sat. "Ruth, Louis Dakis, your adjunct professor or whatever his title is, had in his possession an icon that had a bit of…an anomaly, you could say."

Ruth swiveled gently side to side in her chair. "An anomaly? What sort of an anomaly? And why would the *intelligence community* be interested in it?"

"It is an anomaly that is very out of place."

"Charlie…can I call you Charlie? That statement is silly. It's a tautology."

"Life is a tautology." Charlie grinned.

"That was very deep, Mr. Garland."

"You think? Would you say Proustian?"

"No, but nice try."

"Freudian, then?"

"Maybe, but not in the way you mean it."

"Will you two cut it out? I feel like, what's his name, the old comic, Jack Benny."

"Okay. The icon carried something it shouldn't have and which connects it to people who are not nice generally and a potential threat to my employer, specifically. We are here to tell you that Ike has gotten himself into another mess and we—that is the FBI and myself, figuratively speaking—will be hanging around for a while until the bad guys are caught, expelled, or dealt with in some appropriate fashion."

"All that for a break-in? Wow. I'd hate to see you guys when there are nuclear devices gone missing or—"

"No, you wouldn't." Charlie wasn't grinning any more. Ruth's jaw snapped shut.

"Thank you for the heads-up. I will take out my anger on the sheriff there if it's all right with you."

"My pleasure."

"No, mine. You should see what she does with plum sauce, Charlie…"

"Ike, you are skating on very thin ice here. Charlie, while I have you here, I want to know what your people are up to in my old storage facility."

"Up to? Nothing important enough to bother you."

"Nonsense. You and your pals are in my building hatching dark schemes and plots. I leased that building to you back when the college found itself over a financial barrel. We are better off now, but I do not want to come to depend on that rent for ongoing expenses."

"And why is that?"

"I have this awful feeling that whatever passes for an investigative reporter nowadays, which isn't saying very much, I know, or God forbid, Michael Moore, will find his way in and do an exposé. And I will end up feeling like I popped up stark naked in the middle of the half-time show at the Super Bowl."

"An arresting image. You're a lucky man, Ike."

"Cut the crap, Charlie. What's going on in there?"

"Sorry, can't say."

"Can't or won't?"

"Let me allay some of your fears. In fact, some of those would-be investigators have tried and come away empty-handed, alas."

"Who? When? Why didn't I know about this? Ike, Did you know?" Ike raised his eyebrows a quarter inch and shook his head.

"About every six months or so, *The New York*

Times or *The Washington Post* receives an anonymous tip from someone down here suggesting that the things you fear most are, indeed, going on in your building. You have at least one disgruntled employee on your payroll, I gather. No doubt a faculty member passed over for tenure, a rival for your job, who knows."

"Comes with the territory, Charlie. So what then?"

"Anyway, the paper then sends somebody down here, they snoop around and find nothing. Don't worry, Ruth, you are covered, you could say. You should have no fears about being naked on national TV, so to speak. Unless...well, not on our account, anyway. I put to you a question, how did you use that building before?"

"As a storage facility, for art objects. You know, it held the Dillon Art collection, or part of it."

"Then, there you are, it still is a storage facility. Not for art, however."

"A storage facility? The truth?"

"Indeed. So, you need not fear Michael Moore, Mary Tyler Moore, or Saint Thomas More. Super Bowl. My, my."

"Why don't I feel reassured?...Agnes?" Ruth barked.

Agnes Ewalt stuck her head around the door jamb, "Yes?"

"Coffee and some of those Danish things left over from the Building and Grounds Committee meeting, and why don't you join us."

"Right away." Agnes hustled off smiling.

"She's terribly disappointed, you know, Ike. She expected a real spy. She got Charlie."

"What's wrong with me?"

"Charlie, with respect, you are not Matt Damon, Sean Connery, or even Frank Lovejoy."

"Frank Lovejoy?" Ike asked.

"You're the classic film guy. *I was a Communist for the FBI,* that Frank Lovejoy."

"I know who he is. I'm surprised you do. I'd say Charlie was more on the lines of Rowan Atkinson."

"Mister Bean, yes, perfect."

"I drive all the way down here to help my friend yet again, to snatch him from the jaws of defeat and imminent disaster, and what do I get? No respect. If I weren't so attached to the two of you…I include you now, Ruth, as I realize the labor it must have taken to salvage this man…if I weren't, I'd pack up and leave this moment."

"But you won't. You will spend the night. We will have a fabulous dinner on your expense account, imbibe too much, and—"

"Sorry, can't. Change of plans, Ike."

"Tommy Wainwright?"

"Yes. I think he may have been connected."

"To this business?"

"As I say, I think so, and maybe to your murder as well."

"That's not good news. Why don't you ever bring me good news?"

"I'd rather bandy words with your future bride, Ike."

"You're not telling me something, Charlie."

"Later, perhaps. I need to check a few things."

"Can you at least stay for a quick dinner?" Ruth asked, her face serious.

Charlie shrugged. "An early one, but in a real restaurant. I saw the effects the local diner had on Ike's colleagues."

"I will rustle us up a salad and Ike will turn some otherwise perfectly fine Angus beef into charcoal on the grill on my back porch. Okay? Ah, here's Agnes with the coffee. Tell her some lies, Charlie. She had such high hopes."

Chapter Twenty-one

After they'd said their goodbyes to Charlie, Ike and Ruth retreated indoors. The evening had been warm enough for them to have enjoyed their brief meal outdoors on the porch, but the March chill arrived as the sun set and they'd fled inside to the den and a fire.

"So, how did you like Charlie?"

"I like him, Ike, and I hate him, too. Sorry, that's a contradiction, I know, but there you are."

"It's a paradox. I think we worry too much about absolutes."

"If you say so. I have no idea what you're talking about, but don't stop. We have precious little time together as it is. Opine away."

"Thank you. So, why do you hate him?

"Because he represents many of the things I find disagreeable in this world, covert plotting and scheming, geopolitical posturing, dark, perhaps not very ethical, operations about which nobody gets a say and over which there is no oversight, and—this is the real reason—he regularly puts you in harm's way."

"Regularly is too strong a word. I help him sometimes. He helps me sometimes. We're friends. That's what friends do."

"Okay, I understand that, I guess. I don't like it, but I understand it. Anyway, before you ask the next question, I like him, I think, because in spite of all the bullshit you two get off, he genuinely cares about you. I wouldn't want to bet the rent on it, but I'd wager he'd take one for you. And you for him."

"Probably. You never know what you will do until you're called on."

"So there's my contradiction. I like him and I don't. What do you mean paradox?"

"Paradox is defined, not very well I think, as a 'seeming contradiction.' It's another hobbyhorse of mine, Ruth. If I didn't know it beforehand, I learned in the police business that we deceive ourselves with 'either/or' situations. Contradictions do not allow for alternative views. It's black or it's white, period. All the 'if you're not for us, you're against us' crap, 'if this, then that' and so on."

"Syllogisms."

"Them, too, yes. The world does not operate in that kind of reality. That's the world of polarized positioning and the fundamentalist thinkers who inhabit those poles, Jihadists, academics, lawyers, evolutionary psychologists, all the people who would shape our culture whether we want them to or not. The truth is that between black and white there is not just gray, but infinite shades of gray, and beyond that lies the distinct possibility that neither position is correct or perhaps both are correct, but in opposition to one another. Paradox."

"Like?"

"Take an issue, any issue: gay rights, animal rights, whale hunting, global warning, water boarding, the make of car you drive, for God's sake. Some idiot social evolutionist, whatever that is, declared driving a Cadillac indicates its owner's lowered educational values; Saab or Prius owners, he opined, would be the quite the reverse. Moronic classism all wrapped up in pseudoscience, and you don't have to be a rocket scientist to figure out the make of car that bird drives. We do not speak to each other with either civility or patience. If you don't agree, you are either condemning or you're condoning—either, or. No gray."

"Okay, okay, enough. Don't *you* start. We sent Charlie packing, and now you are about to push me down the slippery slope of metaphysical double-think."

"It's not metaphysics and it's not double-think. Try this. Linus Pauling, a Nobel Prize winner twice over, no mean feat by the way, publishes a paper extolling the use of megadoses of vitamin C to treat the symptoms of the common cold. People try it. It seems to work. Break-through medical intervention! A professor at the University of Maryland, School of Medicine mounts a controlled research study and finds that vitamin C in large doses has no effect greater than a placebo on cold symptoms. Who's correct?"

"Scientific method wins, I suppose."

"Do you take three or five thousand milligrams of C when you feel a cold coming on? Don't say no, because I know you do. Why?"

"Because it works. But it shouldn't."

"Consider the possibility that Pauling and Hornick, that was the professor's name, are both right, that the scientific method, as good as it is in sorting out all sorts of things, does not reveal all, that we do not have a single, certain path to truth, and that the psychiatric maxim that holding two opposing views simultaneously is a sign of madness is untenable, but rather a nod in the direction of acceptable uncertainty—paradox. We allow they both may be correct. End of rant."

"Michael Specter would say you have succumbed to 'denialism.'"

"So, another county heard from. As I said, end of rant."

"Thank God. You are beginning to sound too much like the head of our physics department and his discourse on quantum mechanics and Schrödinger's Cat. I am weary of intellectual gymnastics. Besides, Scott Fitzgerald, among others, said that to hold two…whatever you said…was a sign of genius, so there.

"I'm with F. Scott."

"You would be. Ivy Leaguers always stick together. Anyway, people don't like uncertainty, and analysis of that the sort can only cause major headaches for a world clamoring for absolutes. Besides, I'm tired and I want to go to bed."

"I thought you'd never ask."

"Whoa. I'm not sure that's such a good idea."

"You don't want to go to bed? We could watch television instead. The classic movie channel has *The Great Escape* on tonight."

"No television either. I have a busy day tomorrow, meetings starting at seven in the morning. That means I'm up no later than five-thirty."

"Gotcha. I will retire to my own quarters, watch James Garner, Richard Attenborough, and Steve McQueen tunnel out of the Nazi prison camp by myself. Perhaps I'll even go on the Internet and look up Schrödinger's cat"

"Give him my regards. Now, give Mommy a kiss and then shove off."

Essie wig-wagged to Ike as he pushed through the door. "You're late again, Boss. You weren't fooling around all night with Miz Harris, I hope. You need to be some discreet, you know."

"For your information, Mrs. Sutherlin, I was at home alone last night enjoying television and a cup of hot cocoa."

"Movie, maybe; cocoa, not."

"Either way, you can update the town gossips. I spent a chaste evening alone. What beside *tsouris* have you got for me today?"

"The D.C. Metro cops called about a cell phone that went missing that their techs have located somewhere around here. They want us to pick it up if we find it."

"They don't expect us to go looking, do they? We are not a big-city outfit and we are not deluged with the antics of gangbangers, bad guys, and politicians gone wild, but we still have a full plate."

"No, I don't think so. They thought, you know, if we ran across it and all."

"Did they give a name or specifics?"

"Nope, just a heads up."

"That's not much help. Okay, if anyone reports a lost cell phone or turns one in, you can let them know. In the meantime, give them a call back. We need a name at least. Where's Frank?"

"He went to interview a couple who were at the clinic place but had left and then were out of town. He thought they might have seen something. He'll be back in a bit. There's fresh coffee. I made it myself, and there's some pastry leftover from yesterday."

"Thanks, but no. I need to check the Picketsville grapevine for news. I'll be at the Crossroads for breakfast and my morning abuse by its proprietor. You can reach me there."

"Good luck with that."

Frank Sutherlin sat across from Brad and Jessica Phelps and waited. The two were painfully young and she obviously pregnant, a condition he guessed to have been the unanticipated outcome from a poorly executed honeymoon.

"So, what can you tell me about Friday night?"

She looked at her husband and started to speak but he held up his hand to silence her. "We won't get into any trouble will we? I mean, if the men we saw find out we identified them, they might come back for us."

Too much television, Frank thought. The cop's bane: *CSI.* "Why would you think that?"

"Like, if they were involved in a murder and they thought we might testify against them, they could try to silence us, or something."

Frank suppressed a sigh. "Well, in the first place, we don't know who or what happened. Secondly, many people were there that night and they certainly couldn't hurt them all, and finally, believe it or not, that isn't the way things happen, generally. Bad guys are arrested, tried, and put away. Period."

"Okay, but we want police protection if they are caught."

Frank tried not to roll his eyes. The next thing they'll probably ask is; do we want DNA samples?

"No problem, tell me what you do remember."

"Ask him about the DNA," Jessica said.

"Yeah, well, Okay…that night, Jess was having what she thought were labor pains so we went to the urgent care place only it was full of sick kids. The nurses and all they, like, blew us off. You know, Jess is in labor maybe, and this nurse person, or whatever, not a real doctor, for sure, asks, like, three questions and says, like, go home, you know?"

"I see, well they generally know what they're doing. Were you in labor?"

"No, it was gas." Jessica reddened at the memory. "But, hey, I mighta been."

"So you were saying?"

"Oh, yeah, so we were trying to figure out what to do, you know, like ask for a second opinion or something, when these two guys drag this other guy in and sit him down."

"Yeah, and they see us looking so they say, he's been drinking and maybe has a heart attack. Then we left."

"You didn't see if they went to the desk to sign him in?"

"No, we up and left. All those kids spitting up, it was making me nauseous, you know?"

"Do you think you could give me a description?

The two thought they could and between them managed to describe two men who could have been Al Pacino and Robert DeNiro.

Or not.

Chapter Twenty-two

The news at the Crossroads added little to Ike's information base. Most of the morning denizens wanted to know where and how all those kids got sick, how could they all come down sick all at once, and was there any truth to the rumor that the town's water supply had been tampered with. Buster Hawkins allowed as how he heard of something like that happening in Pennsylvania somewhere, too. Ike's statement that most of the kids were from families on private wells had no impact on their speculation about terrorist plots and the general decay of the American way. Nor did it change their opinion. He hadn't expected to learn much, but he knew that once in a while, somebody knew or heard something that was sufficiently eccentric to head him in a new direction. Not today. Still, breakfast never failed to cheer. He entered the outer office and confronted his staff of deputies.

"You are here, not out serving and protecting.

I must assume you have things to tell me. Otherwise, I want to know why you are, in fact, here not there." He jerked his thumb toward the door.

"I have a name," Essie said. "I called the D.C. cops and they told me. They said they were sorry I had to call back. Something about a new dispatcher. Don't that just bake your beans? Anytime somebody messes up a message they blame it on the dispatcher, right?"

"Essie, you can't know that for sure," her husband, Billy, said.

"Oh, I can. How many times you done that to me before we were married? And Ike here ain't above it either."

"Point taken, Essie," Ike said.

"I'm just saying."

"Okay. Got it. What name are you talking about?"

"The missing cell phone thing, that guy. Oh, that's the good part. It's that the one you all been trying to figure out who he is."

"What?"

"Zaki, Sacci, whoever. The D.C. cops called him Sacci, though. They said his fiancée reported him missing."

"Does she have a name?"

"Oh yeah. You ready for this? Lorraine Dakis."

"Louis Dakis' wife, or ex, or whatever?"

"They didn't say, but what's the likelihood it's a, you know, coincidence? I mean how many people called Dakis can there be in the world? And in the same area?"

"Dakis is a fairly common Greek name, Essie, like Zaki is a common Egyptian name. Admittedly, not one you hear around this neck of the woods." Ike started to pour a cup of coffee, caught a whiff of the too-long-on-the-burner aroma, and put the cup down. "But you are probably right. Frank, this is your baby; call the D.C. police and explain to them about the death here. They can notify the lady. They'll be happy to close a case. Then tomorrow, call her and ask her to come down and identify the body. She can make arrangements for the funeral or whatever. Billy, you set up a meeting with your Dakis for about the same time she gets here. I want to see the reaction when they meet."

"You don't think he shot Sacci/Zaki, do you? What are we going to call this guy?"

"Let's stay with Sacci. That's what he's known as in the States. If he has ID that will probably be the name—credit cards, the whole business. And, to answer your question, no, I don't think he killed our guy. Unless, of course, he's not telling us everything. He may have taken a shot at a retreating figure, maybe. The guy doesn't realize how badly he's hurt, gets his buddies to take him to the clinic and…So, if Dakis' had a gun and if it isn't registered, he may not have wanted to mention it."

"I checked it out, Ike," Frank said. "He has a Virginia concealed weapons permit. He applied for it when he ran an art store and was transporting expensive things around. It will expire in four years."

"Did you get the caliber of the piece?"

"He had several handguns, but yes, one of them was a small caliber pistol.' Frank flipped through the pages of his notebook. "A .25 caliber Beretta 21 Bobcat."

"That would do it. Do we have any ballistics back?"

"Nothing yet."

"Let's get on that. Anything else? So far, Essie, you win the donut."

"We have donuts?"

"Figure of speech. Where's Sam and Karl?"

"Um…" Essie gave him the look.

"Call them and say I want them, well, I want Sam anyway. Karl is on someone else's payroll. Tell her to come in this afternoon. I want to dig into some Internet sites, and she's the one to do it. Also, I need her to teach me about electronic encryption and so on."

"Does this have anything to do with the case? I guess it is one case now, right?" Billy said.

"Yeah, I'm afraid so. Unless this Lorraine

Dakis is no relation to Louis. The question Charlie Garland and I wrestled with over coffee last night was 'why?' Why use this old spycraft, microdots, to transfer information when the Internet is so easy and so available. Sam can help with that. Charlie will call when he gets his people to answer the same question."

"We gonna go after spies?" Essie asked.

"Not if I can help it. That's the Bureau's job, or Homeland Security, or some task force. All we're after is a murderer and a B and E perp. We get them and we're done. No spies, no international intrigue, no Robert Ludlum. Sorry. I want this business tied up in a neat bundle and all the spooks, spies, and miscellaneous Federal employees the hell out of here."

Billy looked disappointed.

Charlie Garland studied the papers on his desk. He had a permanent furrow between his eyes, a crease developed from twenty-five years of service in the CIA. He shuffled the papers back into their original order and tapped them into a neat stack. His name was not on the routing slip. It never would be. He was ostensibly assigned to the Public Relations Office and therefore had no need to see its contents. The fact that his office was in the basement, well away from the rest of the PR folks, was noted, but in an organization given to secrets and deception, never mentioned.

What possessed Tommy Wainwright to go to Rock Creek Park? According to the information in the report he'd been assigned to one of those interagency task forces that were supposed to facilitate communication and cooperation between the several intelligence services. That they rarely worked that way did not alter the practice. Usually, instead of linking Quantico and Langley, they merely created another element in the mix of nonaccountability. It was possible someone in the Hoover Building or out in the wilds of West Virginia knew the answer to the question, but he did not and he needed to. Tommy was one of ours and he went down. The director wanted to know why. Charlie leaned back in his old-fashioned swivel chair and contemplated the water stains on the acoustical tile in the ceiling. One looked like a silhouette of the President, big ears and all.

Something was not quite kosher here. The task force bit was a cover, he knew. Tommy was after someone inside. He flipped through the papers again. The routing slip. Could that be the missing piece. Who is on it that maybe shouldn't have been? Who held the papers for an unusually long time? Would the copy center know if duplicates had been made? He checked the time stamps and then sat upright and punched buttons on his phone. He waited and when connected asked the person on the other end of the line for the financials of the Mid-East section, Tony Fugarelli's bailiwick. The guy was close to retirement and he got a mention in the report. What was he up to? The best way to know a man's priorities was to look at his balance sheet, his assets to liabilities ratio. The notion that intelligence officers were turned because of political scruples, or moral convictions, was mostly a myth.

It was about the money. Always.

Chapter Twenty-three

Two D.C. Metro police stood shuffling their feet in front of the small counter area where customer orders were rung up, inquiries answered, and the day-to-day business of running a high-end boutique were managed. Lorraine Dakis stood frozen in place across from them. She'd received the news but had difficulty taking it in. It couldn't be true. Franco couldn't be dead. The police must have made a mistake. He went to New York, got delayed, that's all. He was never very good at phoning and… No, they had to be mistaken.

"Where did you say this happened?"

"Picketsville, Virginia." It sounded familiar but then she wasn't thinking straight at the moment. "An officer from the Picketsville," he consulted his notes, "Sheriff's office will be contacting you shortly to identify him."

"Picketsville? Where exactly is Picketsville?" She ought to know. Virginia wasn't that big, and she'd attended the College of William and Mary. Picketsville…?

"Shenandoah Valley, ma'am, near Lexington or Natural Bridge, I believe."

She'd been to Natural Bridge, but that was a long time ago. There used to be a big, old-fashioned hotel there, and the huge stone arch that carried Route 11 over it. And George Washington had scratched his initials in its face, near the base… was that right?

"Someone will contact me?"

"Yes, ma'am, Sorry for your loss."

The cops left, relieved to be finished with the one duty none of them liked. News of death was never easy. To compound that bad news with the possibility of a violent death, accident, murder, or tragedy of any stripe, made it doubly difficult. The bell over the door clanked as they filed out.

Elaine remained stock-still. Picketsville? Then it hit her, Louis said he was in that place. A school, or college, or something he'd said. She should have paid closer attention. Did Louis—could he have?

Louis Dakis' ears should have been burning. They weren't. He applied the last coat of Craquelure to one of the two varnished icons of the Virgin. When it dried it would craze. He could have brushed on egg whites to produce the same effect, but the commercial product was quicker and easier. When it dried and cracked, he would swab burnt umber across the surface, wipe away the excess and the paint caught in the crazing would age the icons a century or more. They would not exactly match the original. Those cracks had developed over many years and were deeper and clearly different than these produced artificially. But, either way, to the untrained eye, it would be close enough. He called the rector of the Episcopal Church and told him he would bring his icon around the next day. He was about to call the sheriff with the same news when the phone rang.

The sheriff's office was calling him. Nice. Yes, he could come in tomorrow or the next day in the afternoon. He said he'd probably drop the Sheriff's icon by tomorrow afternoon. Good. Job done.

He plugged in the hair dryer he kept on his work bench and began to sweep hot air across the icons' surface, hastening the drying process. Half an hour later he rubbed burnt umber in the new cracks, added a touch of earth red and wiped off the excess. He applied one last coat of varnish to each and put the two icons aside to dry while he made his lunch.

Louis moved to the back porch to eat. He twisted off the cap of his light beer and lowered himself to the stoop. As he ate his sandwich he wondered about Lorraine and her boyfriend, her boy toy. And he also thought about Annescott Jacobs and what she'd said. It wasn't fair of her to dump all the blame on him. How else were they ever going to break into the high-end art market unless he worked his butt off? A little gratitude would have been in order. Still, maybe she had a point. Did Lorraine think he didn't care about her? And a baby…now that wasn't going to work, surely she must have realized that. But she evidently didn't. Hormones did that to you, he'd heard. He wondered if Annescott had called Lorraine after all. If she had, what had Lorraine's reaction been? Two women boo-hooing over martinis, if he guessed right. That wasn't fair. Well, life isn't fair. Get used to it. Who should, Lorraine or him? Both. He shook his head to clear it and concentrated on the pastrami and pickle on rye. He wished there was a decent source of feta in town. It would have helped.

He heard the phone ringing inside, glanced at his watch, and decided to let it go to voice mail. If the call were important the phone would ring again.

Lorraine slammed the phone down and looked at her watch. Where was he? Eating lunch in some expensive restaurant, probably, while she had to run the shop with half her inventory gone, and the best half at that. She'd kill him. No, oh my God, no, a figure of speech, that's all. Did Franco go to Virginia to retrieve some of the icons and maybe the two fought and then Louis shot him? Louis had a gun; several, in fact. Where were they? She stamped her foot in frustration. And on top of everything else, she was late. Finally a chance to…but now, with Franco out of her life, what would it mean? What would she do with that? She suppressed an urge to flop down on the floor and cry. After years of deferring this and that, everything, she'd an opportunity for something and now it was gone. Ashes. Damn men, damn them all.

She wiped her eyes and looked at the slip of paper the cops had left. The phone number of the Picketsville sheriff's office was on it. What kind of town has a sheriff? The Shenandoah Valley sat smack in the middle of Virginia, not the Wild West. Sheriff Isaac Schwartz. Isaac Schwartz? A sheriff named Isaac Schwartz. This was getting weirder and weirder.

She hesitated, picked up the phone, put it down, then picked up again.

Charlie Garland paused outside Eastern Vision and checked the address. He had the place. Icons again. That had to be the connection. Ike's icon? Another?

He pushed in and waited for the woman behind the counter to replace her phone. She looked distraught, he thought. But then, she'd probably just found out about her friend's death.

"Yes," she said finally. "I was about to close. Is there something special you want?"

"Just some information."

She blew her nose in an already soggy tissue. "Are you the police? I just now spoke to two policemen. They told me about the murder."

"Ah," Charlie mulled over his options. "I won't be a minute. I wonder if you can recognize either of these two men?" He withdrew photographs from his pocket.

"Who are you again?"

"Sorry, I'm with..." Charlie had rehearsed his approach but he reconsidered. The police had already called. "FBI Special Investigative Branch, Art and Artifacts." He flashed his CIA ID quickly. She could see the USA and Official but that was about all. He laid the two photos on the counter and looked up at her. "A quick follow-up is all. Do you recognize either of these two men?"

She looked at the photos. Charlie waited. It would not do to force her into making a quick identification. He needed to be absolutely sure. And even then, it would still be a maybe. She pushed the pictures around with her index finger.

"Art and Artifact? Does this have anything to do with Franco's murder?" The last word came as more a sob.

"There is a report of an icon, very old and worth some money. We're interested, you see?" She didn't. "There have been some developments and, ah, we need to figure how they fit together before we can determine what happened to your friend." Stay vague. Don't spook her.

She pushed one of the photos toward him.

"This one came by a while back, I think, a week or ten days ago. I can't be a hundred percent sure. He wished to see an icon, as a matter of fact. We had the one he wanted in our inventory but not on the premises. But, well, I didn't pay that much attention to what he looked like. I could have used the sale. I told him where it was at the time but that I could get it for him in a few days. He said he'd be back, but he never came."

"I understand. But as far as you can be certain this man was here, and did ask to see a particular icon, not just some icons, but a particular one."

"Yes."

"Would it have been this one?" Charlie placed a photo of Ike's icon on the counter beside the two head shots.

"Oh, my God, yes. That's the one. Everybody wants that icon. I don't have it. My husband, my ex-husband that is, has it. I think Franco may have been looking for it. Is that why he was murdered?"

Charlie equivocated. He did not want to alarm her or set in motion another sequence of events that would produce more bodies. "I don't think so, no, but it is remotely possible it might have been, as I indicated, connected."

The woman's eyes glazed over. She apparently had slipped into information overload. Charlie picked up his pictures, excused himself, and left.

It was a start. Fugarelli.

Chapter Twenty-four

"Sam, what I want to know is why would anyone bother with a microdot when the Internet is available and, if I understand it correctly, one can send encrypted messages that are practically undecipherable?"

"Can't answer the first question, but you are right about the possibilities in the second. The levels of encryption are so sophisticated that if you use the technology you can send messages, and they would be nearly locked up tight."

"Just nearly?"

"Well, you remember the old GIGO formula, garbage in, garbage out? Well, technological advances are like that. Whatever one guy can dream up, eventually another will top. So, if some dude in Pakistan puts a message into heavy encryption, there's no assurance that some equally sharp guy at NSA won't be able to unravel it but, and this is the important part, the very fact it *is* in code is a tip-off that it's probably from someone we're interested in, the bad guys *du jour,* so to speak."

"But I thought they could route the messages through multiple servers or whatever they're called and you'd never know what or who sent it or from where."

"As I said, what one guy can come up with… Besides, like the encoding, the fact it's tied up in routing knots is a dead give away. The idea that you may or may never trace it to the source does not mean you can't go after the message. You follow? Police, fraud investigators, people like that, want to know where it's from and where it's going. NSA and the intelligence community want to know what it says. Different priorities."

Ike scratched his head. The world of satellite communication, electronic surveillance, and even the now ubiquitous Internet hovered outside his willingness to comprehend.

"Then, and more important," Sam continued, "you have the sender/receiver compatibility issues. For example, if I send a heavily encoded message to you, you would need the same computing power, software, and so on, to un-encode it. That unbreakable coding you've heard so much about requires capabilities so sophisticated that it isn't practical for a receiver, a terrorist on the move, say, to lug around."

"Okay. So, you're saying that fancy codes are

not all that practical for the average miscreant."

"More or less, yes. And even if we can't decipher it, we can always corrupt it."

"Say what?"

"We could intercept the message as it moves through cyberspace and re-code it in our unbreakable system. The baddies still get the message but now they can't unravel it. Neat, huh?"

"That still doesn't tell me why a microdot."

"As I said, I can't help you there, Ike. You'll need a bigger brain than mine to figure that one out. Maybe, it's about something that even if it's an out-of-date technique, is simpler, or easier to manage. Or, maybe it has to do with what's on it. You know, maybe they used old spycraft because it *was* old spycraft. Maybe plans or drawings left over from the sixties or something— a dam, a railroad terminal, floor plan of the capitol, who knows? Have you considered the possibility that the thing is left over from another day and has nothing to do with anything we're looking for, that the thing was happenstance and coincidental to the rest of the business? Do you know what was on the dot?"

"No clue. Charlie was supposed to call me. Apparently he's been side-tracked on another matter. I'll call him tomorrow, if I don't hear from him sooner. I doubt this is happenstance. The thing was what prompted the break-in."

"If you say so. Okay, you said you wanted me to poke around in some data bases. What were they and will I risk federal prison if I'm caught?"

"Ah, yes. As to that. You found Sacci in the FBI base. Try to find Zaki this time, but be careful. They'll be waiting for you. Then, if and when you finish that, hit the site Charlie gave you. By the way, do not be taken in by a phony willingness to accommodate. Unless I miss my guess, it is a back door the Agency keeps open for hackers, snoops, and other intelligence bodies trying to sneak in their backdoor. It'll be hard enough to get in, but you can bet your boots that all the data in there will be disinformation. You may have to search for another portal. Anyway, if you do find your way in, I want to know about one of their people named Thomas Wainwright. Find out what he was up to, if you can. Charlie hinted he might be in the picture here somehow. If you can get a photo or an image of him, that would be a big help, too."

"That's all? You're sure you don't want to know what Internet sites the President is logging on to, also?"

"I would, but we'll save that for one of those rainy days when nobody in our jurisdiction feels criminally inclined."

"Okay. But it would help if we knew what was on the microdot."

"I'll call. Be careful out there in cyberspace. Lots of weird people lurking there."

"I'm not sure I like being referred to as weird, Ike."

"I wasn't talking about you."

"Unfortunately, you were. All of us who live in the neighborhood have more in common that you might want to think. NSA geeks, FBI geeks, CIA geeks, evil geeks, and geeks like me. We love it."

Sam retreated to her office to plunge into the inky waters of electronic crime.

The phone rang. Essie wagged the receiver in Ike's general direction. "It's for you. It's Miz Harris. Hey, how you doing there, Miz…um, Doctor Harris. We celebrated your good news here yesterday. We're pumped. What? Okay, here he is… She says she's on another line. Ike, so she can't talk much and she's tickled pink."

Ike picked up. "Yes, ma'am, this is friendly Sheriff Schwartz here to serve. Do you have a problem that requires police presence, and when did you start saying things like *tickled pink*?"

"Since I met your loyal, but rural staff, Schwartz. When in Rome speak Latin, or in the case of fair Picketsville, speak redneck. Listen, I have another call on hold and I'm swamped. So we're off, if you catch my drift. I can't do anything more with you this week, sorry. However, there's a cocktail reception for retiring faculty Friday evening. I thought you could come to it, with me, and we could, you know…"

"Know? Know what?"

"Sheesh. I thought I'd sort of flash the rock around, answer the inevitable questions, and that would get the ball rolling on the, you know, the… you know."

"The word you're having such a hard time getting your tongue around is *engagement*. I doubt seriously that anyone on the faculty of yours has not already heard about it in grisly detail."

"I find *grisly* a bit over the top even for you, Bunky. And how would they?"

"Ingenuousness does not become you, ma'am—Agnes, of course."

"Oh, yeah. Agnes would have told at least—"

"Everyone who came into your office, the cafeteria, her canasta club, you name it."

"She doesn't play canasta."

"You're sure? She strikes me as a canasta person, Extreme Hand and Foot. Quilting bee, then. Has she been to quilt camp lately?"

"I don't know, probably; and don't call me ma'am. Makes me sound like dried-up old spinster schoolmarm."

"You are a schoolmarm, if you must know, but definitely not dried-up."

"Okay, enough. You come to the do, wear your dark suit, and get a haircut. You look like Cousin Itt with that mop in your eyes."

"Suit, haircut, shower, shave, a dab of Hugo Boss, the works. I'll even get the car washed. What time?"

"Seven-thirty. It should be over by nine and then we can take off for the A-frame."

"I like it. Not the suit and cocktail part, but the get-away to the A-frame."

"Okay, and this time try to play nice with the faculty. They have fragile egos and succumb to a bad case of the heebie-jeebies when you insist on destroying their carefully constructed preconceptions."

"I'll be good. I'll only beat up the bullies and leave the junior faculty alone."

"Thank you, I think. Seven-thirty, Friday, haircut, suit, bye."

Chapter Twenty-five

Ike parked in Lee Henry's driveway. He'd discovered her in his first year as sheriff. Besides giving the best haircut in the area, she remained a fount of gossip, news, and stories. He depended on her to keep him both groomed and informed. A new, hand-lettered sign hung on the door that led to the part of her house she'd set aside for her salon business.

"What's up with 'Moving to a New Location,' Lee?"

"Well, ain't you the observant one. You like my sign?"

"I don't know. It depends on where you're planning on relocating. If it's out of the area, I may have to hold you on some charge. Don't plan on losing you."

"What charge would that be? And would it involve a strip search? I might give you a discount for that."

"Promises, promises. Where're you going? We'll settle on searches later, but a word of warning, new state law says I have to have a person of the same sex do the search, so unless you're holding out on me, someone else would be doing it."

"Shoot, that wouldn't be no fun. Sit down and let me see what you've done to your head since the last time you come in."

Ike eased into the chair. The place reeked of wet hair, an odor not quite masked by the combined over-scents of hair spray, shampoo, and something chemical that Ike assumed had to do with perms, or coloring, or both. He knew better than to ask.

"You still haven't told me where you're going. Do I need to worry?"

"Lord, no. I'm moving up, not out. See with the economy in the dumpster, I figure it's time to take advantage of cheap real estate, and people needing some help."

"Okay. So, what does that have to do with relocating? You buying a new house from a desperate real estate agent?"

"No, nothing like that. See, there's a storefront on Main Street that's empty. It used to be a coffee shop. Before that, it was a craft store, and before that, it was a pretzel and cookie store. You know which one I mean?"

"Yes. It's down the street from the office. You moving there?"

"I'm buying it. There's an apartment over it where I can live. I'll sell this house when the market's right, rent it 'til then. My kids is all grown and gone. I'm single, more or less, and I need to move on, you know?"

"But a salon? You said it, the economy is flat. How are you going to make it work?"

"That's the good part. See, there's a bunch of women in the area that, like, is needing extra money. They're hairdressers and all and some of them work, like me, out of their houses, and some ain't worked for a while but need the extra money now. I'll fix up the store with maybe five chairs, like this one you're sitting in, and rent 'em to them gals. They don't have to, you know, work in their house, lay out a bunch of money they ain't got to start up, and can maybe get some walk-in business on top, and all like that. It's a win-win."

"Well, it'll make my trips to get a haircut easier."

"I ain't cutting your hair, handsome, I'm styling it. There's a difference."

"I'm a guy, Lee. For men that's a difference without a distinction."

"If you say so. Just don't let your Honey hear you say that. Say, I hear you and the beautiful lady president has got yourself engaged."

"We have."

"All the single ladies for miles around just went into mourning, Ike. You done broke a lot of hearts."

Ike exhaled. He daren't shake his head. Lee's scissors could be lethal. She rubbed his shoulders and slipped the black plastic sheet on his lap and around his neck. "Hey, your muscles feel like rocks, Ike. You under a bunch of stress?"

"I'm a cop. Of course I'm stressed."

"Listen, I'm going to have me a massage person in the new place. You know, therapeutic, Swedish, and like that. No hanky-panky though, no 'happy endings.' You should sign up for one. It'd do you some good."

"I'll think about it. Who's the masseuse? Do I know her?"

"What makes you think it's a her?"

"I can't see you working with a man under foot. That's why."

"Well, you got that part right. You know Georgie Tice's wife?"

"Marge? She's the masseuse?"

"Yep. Her kids is all pretty much grown up, too, and she's at loose ends. And I'm thinking things ain't too smooth at Georgie's bank either, so she got herself certified and licensed."

"Marge Tice. Well, well, I may have to take you up on one if only to see Marge again."

"You do that."

Blake Fisher walked in and took a seat in one of two plastic chairs.

"Afternoon, Rev. How're you and your new missus gettin' on?"

"Can't complain, Ms. Henry, yourself?"

"Just dandy. No prospect of any little Revs any time soon?"

Blake flushed and reached for a year-old magazine.

"Okay, so did you-all hear about the old guy who goes to the doctor and is told he's got twenty-four hours to live?"

"Nope. Is this a true story?"

"'Course it is. Only kind I tell. Only I have to clean it up a bit for the Rev."

"No need," Blake said.

"Yeah, well, I ain't used to talking a certain way in front of preachers. So that's it. Okay, so this old guy, his name is Irving, goes to the doctor and the doctor says, 'Irving, you got twenty-four hours to live.' So, Irving comes home from the doctor and tells his wife what the doctor has told him, that he has only twenty-four hours to live. On account of this, he asks his wife for, you know…"

"Sex? I'm not going to be embarrassed by this, am I?"

"Shoot, that'll be the day. Cover your ears, Rev." Blake only grinned. "Yes, sex. So, naturally, she agrees and they make love. About six hours later, he goes to his wife and says, 'Honey, you know I have only eighteen hours to live now. Could we please do it one more time?' Well, she says, 'okay,' and they do it again. Then later on, when they go to bed, he looks at his watch and realizes that he now has only eight hours left. He touches his wife's shoulder and asks, 'Honey, please…one more time before I die.' She says, 'Of course, dear,' and they make love for the third time. After this, see, the wife falls asleep.

"But old Irving is thinking about how his time on earth is running out on him and he tosses and turns, until he's down to, like, four hours. Then he wakes up the wife. 'Honey, I have only four more hours. Do you think we could…?' So, the wife sits up and says, 'Listen Irving, I have to get up in the morning, you don't.'"

Ike and Blake laughed with Lee, who clearly enjoyed the story more than they did.

"Speaking of dead guys, what do you hear about the one we got from the urgent care center?"

"I cut the hair of Jessica Phelps. You could say she is up-tight about what she and her husband saw that night. Says she's afraid the killers will come and get her. She's thinking of asking to be put in the witness protection program."

"That's idiotic. She watches too much

television. As near as we can determine, she couldn't identify them if they lived next door to her."

"Yeah. Well, here's a tip. You might want to pull her in again. She didn't tell you everything."

"You think?"

"I know. She told me that she and her husband might have got part of a license number."

"Thanks. Anything else?"

"Nope, sorry."

Blake looked up from his magazine. "Well, if you believe anything Buster Hawkins says—"

Lee interrupted "Which I don't. He's about the biggest liar in the county, except for my ex, of course."

"Yes. Well, he told Mrs. Craddock, that'd be the younger one that lives out on the highway, that he was sitting on the stoop of his house smoking. His wife doesn't let him light up in the house apparently, and he said he heard a shot in the motel next door to him."

Ike sat up. "That would be the Dogwood Motel?"

"That's the one. And he had the day right, too, but you know how he likes attention."

"Maybe. But it's worth a look. Thanks. So, when do you move, Lee?"

"Maybe next week, week after that. Depends on how quick I can get all the stuff together and the remodeling finished."

Chapter Twenty-six

The Dogwood Motel sat back from the road surrounded, not surprisingly, by dogwoods. Constructed in the late sixties, it had been built adjacent to the then newly constructed Picketsville by-pass, a road which rerouted the traffic on Route 11 away from the downtown area. At the time, the project met with stiff resistance from the town's chamber of commerce but was supported by the police, the college, and the local school district. In the years that followed, I-81, built a mile east of Picketsville, took most of the through traffic away from the by-pass and the motel fell into general decline. It had begun its life as part of the Holiday Inn chain. It then shifted from one franchise to another as it aged and decayed. Finally a local businessman bought it, remodeled it, and turned it over to his wife to run. He called it her hobby job, something to keep "the little woman" busy and out of his affairs. Unfortunately, at least one of his "affairs" became public and the subsequent divorce settlement specified she receive the house, the motel, and enough cash in lieu of alimony to secure her future for the rest of her life. She moved to Hilton Head and left the motel in the uncertain hands of her prematurely pregnant daughter and reluctant son-in-law.

Dogwoods are known for their lovely blooms in the spring, but not for seeds. The Dogwood Motel, never-the-less, had become a very seedy establishment. A cow bell had been attached to the office door frame and it clanked a welcome of sorts as Ike stepped in. The aforementioned son-in-law, Harvey Bristol, slouched behind a cluttered counter which held a registration pad, a stack of men's magazines, two empty beer bottles, and an overflowing, but still smoldering, ashtray.

"Afternoon, Harvey."

"Sheriff?" Harvey seemed disconcerted by the sudden presence of the police. "Trouble?"

"No, Harvey, only a question or two if you don't mind. I'm interested in some guests you may have had this past weekend, Friday and maybe Saturday."

"Well," Harvey shuffled papers around on his counter. His eyes never quite met Ike's gaze. "Anybody in particular?"

Ike slid a picture of Sacci across the counter's gritty surface. "Him for one." Harvey tugged at his collar and swallowed. "The reason I ask, is one of your neighbors reported hearing a possible gun shot on Friday night coming from this motel."

"That would be Buster Hawkins, I expect. Buster hears all kinds of things. And he talks too much."

"The picture, Harvey. Do you recognize the man?"

Harvey held the picture to eye level and squinted. "Could be. I think his name was Italian or something; foreign, anyway. I need to check my cards." He lifted a battered box to the counter top and pulled out a stack of creased registration slips. He sorted through them and replaced all but two. "Friday was slow. We only rented two rooms and, looka here, this one says Sacci, Franco Sacci, like I said, Italian."

"Who else stopped that night?"

"Okay, now I remember. Like, it was slow. I told you that already, right? Okay, so two cars pulled in. Three guys in one, one guy alone, but they was together, you know?"

"They were traveling together?"

"Like as. And they took two rooms. See, here's the other room. The guy who signed for it was somebody named Avriam Kolb. What kind of a name is that?" Anyway, the rooms both had twin beds so two guys went into each, right?"

"Did you hear a shot?"

Harvey's line of sight shifted into the distance. He wiped his nose with a dirty handkerchief. "Hear all kinds of things around here. Don't usually pay them no mind. Ain't none of my business what people do."

"It is if what they do can cause trouble with the law. Can I see the rooms these four men used?" Harvey hesitated and looked uncomfortable. "I could get a warrant, but I'd rather not disturb the judge. You know how testy he can be. He doesn't need to hear about another problem at your motel, does he, Harvey?"

"Um, no I guess not. I gotta warn you, though, things been pretty slow, like I said, and I had to back down on the cleaners and all."

"What you're saying is, the rooms haven't been cleaned since Saturday?"

"Things have been—"

"Slow. So you've said— repeatedly. Take me to the rooms."

Harvey ushered Ike along the cracked sidewalk to rooms at the far end of the line. Ike noticed the chipped and weathered paint on the stucco's surface, the weeds pushing up through the fissures in the concrete sidewalk, and the odors, mildew mixed with garbage and petroleum rising from the numerous oil stains on the parking lot's gravel surface. Harvey unlocked the two adjoining rooms and started to shuffle away.

"Not so fast, Harvey, I'm not done with you."

"Look, you can see the rooms. Okay, I ain't cleaned them. I told you business was slow and I had to lay off some of the cleaners."

Slow didn't come close to describing Harvey's business. Dead would be better. The rooms were stuffy and reeked of dead air and the aforementioned mildew.

"Which room is this one?"

Harvey consulted his cards. "This is the one with the Kolb guy and one other man."

"What's the other man's name?"

"Brown, but that can't be right. He didn't look like no Brown I ever seen."

"Exactly what do Browns look like?"

"I don't know, but this guy looked like he came from Iraq or one of them places. Say, do you think he was a terrorist? Maybe there's a reward."

"Don't hold your breath. So, Kolb and Brown were in this one. That means Sacci and…who, were in the one next door."

"Right. He said his name was Paul Wentz, but I don't think he was a—"

"A Wentz? Because he didn't look like any Wentz you'd ever seen?"

"Exactly. He coulda' been another one of

them. Is that why you're here? Are there terrorists loose around here? Buster Hawkins said they were talking about that up at the diner, how they can get at the water supply and bring down the whole town. I didn't pay him no mind at the time. You know Buster, but holy cow. I guess we got ourselves a problem after all."

"No terrorists, Harvey, four guys, probably bad guys. One of them managed to get himself killed by one of the others and therefore, you have a crime scene, not an international plot. I'm taping off these two rooms and calling it in. Evidence Technicians will be here soon. You leave them and these two rooms alone 'til you hear from me. You got it?"

"You mean CSI will be here? Wait 'til I tell Dottie. She'll be stoked."

"You call no one except me, you got it?" Harvey nodded his agreement but the idea of making a picnic out of this new-found notoriety lurked in his eyes. "I mean it, Harvey, you don't want me talking to the judge about another problem in your motel, right?"

Harvey grunted his acceptance and wandered back to his office, ash tray, and magazines.

Ike stepped carefully into the rooms, careful to touch nothing. In the second room there were stains on the shabby carpet that could be blood. He thought he smelled the residue of cordite, impossible after a week, of course. He spun three hundred and sixty degrees memorizing the room and its contents. The beds were unmade, the bathrooms cluttered with towels thrown on the floor, that is, except in the second room, the one with the stains. There were no towels in it at all. Ike shut the doors of both rooms and walked back to the office.

Harvey had resumed his place behind the counter, a fresh bottle on it, and a new cigarette dangled from his lips. He swiveled around.

"Now what?"

"Your trash, Harvey. I see you have a dumpster out back. When was the last time you had a pick-up?"

Harvey looked confused, fiddled with his cigarette, and tapped ashes in the general direction of the tray. He missed. "I don't use that service no more. Times are hard. I generally let her fill and then I get one of the locals with a pickup to empty it and haul it to the county landfill."

"Am I correct in assuming you haven't emptied that thing since sometime last week?"

"Well, yeah, I guess. See—"

"Things have been slow, I know. Good. Leave it alone as well. Until we can check out where all your towels went, it's part of the crime scene as well."

"Towels? What towels? Someone stole my

towels? Damn, I'm sending them a bill. I got their credit card number right here and—"

"You have a what? You have a credit card number? I'll need that, too, and thank you Harvey, you just made my day."

Some law enforcement units were blessed with the latest in hi-tech equipment, elaborate computer links to national and international agencies, and personnel. Other, smaller and more poorly endowed departments, require outside help, even Providential.

This day Picketsville, that is to say, Ike, was plain blessed.

Chapter Twenty-seven

Charlie called as Ike walked in the door. Essie handed him a stack of pink call-back slips, and Sam started talking to him, fourteen to the dozen.

"Whoa. Stop, give me a break. I'll take those slips, Essie. You sure you edited out the crap?" She nodded. "And Sam, I need to talk to our friend in the Puzzle Palace first. Then you and I can chat. Where's Karl, by the way?"

"He's been called back to D.C. He couldn't convince them he needed time here. Anyway, this is about the…what did you call them?"

"Never mind. Sorry about Karl, but Charlie first." He waved her into a chair and picked up the phone.

"Okay, Charlie, you have my complete attention. What can you tell me?"

"Remember I said I thought the microdot was bigger than normal, if there is a normal for this stuff."

"Yes, and I said it might have been an extremely old one."

"You did, and you were wrong. So was I."

"A rare confession from you, Charlie."

"Don't start. This is serious."

"Okay, sorry. Go on."

"I was wrong because I said it was a microdot. It isn't. It looks like one but it's something dicier."

"Are you going to tell me? Better yet, do I want to know?"

"You might want to know, but I can't say anything now. Here's the immediate problem. It's a micro chip, a piece of miniature electronic business, not micro-photography, that's been embedded in a small disc. That's why we mislabeled it. It's a look-alike."

"Not a microdot."

"No, and because of that, you can't use the bogus ones I brought you earlier. If the guys looking for this stuff are even slightly sophisticated, they'll know right away they've been had. I can fix you up with a better substitute but it will take some time. We have to find a similar chip and write to it. The properties people may have what we need. They may not. The techs here say this one is Chinese and different. How different, I can't say or even if the people who're after it will know either. Can you buy me a day?"

Ike scratched his head. "I can. I'll put a car outside Dakis' house twenty-four-seven. That will hold them off for a while. I'll let it out that we're closing the investigation tomorrow and that should bring them back into play right after that—that is if they're still local and listening."

"Good. We'll ship you a dummy chip by helicopter ASAP."

"I'm impressed. This must be pretty hot for the agency to pony up for a chopper."

"It is. Okay, I need to talk to Sam, your hacker and—"

"She's right here. I'll put you on speaker phone. Okay, go."

"Ah, Ms. Ryder, you are to be congratulated. The security boys in the basement said you got into the back door faster than anyone, set a possible record, in fact. The gang in the anti-hacking division put your name up on their bulletin board. Not everyone gets that sort of recognition."

"You knew I hacked in?" Sam looked chagrined.

"Oh, yes, but don't let that get you down, They were impressed at the way you worked and, in fact, it was all they could do to keep you from breaking in deeper. You know we have the 'hacker room' for people like you and not nice people who want to steal our stuff. Most are satisfied to take what we give them. It's very useful for us that way and we get to meet some interesting people. Except in rare cases, yours being one, hardly anyone attempts to go farther."

"I thought I did, go in farther, I mean."

"Did you, indeed? Why do you say that?"

"Well, Ike asked me to poke around and dig up anything you might have on Sacci/Zaki, and some other things." Sam squinted her eyes at Ike, seeking advice as to how much she should tell Charlie. He nodded. "So I went into your personnel files looking for Thomas Wainwright."

"You didn't."

"Yes, sir, I did. Got him, too."

Charlie fell silent. Ike thought he heard paper being shuffled in the background.

"I'm listening," he said finally.

"I managed to find his personnel file, I think. It had a number but I don't remember that part. I read it, took some notes and—"

"You didn't download it, I hope."

"No, sir, I didn't, but I could have. I did retrieve a picture of him though."

"That's it?"

Sam thought, scrunched up her face, an expression Ike recognized as her "liar's face" and said, "Yep, that's it."

"Okay, good. Don't go there again, you hear?

It could be dangerous for you and…you listening, Ike? You keep her out of our files. I mean it."

"I hear you, Charlie. Now, what are you not telling me?"

"You have everything I can share at the moment."

Ike stared at the phone and scowled. It was not like Charlie to be circumspect. Something was up. Maybe Sam knew.

"Okay, we're done here. Hurry that chip along, will you? I want to close this thing and get back to the real business of sheriffing."

"Breaking up teenage keggers in the woods?"

"That and setting up speed traps. The town needs budgetary relief, and I need to make some new friends. Goodbye, Charlie."

Ike hung up and swiveled to face Sam. "All right, Sam, what didn't you tell Charlie and what didn't he tell me?"

"Well," Sam rifled through a sheaf of papers she held in her hand, "I have his picture."

"So you said."

"And, this is the screwy part. Didn't you say Wainwright was tasked to Homeland Security?"

"That's what Charlie said, yes."

"Not so. It didn't make any sense at first, his assignment, that is. It was, like, in code. So I searched around…remember, I didn't dare stay too long, and I found a key, a coding key, you know what the numbers stood for. I could see, for example he'd been assigned to the Near East in the past, Egypt, and so on. The last assignment code meant Mossad. Does that make any sense to you?"

"It might and it might not. I'll have to think about that for a while. I have a simpler, safer task for you to do. I have some credit card numbers. See if you can find out to whom they belong and anything else you can turn up. And, whatever you do, don't mess with the CIA's database. At least not for a while."

"Right. I'm on it."

Sam scurried from the room. Ike studied the picture of Tommy Wainwright. "I wonder," he said and placed the picture next to Franco Sacci's. "Do you two know each other?"

Chapter Twenty-eight

Charlie Garland dropped the phone into its cradle and tapped his foot on the side of his desk. The varnish had been worn away from the spot from years of similar tapping, and there was a notice-able dent in the desk's surface where a portion of the institutional desk's oak veneer had been worn away. He reviewed what Ike and Sam Ryder told him. He'd heard the small, very small, quaver in her voice when she denied knowing anything more. She was lying. What had she found? Ike had good people. And loyal as well. She'd tell Ike and Ike, in turn, would tell him. Maybe. He might hold out for a favor. What to do?

He could tell the Director. And as much as the Director admired Ike, he wouldn't hesitate to send a squad of interrogators down to Picketsville and extract Ryder. Then, Ike would go off like a new bomb and there'd be hell to pay. He'd need a better strategy. A clerk knocked and entered to drop off a file he'd asked for. Wainwright's as it happened. The clerk seemed very young to work here, he thought, and she left a scent behind. Lilac, but not the lilac his maiden aunt used to wear. It reminded him of Francine…that was long time ago. Can't go there, need to focus. He picked up the phone again this time to call his contact at the NSA. Alternatives. Life was about the correct selection of alternatives.

He liked that. He would write it down.

Life is about the correct selection of alternatives.

Ike set up twenty-four-seven surveillance on Louis Dakis' house, making it clear that the cruiser should be parked out front and in plain sight. Then he called Frank and told him about the license plate number that the Phelpses might have for him. He asked him to call on them, get the number, and trace it if possible.

If Sam was able to put a name to the credit cards, and Frank to the plate, with any luck he'd have a name or names soon. Names and a direction to go.

His next call was to an old contact in the Mossad. He didn't know if the contact was any good any more, and even if it were whether Shmuel would or could answer his questions. Worth a try. If Wainwright wandered into their territory, Shmuel's friends would know. An answering machine took the call. He expected that. The time difference would have his old friend at home and asleep. That is, if Shmuel ever slept. Ike had his doubts. He hesitated a moment and finally asked Shmuel to call him back and left a cell phone number. He scooped up the two pictures and headed back to the Dogwood Motel. Things were beginning to get interesting.

Harvey was in exactly the same place he'd left him two hours earlier. Only the pile of ashes in the ashtray was deeper and three more empties cluttered the counter. Ike noted the evidence techs had arrived and were busy in the two rooms at the far end of the motel. He would check with them later.

"Harvey, I have another picture for you to eyeball." He slid the photo of Wainwright across the counter.

"That's him. That's the guy with the funny name, you know—wait a minute, I'll get it."

"Kolb, you said."

"Yes, Kolb, that's the guy. Tough sumavagun. At least that's what I thought. You know he had them hard flinty eyes like you see on the bad guys on the TV. Not much of a picture, though."

"Thanks, Harvey. You've been most helpful."

"When are those people going to be done with my rooms? I gotta business to run here."

"Harvey, those rooms stood empty and not cleaned for nearly a week. What are the chances you're going to need them anytime soon."

"Shoot, you never know. A bus could pull in here any minute and then where'd I be?"

"Again, what are the chances? You want busses to stop. See if you can persuade the AAA to star your motel. Before you do that, you might want to fix up this place first. God only knows what the Health Department would say about your plumbing. In the meantime, relax. They'll be done when they're done. If I'm right, you have a murder scene here, Harvey, so get used to the inconvenience."

Ike phoned Sam. "Sam, another thing, did you happen to pull our friend's fingerprints when you were snooping?"

"I wasn't snooping, I was following orders."

Ike chuckled. "You're a quick study, Sam. You stick with that when the goon squad from the CIA arrives, if it does. But you haven't answered my question."

"Am I in trouble if I did?"

"Not with me, but maybe with the Agency. Did you?"

"Get a set of prints? Um…well, I did. I don't know why but with everything all mixed up around the shooting and the breaking and entering, well, I guess I thought why not."

"You've got good instincts, Sam. I'm going to miss you."

"Miss me? You know something I don't?"

"No, but Karl and you can't keep going on this way forever. One of you will have to bolt and I'm guessing it'll be you."

"I love my job."

"I know. And you're good at it, but…listen, put the fingerprints in a folder and bury them where nobody will think to look."

"You think someone will come after them?"

"Maybe. Then, tell you what, you have files and whatnot downloaded on your hard drive, right? Leave it there. If they know you have the file they'll want it. It would be best to let them find it, but first, make a copy on one of those stick whatchacallems and hide that."

"USB Flash drive."

"That's the thing. And stay way away from the CIA."

"You already told me that."

"This time it's for emphasis." He hung up and sauntered down the row of rooms to the crime scene tape. He nodded at the lead tech and waved to Henry Sutherlin, who had an internship with them before entering the academy and ET school.

"What have you found for me?" he asked.

"Well, you called it, Sheriff. We have blood

trace in one room. Not much, but enough to sample and type. It appears that an attempt was made to clean it up, but either they were in a hurry, were careless, or plain didn't give a hoot. It's still early. If this room was ever cleaned, it sure wasn't lately, so fingerprints are all over it, dozens, some of them too old to lift. Is this a murder room?"

"It is."

"Yeah, so the other room wasn't wiped down either and we have a lot of prints in there, as well, maybe too many. We'll process them and shoot over what we find."

"I have some prints I'd like you to match if you can, the victim and one other set."

"Sure send them over. We'll have a look-see."

"How about the dumpster?"

"Godawful mess. Found some towels and a torn shirt. Let you know about them, too."

Ike watched for a few more minutes and then headed back to his office. He should have some new information by now.

Sam watched as her computer screen flashed. Files appeared and disappeared. Its cursor swept back and forth busily opening and closing files. It would have been a normal afternoon except her hands were not touching the key board. She had a hacker.

The tables had been turned and she was the hackee. Cool. She pushed the on-off switch repeatedly but the intruder somehow overrode it and kept searching. Finally, whoever was at the other end of this operation found what it/he/she was looking for— the data she'd gleaned from the CIA—and opened it. There was a brief pause and then, in less than a second, the file was deleted. It continued to search then paused again, and inspected the computer's logger, the record of her most recent actions. Sam held her breath. It passed on, sampled her back-up files and then the screen went blank and the machine shut down with a whir and a click.

"Wow," she muttered. "Those guys are good." She clutched the flash drive in her hand. "But you have to get up early in the morning to nail this nerd."

Before she'd copied the files, she'd disabled the logger. She'd copied the data to a flash drive, then shut down and rebooted and enabled the logger again. Its record would be seamless if anyone were to look. Apparently, someone had.

The car had been parked a block farther down the street from Dakis' house. Amos had noticed it, jotted down its license number, and put it in his report. It would only be important if he could make a connection between it and Dakis. He couldn't. At least not until it pulled away from the curb and followed Dakis when he left the house in the afternoon. Amos left a message for Ike with Essie.

Chapter Twenty-nine

Louis Dakis arrived at the sheriff's office after three. He'd made a stop beforehand at the church, and delivered the first of his two newly created icons to the Reverend Fisher. The clergyman seemed very pleased with it, his wife, less so. She mentioned, by way of explanation, that she was raised a Methodist. He supposed that meant something to her. Not to him, however. He waited until the icon had been installed temporarily on a stand on the left-hand side of the church, the Gospel side, the Reverend Fisher had insisted, and left. He did not notice the car that had followed him to the church and then to the sheriff's office. Even if he had been suspicious, the fact that the car continued south on Main Street when he turned into the town parking lot would have allayed any thoughts he might have had about it.

What he did notice was a familiar looking Volvo pulled up to the side when he'd turned in, but its full significance wasn't apparent until he walked in the door. Lorraine glared at him as he entered.

"You bastard, you killed him." Lorraine Dakis launched herself from her chair and charged across the room, hands high and, he supposed, nails at the ready to claw out his eyes.

"Killed who? What are you talking about?"

"Don't play stupid with me. Franco came here to retrieve the Virgin of Tenderness that I bought in Egypt and you…what? You argued and you killed him. Sheriff, this man killed Franco Sacci. Arrest him."

"I might do that," Ike said, "But not right now. There are some things that need clearing up first."

"Like what?"

"Well, like how he managed to put Sacci's body in the urgent care waiting room without anyone seeing him. Like how he managed to do that in the presence of two or three other men at the Dogwood Motel. There are a few other problems with this, but you get the picture."

Dakis had listened to Lorraine and then Ike. "Will someone please tell me what's going on? Franco Sacci is dead?"

"What other men?" Lorraine said. "He had help?"

"I don't think so," Ike waved Frank Sutherlin and the two of them into his office. "You two take a seat and we'll sort this business out eventually. Frank, do you have some names for me?"

Frank deposited a slip of paper on Ike's desk and positioned himself in the corner where he could monitor the two Dakises.

"Now, Mrs. Dakis, why would your husband want to kill Sacci?

"Estranged...not husband anymore."

"Sorry to hear that. Estranged husband, then, Why would he want to do in Franco Sacci?"

"Isn't that obvious? We were getting a divorce. Louis didn't like that. He was jealous. He was trying to ruin my business. He was—"

"Our business, Lorraine. No matter what was going on between us, between you and the creep, it was and for the time being remains *our* business."

"We, Franco and I, planned to buy you out."

"And I told you my half wasn't for sale even if you could raise the purchase price, which you can't." Louis Dakis leaned forward and addressed Ike. "You see how it is. She will accuse me of anything. This Sacci guy was like having termites in the basement. Left alone, the whole business would have collapsed. I didn't want that. There's a right way and a wrong way to take a business down. They," he jerked his head in Lorraine's direction, "would have ruined it."

"We would not. You see, Sheriff, he's insanely

jealous. For years I'm like a doormat and then, when I do something about me, he goes nuts. Besides, who else could have any reason to kill Franco?"

Ike picked up the paper Frank had placed on his desk and studied it. Lorraine Dakis opened her mouth to speak again but Ike silenced her with a raised hand. He reached for his telephone, grumbled something about buttons, selected and punched one of them on the phone's base and picked up.

"Sam, what did you get on the credit cards?" He listened and then made a check mark on the same piece of paper. "Thanks. If he hasn't left yet, why don't you slip home and say goodbye to Karl." He turned his attention back to the couple.

"To answer your question, Mrs. Dakis, the list of possible killers is as follows: Avriam Kolb; two other men, to wit, Sandor Brown and Paul Wentz; and a possible third who calls himself Bob Smith. I wouldn't hold out much hope on the last one. It's a phony and belongs to either Brown or Wentz, or to yet another party we don't know about who could be complicit but not present."

Lorraine Dakis sat with her mouth open. Then, something approaching comprehension crossed her face. She wheeled on her husband. "You hired thugs to kill Franco. You couldn't do it yourself and so—"

Ike held up his hand. "Not likely, Mrs. Dakis.

Possible, but not likely. There are things at play here we do not yet understand, but I think for the nonce your husband, irrespective of how he might have felt about Sacci and how much you might wish it to be so, did not have anything to do with his death. We might have to revisit that later, Mr. Dakis, but for now I think you are in the clear. I want some information about your gun collection and may want to see it in the future. Now, what can you both tell me about this icon?" Ike held up The Virgin of Tenderness.

The two of them began to speak at once. Louis Dakis cut his wife a look. Thin-lipped, she nodded to Dakis.

"We were lucky with that one. I had a contact in Cairo who heard it was coming on the market and e-mailed me the catalog from the sale. Lorraine was in Rome at the time, and she hopped on a plane, flew over to Egypt, and scooped it up before the catalog was widely circulated. It was a coup, I can tell you."

"Did you have a buyer or one in mind?"

"No, but an icon of this quality will sell quickly. There's no doubt about it."

"I've had several inquiries in the last week," she said, and scowled at her husband. "I could have sold it a couple of times over, except he," she pointed at Louis, "took it with him when he ran off to this jerkwater town."

"We think it's a very nice town. The only real problem we seem to have here has to do with strangers coming in and getting themselves murdered. It could be worse. We could be losing locals, but so far we've been lucky that way. Tell me, do you have any idea why someone would want to steal it, Mrs. Dakis?"

"It's very valuable. Why wouldn't they?"

"So how does Sacci fit into the picture?"

Louis hung his head and glowered at his wife. "Sometime before she was due to return to the states, that guy showed up and..."

"We weren't getting along all that well, Louis and I," she said, "he was always working or at the shop doing this and that. We never...Well, you don't need to hear all this, but then Franco showed up and I don't know, I...I don't know..."

"Swept you off your feet?"

"It's a terrible cliché, but, yes, maybe you could say that."

"How well did you know him before you were 'swept,' would you say?"

"Not very, but, well you know about those things instinctively, don't you? I mean things clicked, and, you know how those things happen."

"It's possible. You vouched for him to obtain a visa, is that right?"

"Yes. What has this to do with his murder?

Since you insist that he," she wagged her finger at her husband again, "didn't have anything to do with it, have you made any progress? I mean who else would want to?"

"Well, we're not sure about that yet, but we have some ideas. But back to Franco Sacci. Were you aware his real name was Farouk Zaki?"

"What? No. That's not possible. I saw his passport. I had to if I wanted to obtain the visa. His name was Franco Sacci. He's Italian, born in Milan and—"

"His name was Farouk Zaki. He was born in a small village in the Sinai near Gaza. His father was killed in the Six Days War and he has been connected to groups that are suspected of or associated with international terrorism. He was on the Homeland Security watch list. Your sponsorship provided the only way he was ever going to enter the country."

"No!"

"Sorry, but yes. Now I have to ask you again, how well did you know this man? Were you in on his plan to slip into the country and if so, why?"

"In on, I don't…You're saying I was used? I don't believe you. This is a mistake. His plan to slip into the country? What does that mean?"

"Mrs. Dakis, I know all of this is upsetting but this is important. Did you two enter the country, the US, together?"

"No. He had some mix-up with his visa or something. He flew in a week after I did."

"But you brought in the icon, I assume. Did you have any difficulty?"

"The icon? No...well, the usual . . I had to show the bill of sale and so on. Egypt, like so many Middle Eastern countries, is pretty careful about their antiquities. But this icon was originally from Russia, so they had no problem with letting it go. I've done this many times before and they know me by now."

"So, let me venture a guess, your husband was aware of your intention to split up before you arrived. Is that correct Mr. Dakis?"

"Yes, but I don't see what this has to do with anything."

"Possibly it is immaterial. How long after your wife arrived did you remove the icon from the store, Mr. Dakis?"

"Oh, a day or so, I think. Yes, two days later. She said she didn't want me to...well, I don't trust the legal system and so I took what I considered half of the assets. Not half of the stock but enough pieces to make up for my half in terms of monetary value."

"He took all the pieces worth anything."

"I see. And when Sacci arrived, how did he react to the icon having been taken?"

"Same as me, Sheriff. He was furious."

"About them all or this one in particular?'

Lorraine's lower lip began to tremble. "I don't know what you're implying."

"Leave her be," Louis said and patted Lorraine's arm. "She didn't know. No one did. Besides, what has this to do with us?"

The two men sat in the parked car three blocks from the Town Center Building, home to Picketsville's municipal government, the Sheriff's Office and sundry other governmental services. The driver kept the building in sight in his rear view mirror. He did not see Dakis enter the building but was sure that he'd gone to the police. What now?

"He took a flat package into that church." His companion said. "If the icon wasn't in his house, do you think he might have sold it to the priest?"

"But he just now took it in. If he sold it to the priest, what was he doing now?"

"They put them up in pairs, I think. At least that is what I saw in the last church job we did. They put a picture of the woman and baby on one side and the Jesus figure on the other, Sometimes there are more, I think, saints and so on. This might have been the Jesus one."

"We will need to go back to that church and see." He put the car in gear and drove off. "Tonight."

Chapter Thirty

Shmuel Gold listened to the messages in his voice mail. It had been years, how many…sometimes he lost track. There's a reason why retirement eventually becomes mandatory rather than optional. Events begin to run together and only the past remains crisp in one's memory. How long had it been since he'd heard from Isaac Schwartz—Ike? And now, two messages on his machine, one from him and one from Jerusalem about him. He pulled an old briar pipe from his cardigan pocket and filled the bowl tamping the rough cut shreds of tobacco carefully in place. Correctly packed, the pipe would stay lit for an hour or more. It would burn cool and slow. Pack it too tightly and it would go out, too loosely and it would be hot and dump ashes on his slacks which were already singed in places where he'd gotten careless with his smoking. After all, it wasn't like he was in any hurry.

He wouldn't light yet. He'd wait until the strong Turkish coffee he preferred over the weak

English stuff his housekeeper bought finished brewing and the sun came up. Then he would smoke his pipe, read the paper, and drink coffee until they wheeled him out to the main room and he could start his day. No hurry. He didn't sleep much these days anyway. Old people don't. Well, not until they started to disintegrate. That's how he envisioned the process. You grew old, your muscles atrophied, your brain shrank, lungs failed and then you disintegrated, fell apart bit by bit like an old car rumbling down the road with bits and pieces, bolts and nuts, exhaust pipe sections dropping on the ground. He thought of his old friends, lined up in armchairs, nodding in the sun, their mouths agape, a little drool at the corners. Some had Alzheimer's, some were…disintegrating. He hoped when his decline became obvious someone would have the decency to shoot him. He doubted they would, but he hoped. Perhaps that is why his daughter took away his service revolver. Smart woman, Rachael.

So, what was this thing with Ike? And what did Jerusalem want? Somewhere in the desert the Mossad stirred restlessly, ferreting out plots, watching Israel's enemies, its historical adversaries and its friends equally. Everyone had to be surveilled. Everyone had to be assumed to be a threat. Survival meant there could be no surprises, no interference. *Never again.*

It had always been that way. Joshua sent the spies into the land. Rehab, the harlot, revealed the secrets of the Canaanites and the people of Israel crossed over and took the land. Survival. His coffee ready, he poured his first of the day into a small porcelain cup, stirred it, and breathed in its aroma. He liked a little sugar and milk in it in the morning. Coffee, his pipe, and the *Jerusalem Post* because he needed to keep his English current.

Maybe the call from Jerusalem signaled an assignment. Maybe he would have another day "in the sand." That was how he described his early life to his grandchildren. The years fighting in the wars, in the intelligence gathering. The days in the Sinai—in the sand—the old days when things were straightforward, the enemy clearly defined, and the goals certain. These days? Who knew? But not likely. Not from a wheel chair.

He jotted down the phone number Ike had left him, looked at his watch, the battered Rolex Mariner he'd liberated from a Palestinian border jumper in ninety-one, and called his old head-quarters. There was protocol to be followed, after all. Protocol and procedures. He called the local number. He would find out what Jerusalem had to say. Isaac and the United States would have to wait. He would call Isaac afterwards.

Perhaps.

Besides the tech who'd retrieved the data, the only people to see the print-out of the documents on the microchip was the director, his deputy for mid-eastern operations, and Charlie. The tech did not need to be reminded he was sworn to secrecy, and the rest were even now debating whether or not to inform the President of the United States and the Secretary of State. The operative word in the discussion was *deniability.* What the President should and should not know, how much should he be able to reasonably deny? And then, if he were to be told anything, which version of the truth should it be? Charlie wondered, not for the first time, about an institution that withheld information about a sensitive area in foreign affairs from the President in order to protect him from the possibility of political attack by his own people as well as his foreign allies, never mind the country's enemies. Somewhere in the country's history, he thought, we misplaced the kernel of truth that shaped us in the first place.

He stopped thinking in abstractions and concentrated on the problem that had been thrust on the Agency, on him. There was the immediate difficulty—the microchip and its contents— and the larger problem, the originals of the documents from which the documents had been generated.

Fortunately for Charlie, the latter was not his to worry about. The director would either mount a black operation to retrieve and destroy them or he wouldn't. Certainly the Israelis would, or perhaps already had. Indeed, they may have been found and destroyed by now. But that did not mean there were no more copies. He heaved a sigh. At this juncture, Charlie's only task was to keep a lid on the local operation which, in turn, meant keeping a lid on Ike Schwartz. That would not be easy. Ike had that intuitive sense about things that would inevitably take him down the same road Charlie and the Agency were traveling. And unless he could find some device to quickly divert Ike, he was already on that journey or soon would be. Charlie let out an exasperated sigh. Why couldn't things be easy for a change?

He had to assume Ike had stumbled onto Tommy Wainwright's possible involvement some-how. How much he'd turned up remained an unknown, but it was only a matter of time before he'd dig out all of it or at least enough of it to make trouble. Charlie shook his head and grunted. Unlike the President of the United States, Ike could not, would not accept an expedient version of the truth. What to do? Ike was his friend.

He picked up the phone and called the techs that had been tasked to search Ike's computer operation. Samantha Ryder was far too skillful for her own good. He'd been assured that her hard drive had been wiped clean and no data from her hacking into their database remained on it or anywhere else. They had run sophisticated decoding software on all her files to be sure she hadn't encrypted the downloads and hidden them in an innocuous file. They insisted she was clean.

She wouldn't be happy about that when she found out what they'd done to her machine but, what the hell, who said life had to be fair. She and Ike were safer in ignorance. He called the techs and asked them to go back and be certain no copies had been made, and then be sure that if she ever ventured into their cyber world again, they could block her. They assured him that they had her signature and there was no way she could.

Yeah, yeah, do it again anyway. He hung up.

Next, someone had to find out who had outed Wainwright and to whom. Tommy was dead and the question before the house, who or what group pulled the trigger? Charlie did not want to believe it was done by friends, but he couldn't rule out that possibility either.

There were days when he hated his job. Today was one of them.

◇◇◇

Shmuel Gold's eyebrows came together in an exclamation mark. He hung up the phone. He didn't like this. It wasn't a matter of public dissembling. After all, that was the nature of all politics and especially international politics, and among intelligence professionals it was habitual. No, he understood that this particular book needed to stay closed. He'd been part of the team that wrote it in the first place you could say, and well, enough already. But to put into place the suggested sanctions? Overkill, certainly. Yes, the documents had to be found and destroyed. Yes, the person or persons who'd generated them needed to be permanently silenced. All this certainly, but to authorize such an operation in a foreign country, and not just any foreign country but the United States, our strongest and oldest ally? Shmuel remembered May 14, 1948, and the declaration by the Truman administration earlier in the UN to support the founding of a Jewish nation. No, it was as the Americans would say, over the top, a dangerous over-reaction with possibly tragic consequences, and what about Isaac Schwartz? No, it was too much. He no longer worked for SHABAK. It had been years, many years, since he sat disguised as one of them, drinking coffee and listening, waiting. No more. It was not his problem to solve.

He would have to smoke his pipe and think this through.

Chapter Thirty-one

Ike looked at the two people seated across the room from him. Man and wife, well, they were man and wife once, but no more. Is this how it ends? These two had and then lost the thing that so many people sought but never found and would die to have themselves. Marriages are like Humpty Dumpty. Once they fell, they were difficult if not impossible to put back together again, all the King's horses and men from Marriage Encounter not withstanding. Was there enough crazy glue available to ever repair it? He did notice the man had come to his estranged wife's defense. Perhaps there was still hope for them. Were they the victims of too much familiarity? What had Ruth asked? *So, do you think I will pale eventually, become an object of contempt?* It was a conundrum and Ike wasn't sure he wanted to unravel it. He caught sight of Essie on the phone, probably yammering away at Billy. Would that relationship degrade into the familiar, would the two of them take one another for granted, create yet another hum-drum existence?

He pictured Ruth again. He realized she was a person who never ceased to surprise him day after day. But would it last? Would the surprises become expectations? And if they did, what then? Engagements were more than a statement about commitment, they were a move toward permanency. Was he, or was she, ready to go there?

Someone was asking him a question.

"Sheriff," Louis Dakis said, "What about our icon?"

Ike noted the plural possessive. So there was hope.

"I will need to hold it as evidence until we clear this up. It is safe enough here, I promise. Tomorrow I'd like you to come by and bring the one you were making for me, if it's ready."

"I have it here." Dakis lifted the flat package he'd leaned against the desk earlier. Ike had seen him carry in the package but its significance had somehow escaped him.

"Ah, good. Tomorrow I will want you to do something with it, but I will need to explain that later." He turned to Lorraine Dakis. "Mrs. Dakis, I know this won't be easy for you, but I must ask you to go over to the Coroner's Office and formally identify Franco Sacci."

"I thought you said his name was…whoever you said he was. I don't see how that can be. I want to know how he was killed. I want to know who…" She gulped and tears began to run down her cheeks. "I am so confused. What do I do now?"

Frank stepped forward and took her elbow. "Suppose we drop in on the coroner before he closes." He glanced at his watch, "which will be in twenty minutes. We will have to hurry. Then you can book into a motel, or not. I don't think you should try to drive back to Washington now."

"She can stay with me," her husband said.

"I don't know. I don't know," She sobbed uncontrollably. "I just don't know."

Frank led her from the room.

"Tomorrow," Ike said to Dakis who took the hint and followed his wife out the door.

When the room had cleared Ike moved one of the many piles of paper on his desk aside and put his feet up. TMI. No, TDMI, too damned much information, not enough connection. That the murder of Sacci and the break-in at Dakis' house were part of a whole was no longer in doubt. That there were four men in the Dogwood Motel the night of the murder was certain. That one of those people was Thomas Wainwright posing as Avi Kolb, and the second was Farouk Zaki as Franco Sacci was also a fact. Whatever connected these two dead men to one another had to be the key. The remaining two men, Brown and Wentz, their real names unknown, could be anywhere and anybody by now. He had to hope they'd remain on task, that they would return for the icon, and that when they did he would nail them. But what came next? If he could find them, he had a circumstantial case to hang the murder on them, but he wasn't naive enough to believe he could make it stick. He needed something more, and he guessed that something lay buried in the funny farm up in Langley. What was on that microchip? Would Charlie talk? He'd have to find out.

But first he needed some time with Sam and her wonder machine. He needed some answers, and he guessed they were buried deep in some electronic archive somewhere.

Shmuel Gold watched the clock and calculated the time when it would be seventeen hundred in America. He assumed, rather he hoped, that Isaac Schwartz kept the office hours he associated with Americans, nine to five. When the second hand of his battered watch swept past twelve, he lifted the phone from its cradle and engaged the number he'd written on a scrap of paper. He glanced across the room to the Colonel seated behind the table. Only a small lamp lighted the desk's surface, the colonel's face barely discernable, lost in the shadows. Shmuel drew on his pipe and he, too, disappeared from view behind a cloud of smoke. Three rings. Four.

"Hello, Sheriff's office." A woman had answered. Shmuel lifted his eyes to the colonel again. He raised an eyebrow. The colonel nodded.

"Shmuel Gold here," He said. "I wish to speak to Isaac Schwartz, please."

"Who? Who did you say you were and you want to speak to who?"

"Gold, Shmuel." He spelled it slowly as the voice on the other end repeated after him.

"Okay, that's Shoomel Gold and you want to talk to Isaac…oh, you must mean Ike."

"Ike, yes, Ike Schwartz. Tell him Shmuel Gold returns his call."

He listened as the woman shouted to someone else and then the click as a receiver was taken from its hook.

"Hang up, Essie and go home," he heard Ike say. "Hold on, Shmuel, I need to clear the room and I don't have the luxury of a secure phone. Yes, I said go home. See you tomorrow. Take care of baby. Who? Never mind…an old friend. Good night. Okay, Shmuel, I'm here."

Shmuel waved to the colonel who pressed a button and put the phone on speaker.

"You left me a message, Isaac. You wanted to know something and you thought I could help?"

"I did. Perhaps you can, perhaps you can't. If you can, perhaps you will and perhaps you won't. It's the times we live in. It all depends on whether you know the answers to the questions I ask, and whether the Mossad agent monitoring the call will let you if you do."

Shmuel smiled at the colonel and shrugged. "What are you doing playing wild-West policeman, Isaac? Sheriff, what is that?"

"It's a living. It's something I do now. What about you, old man, still smoking that rotten pipe?"

"No, this is a new one. The one you gave me finally cracked and broke. I took it as a symbol."

"What can you tell me about a man who might have been called Avi Kolb or you might have known him as Thomas Wainwright?"

Shmuel took a breath and straightened the paper in front of him. "I am in a position to say only we know nothing about either Kolb or…" He saw the colonel nod yet again. "Wainwright. I am to assure you that the position of this government has been, is, and remains that we do not have any intelligence interests in the United States. We are allies."

He heard Ike laugh and had to smile himself. The colonel did not seem amused.

"You did that very well, Shmuel. You haven't lost your touch. Now, if I could figure out what you all were after I would…" Shmuel heard what he took to be a hand slapping a desk surface. "Shmuel, you *are* on an open phone, I take it."

Shmuel grimaced at the colonel and shrugged again.

"Major, Colonel, whoever you are, you should know that the microchip is now in the hands of the CIA. Sorry about that. I cannot tell you what they will do with it, as I no longer collect my paycheck from them. I would not be surprised, however, if, in a day or two, there are not urgent communications between our State Department and your Foreign Affairs Ministry. But here's the immediate problem: one of ours was killed by someone, perhaps one of yours, perhaps not. No way for me to know. I sincerely hope it was not one of yours. As we both know, keeping a lid on something like that is difficult and will require some complex explaining to be done, by us and by you. In the meantime, I have a small murder of my own here which I intend to clear up. I hope the perpetrators are not connected to you. If they should be, I want to assure you I intend to lock them up and throw away the key, as we say over here. It was good to hear from you, Shmuel, and thanks."

Chapter Thirty-two

Ike replaced the receiver and drummed his fingers on his desk. That cagey old coot. Now, if he could con Charlie into telling him what was on the microchip…No, wait, international intrigue and snooping was no longer Ike's bailiwick. He didn't need to know. He didn't want to know. His job was to collar a couple of killers and arrest them. That's it, period. If the State Department made him cut them loose later, well, that would be too bad, but he wasn't going to push this. That's it. That's final. No more spooking.

He had one more piece to his puzzle, though. The Israelis were in this somehow. Now, if Sam could figure a way to read the replacement chip before he put it on the newly minted icon, then maybe he'd have an answer or two. What the content didn't reveal might tell him what was on the original. Surely they would not put gibberish on the new one. The people who were after the chip would know immediately that they'd been duped and order up another. No, what had been placed on it would be similar to the Agency's database's backdoor, full of official sounding disinformation, but enough like what had been there originally to convince them they had the real thing. He'd call Sam.

He became aware of Essie standing in the door.

"Did you get all that, Essie?"

Essie squinted at the note book she held in her lap. "I wrote down what you all said, but it don't sound like much to me."

"Good. I didn't want it to, if you must know. Leave the notes on my desk."

"You had me sort of mixed up, there, Ike. You said I should go even though Darcie wasn't here to relieve me and then you're wig-wagging for me to stay and take notes. So, what's up with you and this Shmoo-ell Gold guy?"

"He's an old acquaintance from the bad old days. Among other roles he played in the past, he spent some time in the SHAMAK, that's the Israeli Security Service—spooks to you. I wanted to ask him a question."

"But you didn't. Ask him a question, I mean."

"No, that's the interesting part. He answered a question I never asked, you see?"

"Sorry, too deep for me. Here's Darcie. I'm off."

Darcie Billingsley dropped her purse on the floor next to the Dispatcher's desk and traded places with Essie, who waved and left.

"Evening, Ike," Darcie said. She swiveled her chair around and began to contact each of the deputies on duty. They needed to know the second shift in the office was in place.

"There's a note here for you," she said. "Essie must have forgotten to tell you."

"What's it say?"

"Amos took down a license number of a car that had been parked near the Dakis stakeout. He said the car followed Mr. Dakis when he left to come here."

"Check out the registration with the motor vehicle people and then call Harvey at the Dogwood Motel and see if it's the same one that was there last Friday."

"Will do. Where you going to be this evening?"

"I'm going to get something to eat and then see if I can convince Sam to put in some overtime."

In return for the comp time she needed for a long weekend in Washington, Sam agreed to meet Ike early the next morning and try to unscramble the microchip when it finally arrived. She didn't ask why Ike wanted to see the contents of the chip, contents he had to know would be adulterated at best. But she also knew that Ike worked in ways that frequently defied logic. At least until he solved the problem. Then they seemed supremely logical. She realized that Ike wasn't wired like ordinary people. He would have been a great hacker if he'd taken the trouble to learn computers. But he remained determinedly ignorant of the field. Not a Luddite exactly, but certainly not an enthusiast, either.

"When I looked at it, it reminded me of one of the micro-SD card inserts." She said and settled into her desk chair, a modern bit of ergonomic bent teak and leather that Ike could never believe was comfortable. Ike's ensuing silence meant he needed an explanation. "The memory cards for cameras and other electronic devices have been miniaturized so that they are very small but the card slots remain relatively large. The micro-SD slips into a carrier the size and shape of the older, conventional card and then it acts like a regular memory card. The advantage of the new system is you can put the same micro-memory device into a variety of carriers. Swap them in and out, you could say. One of them would be as small as that chip your friend Charlie picked off the icon. I can't be sure if it was one or not. I didn't recognize it, but the technology is changing so fast it might have been."

"All I need to know, Sam, is whether you can

read it before we stick it on the substitute icon."

"I can, if the contacts line up with one of the receiver sleeves. I won't know until I see it up close."

"Could you modify either the sleeve thing or the chip to work?"

Ah ha, she thought, *not wired like ordinary people.* "Possibly, yes. It will depend on how much time I have and…like that."

"We'll make the time. I'll see you tomorrow morning. These guys are getting desperate, I'm thinking, but they'll wait. As long as we keep that car in front of Dakis' house, that is."

Sam hung up and rooted through her desk drawer for memory cards and micro tools and then spent the rest of the evening on the Internet. She needed at least one manual. When she found what she was looking for she downloaded and printed it out. She would need to take a trip to the computer store or a Radio Shack early tomorrow. The rest of her waking time she divided between reading the twenty pages of technical information and e-mailing Karl who, she knew was on assignment and out of reach. He was working to build up comp time as well. It was after midnight when he finally called and she could tell him her good news. Karl did not like the idea of her tinkering with the CIA's microchip, but he was happy with the compensation.

"A long weekend. That'll be great. Be careful with this thing, though. I don't want Ike to get you thrown into federal prison for one of his brainstorms. I swear—"

"It'll be fine, you'll see. Ike wouldn't do anything like that. He'd have my back. You know that."

"Yeah, well be careful."

Chapter Thirty-three

Ike was about to tuck into his hash browns when his cell phone chirped in his pocket.

"Where you at?" Essie sounded frantic. It had become her standard mode lately. Ike hoped maternity and a return to hormonal equilibrium would also restore her normal cheerful presence.

"Across the street enjoying my usual heart attack breakfast and listening to Flora, who has been telling me all about you. That is, all about you back when. She watched you grow up, she says."

"Well, you can't believe everything that old bat says. You want to know about me, you ask me personal-like."

"Did you really pour maple syrup on your third-grade teacher's chair?"

"Ike, I ain't got time for this. There's a snooty woman here who has a package for you and she won't leave it with me. You got to sign for it or something." Essie lowered her voice and, Ike guessed, cupped the phone. "She looks like one of them spies or something like the woman who came by here once to pick up that old telephone you had. Slick and sassy is what she is. You better get over here."

"I'm on my way. Give her coffee and regale her with your tales of morning sickness, cravings for pickles and ice cream, and the unreasonableness of husbands considering your condition."

"She don't look the type to go into that with. How'd you know about Billy and me? Did he say something? I'll kill him."

Ike paid for his half-eaten breakfast, refused Flora Blevin's offer to box up the remains, received a dirty look from her because of it, and left. He expected but did not hear her say something about starving children in Biafra.

Sam arrived as he did. She carried a small satchel and there was a gleam in her eye that he recognized as her geek alert. She had a challenge in front of her and she could hardly wait to tackle it. Ike hoped she would be successful, and then wondered again why he bothered with this stuff. It was none of his business, he could get both himself and Sam in trouble, and when all was said and done he'd have very little to show for his efforts. He was only after the murder of Sacci, right? But his tenure in the CIA and its aftermath had left him permanently irritated with the world of secrets and operations conducted in the dark. National Security was one thing; geopolitical manipulation was another.

After consulting several photo IDs and asking Ike to sign a receipt, Essie's slick and sassy woman handed Ike a package and left.

"Rudest woman I ever met," Essie complained. "Didn't say a word except to tell me the coffee was burned. What'd she expect? It's been in the pot since six."

"Make us a new pot will you, Essie. Sam, have you got everything you need?"

"I don't know, for sure, Ike. I may have to run to the mall. Let's have a look at that thing."

Ike slit open the tape on the package and extracted a smaller box and a slip of folded paper.

"Ha! Charlie writes us a note to wit; 'Do not try to read the contents of this file. It's all lies anyway.' Then he adds this post script, 'I mean it, Ike. The boss is watching.'"

"So what do we do?"

Ike smiled. "Charlie knows that the surest way to get me to snoop for the contents of this chip is to tell me not to. We tackle the thing. Here you go, have at it." He handed Sam the small box and they walked into Sam's office/communications center.

She carefully tilted the contents of the box into her hand and inspected it.

"It looks like a micro memory card like I said. Let's see if we have a carrier." She poked about in the envelope she'd brought and removed an SD memory card carrier and held the two up side by side.

"Will it work?" Ike peered over Sam's shoulder. That sort of close proximity by men made her nervous. Except Karl, of course, and there were times when she'd as soon he were in front of her, not crowding her space. She wondered some times if it was some kind of neurosis. She'd never confided it to anyone else. Maybe she should. She sat straighter, forcing Ike to retreat marginally.

"You're in my light," she lied and Ike stepped back. "The contact points look like they are in all the right places, but this chip is way thinner."

"Can you make it work?"

"Oh, yeah. Remember I told you about people in the intelligence business having to have identical equipment on either end of the sending and receiving system?" Ike nodded. "So here's an example. If they'd used a complicated chip, you know, custom-made and all that, then the person who received it would have to be in possession of the same special equipment. What they've done, and your pals in the Agency have reproduced, is a chip that can be read by the kind of card reader you can buy in any electronics shop, camera store, or on-line."

"I thought you said it was too small."

"I didn't say too small; I said it was thinner. All I have to do, and all the recipients would have to do, is fatten it up with a layer or two of card stock. This will only take a minute."

"So, it's different enough to dissuade an amateur but if you know what the thing is, it's no big deal."

"Right."

Sam used nail scissors to cut three small squares of card stock and carefully glued them on the chip. "We'll have to remove the glue when we're done here."

"That going to be a problem?"

"No. It's school paste. Heck, my little brother used to eat the stuff. It's water soluble. Okay, here we go." She slipped the chip in a carrier and that into her card reader. The file opened up in Adobe, "There you go. Piece of cake."

"I think it would be a good idea if you didn't look at this file, Sam."

"Why? It's got to be junk, like in the CIA's accessible computer site, right? What's the harm?"

"I'm thinking that if the Agency does send in a goon squad, you can say with a straight face, 'No, I didn't read it.' Capisce?"

"I don't capisce...well, okay. But you'll tell me what you think it means, right?"

"Perhaps. Copy all this for me, and then, Karl awaits, so hit the road."

It took Ike less than twenty minutes to read the documents. His Hebrew was nearly nonexistent. It had been a long time since his *bar mitzvah* and he'd not had much use for it since, but he got the gist. The same was true with his Arabic. You use it or you lose it. He lost it. There was an interesting bit in French that he could make out, written by a French advisor to their air force probably. It didn't matter. Now he knew what the CIA intended to quash and what the Mossad wanted to keep out of the wrong hands—the *USS Liberty*. The damn business wouldn't go away and in the divisive political climate that characterized the day, resurrecting it could be a bombshell, true or not.

Undoubtedly, the information on the original chip, now in the hands of Charlie and his friends and copied, analyzed and summarized by a half dozen sub-directorates, formed the thrust of their next move, whatever that might be. Bully for them. In the meantime, the originals were still out in the Near East somewhere, ready to resurface if the senders of this batch wished to try again. The Mossad and the CIA would scour the desert for them. But the critical thing at the moment was to keep a request for another chip or package of some sort from being requested. The recipients of this new version had to believe they had the authentic goods. Ike shook his head at the significance. This bit of history of military bungling could not be worth the lives of two, at least two, and who knew how many more on the other end. Madness.

Ike removed the adapter, slipped the chip from it, and peeled away the cardboard. He didn't bother to clean off the paste. By the time he remounted the thing in its microdot look-alike, no one would notice.

Chapter Thirty-four

Ike finished reassembling the ersatz microdot, fastened it with a dab of rubber cement on the eye of the icon, his icon, spritzed it with a puff of varnish, and called for Billy.

"He's out running some errands, Ike," Essie said. "He'll be back directly."

"Errands? What kind of errands? I don't remember asking him to run errands."

"We needed some things down to the store and since he didn't look too busy at his desk, and all, I sent him up to the Shop and Save to pick up a few little things for dinner."

"Essie, I know you are in an acute state of maternity and your judgment may, therefore, be somewhat impaired, but this is a police operation and on-duty deputies do not, I repeat, do not, slip out to 'pick up a few little things for dinner' unless, and only when, I say so."

Essie blushed. Her jaw dropped. In all the

years she'd worked the dispatch desk Ike had never spoken to her that way.

"I'm sorry, Ike, I didn't think…I'll get him back." She spun in her seat and toggled the radio key.

"You do that."

Ike felt badly for snapping at Essie. There wasn't a disingenuous bone in her body, but hormones or something had changed her from the smiling hard worker to a grande dame, and he needed to nip it in the bud. He'd apologize later. He retreated to his office and began wrapping the icon for transport to Dakis' place. Billy scuttled in the front door, conferred with Essie, shot a look in Ike's direction, and hustled into the office.

"Don't blame Essie, Ike. I was the one who thought I could squeeze the run to the Shop and Save. You were tied up with Sam and all, so…well, I'm sorry. Won't happen again."

"Billy, you know I run a pretty loose ship around here. I am happy for the informality, the lack of…" Ike took in Billy's unorthodox uniform. He'd substituted a Stetson for the standard issue campaign hat and cowboy boots for shoes. Hardly any of his deputies were ever in proper uniform, including Ike. "Convention, and I adore Essie. She has been a loyal, always cheerful, encouraging employee, and friend. It's that lately she's become,"

Ike searched for the word he wanted, "imperious."

"Say what?"

"She is acting like a queen bee. That has a lot to do with her pregnancy, no doubt, but there is a time and place for everything and, I hate to say it, the dispatcher does not assign duties, or dispatch you or anyone else to the store. Not in this office. At home—maybe, but not here. Send her in. I'll apologize and we'll have a coffee."

"Doctor says she shouldn't be drinking nothing with caffeine in it."

"Is that why she substituted decaf in the urn?"

"You knew about that?"

"I used to be a spy, remember? Now, I want you to take this icon out to Dakis. Tell him to put it out where the thieves, if they come, can easily see it without having to tear his place apart, but not to make it too obvious. I wrapped it in a oversize box so that if the bad guys are watching the house, they won't see that an icon is being delivered by the Sheriff's Office. At least that's the hope. Tell you what, have a civilian do it. No, send one of our volunteer auxiliary deputies. And then call and make sure Dakis understands what he's to do."

"Right. Got it."

"Tell him to make a point to be away several nights in a row so that the snatch can be made and he won't get caught in the middle. Tell him one man is already dead because of that icon. Maybe two men. Now git, and send in Essie."

Billy hustled out the door and Essie swiveled out of her chair and heaved herself erect and walked to the office. She seemed so different now. Before Billy, before her pregnancy, she would have swooped into the office. Now she moved slowly, not a waddle exactly, not yet, but definitely not a swoop.

"Ike, I got these messages for you and I'm sorry for being pushy. I guess I been here so long I sometimes think I'm home, like, this has been my home for so long and now me and Billy…well, I'm sorry."

"I got carried away, and I shouldn't have barked at you. The truth is, you are the heart of this department and so, your baby will be our baby. So, forget I said anything."

Essie brushed away a tear and dumped a stack of pink call-back slips on Ike's desk.

"Anything important in there?"

"The usual complaining by the mayor. He's upset you ain't enforcing the uniform dress code like he told you to. The State Highway Patrol people want to know if we have anyone on the force that would like to transfer over. I guess they miss Frank. You think they want him back? And Ms. Harris called and said it was urgent, like, and you should call her. Oh, and thank you for the 'heart of the department' thing. I'll get back to work."

Ruth answered on the first ring.

"What are you doing answering your own phone? Where's Agnes?"

"Busy. We have an emergency. I need your help."

"Is it serious? I'll be right out."

"No, it's not that kind of an emergency. I don't want you to come out here. Well, not until tonight at the party, at least."

"So what is it, then?"

"Mother."

"Your mother is the emergency? How does that work?"

"Never mind. She showed up in the office an hour ago. Agnes is entertaining her in the cafeteria at the moment. My God, Ike, she wants to move in with me."

"Is that bad?"

"Damn, Ike, I told you about her. She's nipped and tucked and…you know. I hardly recognize her."

"And you want me to do what? I could arrest her for impersonating a celebrity. She could move into the jail, but I don't think that's what you had in mind."

"Don't start with me, Schwartz. I want you to call your dad and invite him to the party tonight. Tell him he owes me for showing up at Dolly's debut on short notice. And he should bring Dolly with him, too. I need reinforcements."

Chapter Thirty-five

Ike arrived at Ruth's party as presentable as possible. Clothing, sartorial acumen, he would say, was not his long suit. He managed to own one—a suit, that is—and could, if given enough time, manage a decent four-in-hand knot on his necktie. Left to his own devices, however, his preference went to golf shirts, slacks, and his scuffed walking shoes. But Ruth wanted to show him off at his best and, then, there was her mother, whether to impress, dazzle, or contain, he couldn't be sure. The party seemed in full swing. A string quartet rubbed well-rosined bow over cat gut, and the room rattled with chatter. On his way in he scooped up a martini from the bar set up by the front door, downed it and helped himself to a second. He spotted Ruth in the corner listening to an older faculty member, probably one of the retirees in whose honor the party had been mounted, and worked his way over to her.

"Excuse me," she said to her companion. He

smiled, nodded a greeting to Ike and drifted away. "What are you drinking?"

"Martini. I haven't eaten since this morning, I don't think, and I thought, given your apparent panic, a small buzz might be helpful."

"Oh, that's great. As you predicted, my mother is flirting with the junior faculty, the older ones are giving me the fish-eye over my engagement ring, and you're on your way to getting shit-faced."

"Tsk, how you talk. Your mother never taught you to say shit-faced. Shall I tell on you?"

"Shut up. That's her over there with those two assistant professors. They're new and single. What am I going to do?"

"Ah, you are in a panic. I will limit myself to two of these concoctions—maybe three, but no more fear not."

"Listen to me, Sheriff. Two is your limit or there will be no joy in the morning."

Ike swung his gaze across the room in the direction Ruth had indicated. "That's your mother? Wow, you're right. She certainly has reinvented herself, enhancements and all. I can still see a resemblance. So, that's what you'd look like as a blond. Worth a try."

"Forget it. Can you imagine what my faculty would say if I showed up blond?"

"I was thinking of variety. Maybe a wig, in private. What do you think?"

"Men! Forget it. Where's your father?"

"My father said, and I quote, 'I'll be along directly soon's Dolly has her beauty rest and then puts on her face.' I assume it's the same face she had on the other night, but with women of a certain age, you never know."

"Okay, enough already. It's time to meet Momma." They made their way across the room and stopped in front of Ruth's mother. "Ike, this is my mother. Mother, Ike."

"It's nice to see you again," Ike wracked his brain for a name. He should know it from the old days. Ah-ha..."Paula."

"It's not Paula anymore, but how did you know?"

"I visited your house, the dean's residence. It was years ago."

"Oh, my, you were one of John's 'young men.' That explains a few things. Not why you're here playing at sheriff but...Well, isn't that ironic."

"Yes, you could say so. You say you've changed your name? Retaken your maiden name or..."

"Maiden name, how quaint. No, as I am now an author, I have a *nom de plume*. I am Eden, Eden Saint Claire."

"I see. So you're a writer? Ruth didn't tell me. What are you writing?"

"An exposé. The dark side of academe. I'm calling it *Ivy League Peyton Place*. What do you think?"

"Very catchy, but I'm not sure many potential readers will get the reference. The TV series ended nearly forty years ago and more years than that since the movie and book."

"Ike knows all this stuff because he watches old movies, don't you, Ike?"

"That's what I've been telling your daughter, but the truth is, you caught me. I'm an eighty-year-old man. I happened to have lived an exemplary and sheltered life as an ovo-lacto-vegetarian, which accounts for my youthful good looks and stamina."

"He also fancies himself a comedian, but nobody believes that either."

Ruth's mother watched the exchange between the two of them and grinned. Ike thought she must have had plastic dentistry; was there such a thing? Implants, caps, or veneers to finish the rest of her makeover.

"So, what shall we do with the weekend?" Eden Saint Claire asked.

Ruth and Ike exchanged looks.

Abe and Dolly made an entrance and bee-lined to them.

"Well, well, there you are Miz Harris, excuse me the Misses Harris." Abe scooped Paula/Eden in a bear hug. "This here is a real pleasure." He released her. Eden recovered and turned her amazing white and straight teeth in a huge smile on Abe. "And I want you to meet Dolly. Dolly Frankenfeld, this here is Ruth's momma."

Dolly and Ruth's mother made a startling contrast. Dolly trim and statuesque, but decidedly her age, platinum, and Eden Saint Claire, gold but decidedly neither one of those other things.

"Mother has come for a visit," Ruth said.

"Her name is—" Ike began.

"Eden Saint Claire." Ruth's mother extended her hand. Dolly took it without batting an eye. Old school, Ike thought. You've got to love it. She'd shake hands with the devil if he was introduced properly.

"I am thinking about settling here," Eden declared. Ruth rolled her eyes at Ike.

"Why that's plain super. Here in Picketsville? Say, why don't you come out to the farm, and me and Dolly can spend the weekend showing you around. You'll love it here. I can show you some places in the valley you'll love and Ike, here, has a friend in the real estate business who could fix you up in a jiffy."

"What a wonderful idea. Mother, you'll love

Abe's place. Country, fresh air...What a great idea, Abe." Ruth sounded a little desperate, Ike thought and glanced at her mother to see if she noticed. Eden Saint Clair looked quizzical but did not lose her smile.

Abe Schwartz winked. Dolly inspected Eden Saint Claire the way a mongoose surveys a cobra. It promised to be an exciting weekend.

Chapter Thirty-six

"Saved by the bell. The cow bell, I guess it would be. Did you put your father up to inviting my mother to his farm for the weekend?"

Ike and Ruth had made it to the A-frame alone after all, as it turned out, and had settled on the deck bundled against the March night chill with down jackets. They were drinking excessively rich mochas in lieu of more alcohol.

"If I had, would there be a reward in it for me?"

"That depends on what you had in mind. Is there anything you lack that I can offer? Well, that I can offer, and not break the laws of the Commonwealth of Virginia?"

"What laws would that be?"

"Well, we have a state law prohibiting 'the corrupt practice of bribery by any person other than candidates' for one, and it is also against the law in Virginia to tickle women. That means you're dead meat, Schwartz. You start anything with me and I call the cops."

"I am the cops. And in my view, tickling you comes under the heading of a carnal bribe, which in my role as potential candidate for public office buys me a pass, so there."

"Politicians, you're all alike. Anyway, I have a more interesting idea along those lines, but you'll have to wait until I finish my chocolate."

Ike smiled in the darkness and stretched his legs. "How about we just admire the view before it pales and so on. No, I'm afraid Pop's invitation was his idea and spontaneous. I think he saw your eye-roll and figured out what he needed to do. He's very fond of you, you know."

"And I of him. He figured it out from an eye-roll?"

"You have a particularly expressive eye-roll, Madam."

"So now I know where you inherited your intuitive genius. How's your investigation going, or don't I want to know?"

"It's gotten complicated. I'm not sure I want to drag you into it. It could be dangerous."

"You're kidding. I could be in danger if you talked to me? How does that work? You're not going to go back and play in Charlie's sand box again are you?"

"No…well, not exactly. As I said, it's complicated and there could be repercussions to the department if it became known you were in possession of certain information."

"Ike, I hate to sound crude for the second time tonight, but bullshit. What are you not saying?"

"Okay. What do you know about the *USS Liberty*?"

"Nothing. What should I know? Oh, wait is it the name of Captain Kirk's starship?"

"No, that's the *Enterprise*, I think. I don't know. Anyway, during the Six-Day War, that would be back in 1967 and you were a mere slip of a girl,"

"Thank you for that. Slip, I like it. Don't know about the mere part, though. Sorry, continue."

"As I was about to say, an American intelligence gathering vessel, the *USS Liberty*, was in international waters off the coast of Egypt."

"It was a spy ship?"

"Probably. No, definitely. The Liberty was a World War II freighter and had been converted into an intelligence vessel by the National Security Agency. It had been given the task of monitoring electronic communications in the area. Very sophisticated for its day. It bristled with antennae and listening devices of one sort or another and was sent to track the Israelis in their conflict with the Arab coalition."

"Are you sure you want to go on? This doesn't

sound like murder and mayhem in Picketsville. This is spook stuff."

"You said you wanted to know about my work, and I need a pair of ears that happen to be attached to a better than average brain, so I talk to you. I'm not supposed to."

"Says who, or is it whom? You know for a university president, I should know that—who, whom—shouldn't I?"

"In this case, the 'says who' are the authorities, both federal and state. Police investigations are supposed to be confidential, not shared higglety-pigglety with civilians. I could get the department in trouble."

"I'm not sure I like the higglety-pigglety allusion. You think I'm fat? And it's a little late in the game to worry about that now, Sheriff. You've been doing it for over a year."

"Right, but I'm covered. Never mind how, you wouldn't like it."

"Okay, I didn't mean to interrupt. Go on. The boat was in the Mediterranean, and the war raged ashore. Have I got it?"

"Right. So, the story goes that on the fourth day of the war, the ship was steaming along in international waters while Israeli armored forces were roaring into Sinai in pursuit of the retreating Egyptian army."

"That was a long time ago. Ike. What's that to do with your murder? I'm missing something, aren't I?" Ruth hitched her cocktail dress closer and retreated deeper into her jacket.

"A long time ago, yes it was, but it won't go away, it seems. At eight in the morning, it is alleged—I have to be careful here, there are rumors and accusations, and then there is the official version. What I am telling you is decidedly not the official version. At eight in the AM, Israeli recon planes flew over the ship, which was flying a large American flag, by the way. Then, at two in the afternoon, Israeli Mystère and Mirage-III fighter-bombers—French manufactured aircraft—repeatedly attacked the American vessel with rockets, napalm, and machine guns. The attacks were quick and over in twenty minutes or so, and were aimed at the ship's electronic antennas and dishes. The Liberty caught fire. Eight of the crew were killed, a hundred or more were wounded, including the captain. Then, as if that were not enough, twenty-five minutes or so later three Israeli torpedo boats attacked it. They banged away at the already burning ship with 20-mm and 40-mm guns. Five minutes into the second attack an Israeli torpedo hit the Liberty amidships, where the intelligence paraphernalia were located. Twenty-five more Americans died and the ship was effectively out of commission and unable to communicate."

"No. This is true?"

"True, false, partially so; you're the historian, you tell me. Some of it, yes. I don't know how much. It's one side of a complex story. In any event, it does not matter. If you are intent on creating division in the country, it is enough that you have the means, true or not. People lap up conspiracies like cats lap milk."

"But not Schrödinger's cat, because he may or may not be dead."

"Are you listening to me? Okay, so the gunboats circled the ship, which was listing and possibly sinking, and fired at the crewmen trying to put out the fires. The captain ordered the crew to abandon ship. The Israeli warships were said to have closed in and machine gunned the life rafts. While all this was going on, a rescue mission by US Sixth Fleet carrier aircraft was apparently aborted. Allegedly on an order from the White House itself."

"That's it? Didn't anybody do anything?"

"They say that some former U.S. government officials, including then-CIA Director Richard Helms, Secretary of State Dean Rusk, and the chairman of the joint chiefs of staff, did not accept the incident as innocent, or a consequence of friendly fire. The administration, however, decided not to dispute Israel's claim that the attack had been nothing more than a terrible mistake. White House documents someone obtained from the Johnson Presidential Library seem to indicate that the Israelis' explanation of how the attack had occurred was not generally believed at the time."

"Nothing happened? They let it go?"

"You have to remember, this happened in the late sixties. A lot of very heavy stuff hit the fan about then—the Vietnam war, an election coming up, Haight-Ashbury, White and Grissom killed in a testing exercise, race riots in many of the major cities…it was a crazy time in our history. The country had enough problems to deal with and we didn't need another, particularly one that would put us at odds with an ally. So, it went away."

"Men were killed needlessly in the Liberty attack, you said. And now, what? Add two more? Doesn't it strike you as odd that if a clean breast had been made, the truth told back then, no equivocating and so on, those two would not be racked up to the incident. Maybe even more—who knows? Ah, well, that's the mess we create when we yield to pride, I suppose."

"*Hubris,* I think. That and institutionalized stupidity, the hallmark of a smoothly running political system."

"Cynical, Ike, very cynical. What has become

of my Boy Scout? I think you need another vacation."

"No, This business takes me back to a previous life and some unpleasant memories."

"Gottcha. So, I ask again, what has this got to do with Picketsville?"

"You remember Charlie's anomaly?"

"The icon thing?"

"Exactly. As nearly as I can figure, the 'anomaly' was a small memory chip onto which various documents authenticating the story, as I've told it, had been embedded."

"I thought you were substituting one with phony information on it. How do you know what the real one said?"

"I didn't see the first one, but Sam fixed it so I could read the contents of the substitute. The Agency reproduced most of the documents, as nearly as I can figure, at least enough to satisfy the recipients that they had the goods, but they fiddled with them."

"Fiddled? How fiddled? I would think they'd put crap on the substitute. A recipe for chicken soup, you know, Jewish penicillin, or something. Why give them what they want?"

"Chicken soup…a happy thought, but not a practical one. No, they had to make it look like the delivery was made. The forgeries, however, all had to have mistakes in them. If they were ever released to the public, they could easily be discredited as such, and the work of fanatics."

"You mean like Dan Rather's documents of Bush's National Guard time?"

"Like that, yes."

"That's very devious. Did you figure that out by yourself or did Charlie give you hints?"

"Charlie doesn't know that I know."

"Wow, this is deep. You were right, I'm not sure I want to know, not that I can help it now. You said I was covered for receiving secrets. How?"

"In the past I said you were a deputy."

"I'm a deputy? I don't remember being sworn."

"Consider it done. Anyway, the Liberty—"

"Where's my badge?"

"Your what?"

"Badge. If I'm a duly sworn deputy sheriff, I want a badge and a piece. I need a piece."

"A piece of what? What are you going on about?"

"A gat, a roscoe, a cannon, a sheep's leg, you know. Isn't that cop talk for a gun?"

"Not even close. You want a gun? You hate guns."

"You're right, I hate guns. They should all be collected and melted down. Make the world a better place. Well, not all of them. You can keep yours. I need you to protect me from the nuts out there who carry—or is it pack?"

"The latent hypocrisy in that statement is monumental, but typical."

"I don't care. So what about your ship, the Liberty. What happens now?"

Ike shrugged. "It's an issue, as I said, that won't go away. It's like your mother's book title. The median age, as of the last census, is something like thirty-six. Over half the people in the country were not even born when the incident happened, and well over that number have no remembrance of it whatsoever, or even the Six-Day War. Vietnam is taught as history to young people who put it in the same category as the Civil War, the Spanish-American War and so on. So, even if the documentation is authentic, it's hard to conceive how it would carry any weight now, but—"

"But, as you keep telling me, we live in a litigious, uncivil world characterized by angry polarized debate where people think it's okay to scream at the President during his speech to Congress. This *Liberty* thing, if placed with the wrong people, could have embarrassing political, or at the very least, foreign policy consequences even now."

"More than that, I think. We have created a small but not insubstantial segment of our society that loves to hate, and the means to feed them what they want to hear. People are obsessed with the secrets of the past and presumed conspiracies. Did Thomas Jefferson sire children by Sally Hemings? What did Roosevelt know before Pearl Harbor? Did the CIA blow up the World Trade Center and fake the airplane crash? Is this another cover-up? And then there is the potential problem this story creates by providing support to the anti-Semitic wing-nuts that always lurk in society's sewers.

So, there you have it. Something like this *Liberty* business in the hands of rabble rousers, whether individuals or media wonks, could very well prove volatile in the society that you said yourself prefers absolutes. It's a small thing, after all. A trifle, in fact. Not something we should be exercised about, but people are dead because of that icon. The anger level in the country does not need any more provocation. It's one more thing. For me, it's about a dead guy in the urgent care center."

They sat in silence waiting for the moon to clear the roof's peak.

"I want a hat."

"What? A hat?"

"As your deputy, I should be issued one of those cute Smokey the Bear hats. I want one."

"No gun, but a badge and a hat. I might have one of each around here somewhere. Come to think of it, I like it."

"You do?"

"Yes, because I realize what I want as a reward for setting up my father."

"You said you didn't."

"I could have."

"As your reward you want me to wear a badge, the hat, and…oh, I see. You *are* a dirty old man, Sheriff, but no blond wig. I have my limits."

Chapter Thirty-seven

Shortly after his marriage to Mary Miller, Blake Fisher switched his days off from Mondays to Fridays. Since his bride had an office job, he figured she would more than likely have her long weekends starting on Fridays than ending on Mondays except, of course, for Labor Day and so he made the switch. It was a change that not all his congregation approved. The sense of it was patently apparent, but change, even something as simple as a day off, is a challenge in a church that measures its time in millennia and this particular parish in centuries, or so it seemed.

He'd also moved out of the rectory, the manse supplied by the church for its rector's residence, to Mary's little house in Chesterfield. A much more obvious change, and also not one well received. A resident clergyman provided a measure of security. An empty house was asking for trouble. And now he could ask for a housing allowance, which was not something the church's budget could swing. So now the empty rectory which stood across the parking lot from the back of the church and which had a view of the office door, failed to provide any measure of security whatsoever. No one was in sight of the church, as he would have been before the move. Added to that, Gloria, the church's secretary, had a dental appointment with her son, T.J., and had taken the day off as well.

Because he was home Friday and the office was closed, it would be sometime Saturday afternoon before anyone realized that the church had been broken into and another hour later, that his office had been, too. The altar guild ladies, led by Dorothy Sutherlin, had come to set the altar for Sunday and Dorothy, mother of two of Ike's deputies, had made the calls—to Blake and the sheriff's office.

Apparently nothing would be missing except one of his newly installed icons.

"I checked, Mr. Garland, like you said. The techs didn't think your friend in Virginia got anything from our database, but there's a slim possibility we may have missed something."

Charlie Garland did not like working Saturdays, or weekends in general for that matter. You'd think after a quarter of a century in the business someone would cut him some slack. He also did not like the idea that Ike's people were skating on thin ice—his thin ice. And he worried that Ike would become entangled in this business and that could create problems. Ike was stubborn and Charlie didn't need any more problems. It was bad enough for intelligence to be leaking from the inside. He didn't need Ike and his friends prying it loose from the outside. This news from the security people didn't sit well.

"Explain to me what *we* might have missed."

"Well, you know we opened red.ryder's, that's Samantha Ryder's cyber name, opened her hard drives. We scanned her computer and deleted all the files she'd downloaded. Then we looked to see if possibly she had made copies."

"I thought you said she hadn't."

"We thought that, yes, but you asked us to recheck and we, that is, I did, and there's a problem." Charlie waited. "See, to find out if she'd copied anything, we had to search her hard drives. Nothing there, we'd purged them once already. Then we inspected her server and logger. Every action the computer does is logged in, and so if a flash drive is plugged in, it will note that and what happened to it."

"So you found she copied files to a removable storage device."

"No. No evidence of that at all."

"You lost me."

"See…" Charlie didn't *see*. They were speaking on the phone, for crying out loud, how could he possibly see anything? The guy must think they were on Skype.

"Everything a computer does is noted on the server's logger unless it's disabled. We think it was and the only reason for her to do that is to hide an action on her part."

"You know the logger was disabled?"

"Yes. See," There was that word again. "According to the log, she never shut down the computer, but there's a gap, a time lapse in the log we can't account for, you could say. And the next thing in the log is a boot up. She might have thought if she disabled the logger, copied files and then rebooted, we'd miss it."

"But you didn't?"

"We don't think so. We've reported it upstairs. The section chief wants to send people down there and take her into custody. You see?"

"Thanks for the heads-up."

Charlie called "upstairs" and talked to the director's right hand. *Talk to the hand.* "Jack, I need a favor.…No, it's important…Can't say…Yes, it's about the chip. I hear you're going to send the goon squad down to Picketsville and hassle a hacker. Can you give me a few days on that, okay?…Thanks."

Charlie hung up. What was Ike thinking? He needed to talk to him right away. All that blather about never, ever, wanting to be involved with the agency again and now this. He tried Ike's cell phone but could only raise his voice mail.

"Ike, listen to me. The boys up here are spiffed with Samantha Ryder's tinkering. They're about to send a gang down there and charge her. I know you and know you're mulish enough to put yourself in the middle. Don't do it. Have Samantha Ryder stand down, and I'll try to fix things at this end. If she doesn't, she…no, both of you, will be in the market for a bail bondsman and an attorney. You must call me, Ike, I mean it. You have twenty-four hours before the dogs are turned loose."

He hung up and drummed his fingers on the worn desk. Another five years and it would be a collectable, like him.

Because Ike had promised Ruth he wouldn't work during the weekend, he'd turned off his cell phone the night before. He'd said he would need to call in from time to time. Ruth said not until after ten. He'd canceled his land line when the reception for his cell became strong enough to use in the mountains. But Ike couldn't wait. Even though Frank was perfectly capable of handling things in his absence, being out of contact with the office made Ike itchy.

Ruth was in the shower, the water was on full blast, and she was making noises she claimed were singing. The first time he'd heard her do that, he went for his first-aid kit. He listened, gauged the probable extent of the as yet unfinished shower— the singing would sound different, worse in fact, when she washed her hair, but working against that—he hadn't gotten around to buying a larger volume hot water tank. He looked at his watch and calculated he had ten minutes, no more. He switched on the phone.

Charlie's message created a deep line between his brows. What to do? He called Sam in Washington and told his very sleepy deputy that she was under no circumstances to return to duty, to Picketsville, even. She was to stay in the city, incognito, and out of sight until she heard from him.

Sam started to argue, but Ike rang off.

He had the phone turned off and back on the chest of drawers when Ruth, wrapped loosely in a towel and wearing her new deputy's hat, stepped out of a cloud of steam and into the room.

"Just so you know, we're out of hot water and you still owe me a badge."

"I'll shower later. I gave you a badge."

"A cast metal badge saying, 'Honorary Deputy

Sheriff, Mayberry, RFD,' and 'Made in Taiwan' on the back, won't play. I want a real one." She sailed the hat onto the bed and wrapped the towel on her still dripping hair.

"Where would I pin it?" Ike said, admiring the view.

"Be creative. Won't Opie be missing his tin star?"

"He's gone on to bigger and better things. I could try two-faced tape."

"No problem too great or too small for our intrepid sheriff. Where'd you get that badge anyway?"

"As I recall, it was a Chanukah gift from Aunt Dolly when I was nine or ten. It's an antique."

"A collectable. I'll cherish it, but you still owe me a real one. What's for breakfast?"

"We have the picture," the shorter of the two, the one calling himself Wentz, said. He handed the icon to his control who took it and inspected the surface. Something was not right. He could swear he smelled fresh varnish. He stroked its surface. It was flat. There was no microchip on it. Never had been.

"Where did you find this?"

"It was in the church. He must have sold it to the priest person."

"This is not the right icon, you idiots."

"It is the one in the picture."

"It is not. The one you were sent for is old. Look at this. It's as smooth as a baby's bottom. Even the varnish is recently applied. You have the wrong one." He threw the icon across the room. It skittered across the carpeting and came to rest next to the motel's trash can.

"Go back to that man's house and this time don't bring me a copy, get me the right one."

Chapter Thirty-eight

At 10:15, Ike called his office. Frank had nothing to report. Dakis' house had not been invaded as of 11:30, and it seemed unlikely it would be any time soon. Maybe that night. They'd had two college students in the tank for extreme DUI. They'd been arrested for driving their cars in reverse through the mobile home park and raising hell in general.

"Oh, and they had a cell phone that didn't belong to either of them. We checked it out, and it was the one that belonged to Sacci, it seems."

"Where did they say they'd found the phone?"

"In the trash bin a block from the urgent care center. No surprise there. They got pretty shirty with me when I asked them if it wouldn't have been appropriate for them to turn it in. They'd been using it to send obscene texts to people they didn't like and some faculty members. I guess they figured the messages couldn't be traced to them. Anyway, we locked them up and gave them a lecture about responsibility, which went over their heads until I told them it was involved in a murder investigation and because it was found in their possession they would be considered suspects—accomplices at least. They sobered up a bit after that."

"So what happened this morning?"

"Like I said we kept them overnight to let them dry out and were about to turn them loose this morning when Essie came in. She'd forgotten her romance novel or something. Anyway, she got on her high horse and made those kids write a 'to whom it may concern' letter of apology to the manager and residents of the mobile home park. It was awesome."

"Better report them to the injured parties who received the text messages as well. So Essie did that. You know, for someone who used to be the life of the party, she sure has come around about one-eighty."

"She's still the life of the party, Ike, but a different party. Also, the lab reports are in from the crime scene at the motel. It will be a month or so before DNA tests can be run. Do you want them?"

"I don't know, Frank. They cost a bundle to run, and our budget is slim as it is. We'll hold on that for a while. I'm hoping we won't need them."

No money would change hands but the lab charged the sheriff's office for work done, and interagency exchanges maintained a paper trail the county needed to keep everyone accountable.

"What did the medical examiner have to say?"

"That's interesting. The evidence technicians at first thought the motel room had been wiped, because they didn't find much in the way of blood. Figured the little trace they did find meant they'd cleaned. But the towels found in the dumpster were nearly clean as well."

"So, this relates to the ME how, exactly?"

"As we figured, the gun was a small caliber weapon, a .25 caliber to be exact. The ME thinks the guy was shot by accident."

"Accident? How does that work?"

"Can't say as to the how, but you remember me telling you about the ME's guess as to the cause of death? Anyway, it's established that Sacci took a single shot on the left side of the chest. The bullet collapsed his lung. That shouldn't have been fatal, but the ME confirmed the slug hit a rib and ricocheted and punched a small hole in Sacci's descending aorta. The guy bled out in his lung cavity with hardly any external bleeding. The ME speculates he died slowly enough for the people who shot him to think maybe he could make it if he got medical attention. I guess they figured that he wouldn't dare to rat them out, considering what they were up to."

"And they couldn't very well sign him in to a hospital themselves, so they dumped him in the clinic and hoped."

"Looks like. I reckon that gives you reckless homicide or a manslaughter charge at best."

"If we catch them, I'll push for man two at least. They had a gun, probably not registered, and were in the act of committing a felony."

"You don't know that, Ike."

"I may not have the evidence, Frank, but I do know it. I'll get the evidence. Call me if anything else turns up."

Ike studied the lighted face of his phone. Ruth, who had made an abortive attempt to sunbathe, stepped back in the room, bundled up in slacks, sweater, and down vest. She still shivered.

"Coffee, hot and a lot of it. How can it look so sunny and warm on that deck and be so cold when you get out there?"

"A better question is, whatever possessed you to walk out there in the altogether in the middle of March? This is the mountains and early spring, not July at the beach."

"Admit it, you enjoyed the view while it lasted."

"Okay, deputy, I admit it, I did. Now, while you warm yourself, here's a puzzle for you. Did I tell you about the Dakises?"

Ruth shook her head, and Ike filled her in on the story, the separated couple, and the icon's connection to both.

"Okay, what's the puzzle?"

"Why ship this bit of information, those documents, into the country this way? For the moment, I assume that the source is Middle-Eastern terrorists or related to them in some way, but having said all that, what I need to know is with all the sophisticated electronic gadgetry available, why ship it this way?"

"I'll need my thinking cap for this one." She left the room and returned wearing her uniform hat. "I think better in character. Deputy Harris reports for duty. Okay, the question was why this way and not the fancier, more sophisticated, hi-tech electronic way?"

"You think the hat will help?"

"Shut up. Of course it will. Give me a second. How about this? The microchip is a response to all the stuff Sam described for you. Too much complexity for what they needed to do. All that's necessary is to send it in on something like the icon, or say, a painting, a tea pot, or a souvenir purchased by someone who is a collector, even a tourist maybe—anything but an obvious threat, someone who is on a list or looks like a bad guy. Then, when it arrives in the States, the people who want it steal the tea pot, or whatever—the icon in this case—or buy it, or grab it. No watch list to reckon with, no TSA or customs problems to contend with. And, if screeners do find the chip thing, the carrier—innocent carrier, in fact—takes the fall. In this case, that would be Mrs. Dakis. No one can connect it or her to the sender or the receiver. So, this gigolo, who wooed and won the Dakis woman, had her be his...do you call them, mules? Whatever. And he figured once in the country he would grab the icon, ship the thing off to the bad guys, whoever they are...don't ask me who—that's your line of work—and skip town. Or maybe stick around. He may have figured that if this maneuver worked, he could set up her store as a permanent mail box. How'd I do?"

"Brilliant. How *did* you do that?"

"Occam's Razor."

"Excuse me?"

"Occam's Razor. You know the philosophical principal."

"Oh, you mean the rationale that posits that when you have two competing theories both of which make exactly the same predictions, the simpler one is the better?"

"*Lex parsimoniae.* Exactly. There are all sorts of possibilities here, I suppose, and you and Charlie and your buddies up in Langley probably buzzed yourselves into serious headaches mulling them over."

"Perhaps, but also keep in mind H. L. Menken, who famously said, 'For every complex problem there is a solution that is simple, neat, and wrong'. Nevertheless, you have pegged it, I think. It is, indeed, simple and very neat, and in this case, undoubtedly correct. I'll find you a badge."

"I solve your mystery—it's the least you can do."

Louis Dakis had returned early from the party the night before. He didn't know anyone and felt awkward in a crowd of relative strangers, and academics at that. Also, the sheriff showed up, and he didn't want to be caught up in a conversation with him. The icon had still been where he'd left it—in plain sight of the front door as the deputy had requested. If anyone had wanted to take it, they would only have had to open the door, take two steps in, and pick it up. They'd told him to make it easy to spot. In addition, and more to the point, Lorraine was sleeping in the guest room. It was her second night in the house, but they'd not spent any real time together. Thursday evening, she'd allowed herself to be brought here, collapsed, and immediately dropped off to sleep in the guest room, her body's response to the stress she was under, he supposed. When he awoke Friday morning she was gone, and he'd assumed she'd returned to Washington. But no. Late Friday evening, as he was leaving for the president's party, she'd wheeled into the driveway, said nothing, refused food, and locked herself in the guest room again.

He'd tried the guestroom door when he returned from the party. It was locked. Either she was sleeping, or, if she wasn't, she still didn't want company, at least not his. He had shuffled off to bed and slept as well, but badly, his ear alert to the noises of the night.

Saturday morning seemed brighter to him somehow, when he awoke. He dressed and settled in the old-fashioned kitchen to brew a pot of coffee. He found the fixings for breakfast and had toast, scrambled eggs, and bacon laid out in a serving dishes when Lorraine peered around the door jamb.

"Can I bother you for some of your coffee?" She looked bedraggled. A poet might have said forsaken, but Louis was not a poet. She looked a mess.

"I made us breakfast," he said. She slid around the door in his old flannel bathrobe and sat across from him.

"We didn't talk last night."

"No, well, I had that shindig at the president's house to go to and...well, I thought you'd want some alone time. You didn't look like you were in a mood to talk. The door was locked when I got back."

"We never talked. That was the problem, you know. What did I look like if not in the mood?"

Okay, forsaken. "Tired and maybe a little confused, I guess. Sad. Here, eat." He pushed a plate toward her. She absently stirred her coffee. Her gaze remained fixed on a spot somewhere over his left shoulder.

"What happens now?"

"Now? I don't know, Lorraine. What do you want to happen?"

She placed the spoon in the saucer and sipped her coffee. "This is a cute little house, Louis."

"Cute? I'm not sure cute is the word I'd use. It's nice enough. I'm comfortable here. I have a place to paint, and I have the teaching gig. It works for me."

She hugged the robe closer. "But it's not the same as before. The store, the trips, the excitement…"

"Excitement is greatly overrated, I think."

"So you're happy here?" She sipped her coffee again and made a face, whether of pleasure or dislike he could not be sure. She was always very particular about her morning coffee.

"Happy? Lorraine, sorry, but that is a silly thing to say. Happy? Everything I worked for, no, that *we* worked for, is gone. Puff of smoke…gone.

No store, no business, no painting…My teaching position here ends in June. I have no contingency plans, no future and you are…Why are you still here? I thought you went home yesterday."

"I intended to."

"Yes, I know, but you didn't. What changed your mind?" Did he want to know? When did enough become enough?

"I was turning onto the highway when I had a little problem."

"A problem? Car problem? What sort of problem?"

"I had to turn around and go to that urgent care facility. That's ironic isn't it? I end up where the deputy told me they found Franco's body. And there I am…same place. Who knows, maybe even sitting in the same chair." She shuddered at the thought.

"You didn't answer my question. What problem did you have that required a trip to a medical facility?"

She sat perfectly still, only her lower lip trembled slightly. He waited.

"It turned out to be nothing. I *was* late, that's all. I thought…It's…I thought I might be…" Lorraine's voice caught and she picked up a napkin and wiped her eyes.

"You were late, but you thought you might be what? I'm not following you."

She shrugged. "Nothing."

"Nothing? Wait, you thought you were late, that kind of *late*...you and Sacci were...and you're not?"

"Does that make you happy?" She glowered at him, her fist clenched.

"Happy? Why would you think that? No. Sad, I think, for you. Lorraine, I never thought that children were that important. Well, not right away, and there was the store and..."

"If you'd only listened to me...oh, never mind. It doesn't matter, and I don't want to fight any more."

"Believe it or not, neither do I. For what it's worth, I'm sorry. I guess I need to work through all the things I probably need to be sorry for, but that will have to do for now."

She blinked and refocused her eyes back to inspecting the spot on the wall behind him "Okay, I guess. What about me? What now?"

"That's the question isn't it? What about you? What happens next for you?"

"I don't know, Louis. The divorce...the store, I don't know."

Louis wanted to grab her by the shoulders and shake her. His world had come apart because of her and her damned now deceased boyfriend, and here she sat looking like Raggedy Ann, only with sad button eyes that pleaded for him to fix everything. To fix her. Well, he sure as hell didn't want to, even if he knew how. She should be the one doing the fixing. Oh, hell, no, that wasn't all there was to it. He needed some reworking as well. He couldn't afford to be angry. But it would take a while, that was certain.

"There's no need to rush anything. You need time to get through this. I guess we both do, you more than me. Let's wait and see." He refilled her cup and gave her plate another shove, the way you might a child's to remind it to eat. She glanced at the food and nibbled on a piece of toast.

"I don't know," she murmured.

Chapter Thirty-nine

Frank called that afternoon. "Here's a coincidence for you, Ike. We got a call from the church, you know, the Episcopal one my mother attends? Anyway, she called, and there's been a break-in."

"How is that important?" Ike was on the edge of being annoyed. Fictional sheriffs and top cops were always called, paged, texted, or whatever technology was *au courant*, by their staffs about everything and anything. But in truth he didn't need to know about everything and anything. He wanted to know the status of ongoing investigations in a timely fashion, of course, but the weekend was the weekend. "It doesn't strike me as an emergency or even very pressing, Frank."

"Sorry, you're right, neither of those, but I haven't told you the interesting part, and I thought you'd want to hear it and then think about it."

"Didn't mean to sound short. What is this interesting thing?"

"The only thing missing from the break-in at the church was…you'll never guess." Frank waited a beat and when Ike didn't venture a guess, continued, "An icon."

"The reverend has icons? I didn't know that. They must be something new. And one was stolen. You're right, it's an interesting coincidence. I hope it doesn't mean—"

"No, no, listen. You're right, it was a new one he'd recently bought. He put it up Thursday afternoon."

"And they only called in a break-in today?"

"We can't be sure when the break-in occurred. Something about Friday is his day off and the secretary, her name's Gloria, happened to take the day off, too, so nobody was in the church until this afternoon. That's not all. The icon that was taken? He bought it from Dakis."

"This is asking too much, but call Dakis and find out what kind of icon he sold to Fisher. Then, check and make sure the one he has is still in place. If it is, there's a better than even chance they'll be back for his tonight."

"You coming in, Ike, in case they do?"

Ike swung around in his leather chair and looked at Ruth curled on the couch up in front of the fire place, a book open in her lap. Sensing his gaze, she looked back and smiled and tapped her sheriff's badge.

"No, I trust you, Frank. You know what to do." He hung up and joined Ruth.

Louis Dakis watched as Lorraine drove away. She'd be back in the city in a few hours. He wrestled with his feelings. As much as he wanted to stay angry at her, he had an equally strong desire to reach out and help her. What was that all about? He stamped his foot in frustration. The Volvo disappeared around the corner and was gone. The sun began its slow descent behind the pines that lined his little street, and he felt as though the temperature had dropped ten degrees.

If their marriage had been a bad one, he could understand, and until this week he'd thought it was good. He'd been wrong about that evidently. She thought she might be pregnant? That came like a bolt out of the blue. How did he feel about that? Not good, he guessed but he needed to let it go. Jesus, it was too much. He turned and retreated into his house. As he stepped onto the porch, he heard the phone ring.

"Mr. Dakis?" One of the deputies. "We need you to make yourself scarce again this evening. We're pretty sure our thieves will be back."

"I can do that. There's a movie in Roanoke I want to see and…yes I can do that."

"Good. By the way, did you happen to paint one of those icon things for the Reverend down at the church?"

"I did, yes."

"Can you tell me what it was about?"

Louis gritted his teeth. Icons weren't *about* anything, they were *of* something, they signified something, they represented a spiritual place. Comic books were about something. Soap operas and mystery stories were about something. Sports were about…"It was a second copy of the one I painted for the sheriff."

"Exact copy?"

"Yes and no. The one I painted for your sheriff had been treated to make it look old, like the original you have locked up. The priest's was not treated like that. It looked new."

"Thank you, sir. That pretty much nails it down. They'll be back. You clear out. We'll be watching."

Louis walked over to the icon he'd created to mimic the original and stared down at it. Something caught his eye. Something was not right. He picked it up and held it as he remembered the sheriff had done. Then he saw it. He squinted at the small bleb on the Virgin's eye. What was that?

He ran his forefinger across it. It had been fastened with some sort of mastic.

This must be the thing that caused all the trouble. It must have been what that Sacci/Zaki person was after. Nothing else made any sense. Lorraine was attractive and all that but…Sacci came to Picketsville. He must have come for the icon, for this thing stuck on the icon, and something must have gone wrong. The icon wasn't in the house when he came and he'd failed. Was that why they, whoever they were, killed him? Louis felt the anger building. His life sent into the dumpster for this? People had to die for this? He wanted to meet the people who so easily destroyed other people's lives. His life, Lorraine's life. What kind of terrible game were they playing? He felt the bile in his throat. He put the icon down and strode to his desk and called Lorraine's cell phone.

"I asked you to call me, Ike. You didn't. You could be in trouble. I can only sit on this for so long and—"

"Charlie. I did get your message and I responded, sort of. Ms. Ryder is on ice where you can't get your hands on her."

"Don't be silly, Ike, I can have her located in an hour or two. I will, too, unless you tell me what's going on."

"A question first, what is the Agency's interest in the *USS Liberty* business? Before you seed the clouds with governmental bombast and cause a metaphorical snow storm, I know your boy Wainwright was here in my town. I know he was with the men who were responsible for shooting Sacci, and I think I know what he was after."

"I won't ask you how you found all that out. What I want to know is why you found all that out. Why did you?"

"I have a murder on my hands, and, as we both know, it's related to the bit of business glued to the icon. I am the sheriff of this here town, and I aim to bring the varmints to justice."

"Very funny. Look, as you also know, it's national in scope. If these guys are located, they'll be ours."

"Yours? I don't think so, friend. First, it's domestic and, therefore, outside your jurisdiction. The FBI can threaten me on this, but not you. Second, if I catch them first you will have to bluff your way in here to remove them. You'll need a high-level court order. And to get one of those, you will need to explain all to someone, and I don't think you want to do that."

"Why wouldn't I want to do that?"

"Number one, as I said, it's domestic. Why isn't the FBI all over this, Charlie? Karl Hedrick was here when you came. It's his call, not yours. Surely you've kept the Bureau in the loop."

"You're being sarcastic. You know why."

"I do and since I do, you and your gang will back off until I have my bad guys under lock and key."

"If you know what I must assume you know, and I have some doubts on that score, you must also be aware that there will be a notification from the State Department informing you that an embassy has invoked diplomatic immunity and the bad guys will be on a plane headed for the Near East inside and hour."

"Not going to happen, and not the Near East, I don't think."

"And why is that, O Mighty Sheriff?"

'Because you, or more properly, your boss, the director, is not going to let it."

"I'm waiting."

"Who shot Wainwright? Not one of these guys. They probably shot Sacci. I'm reasonably sure of that, but Wainwright was long gone, on his way to Rock Creek Park. Do I have that last bit correct?" Charlie didn't answer. "I'll take that as a yes. So, what do your intelligence buddies tell you happened to him?"

"We're working on it."

"Bullshit, Charlie, you know. Someone ratted

your boy out. Someone, if I have the sense of this right, either told someone else who he was and that he'd slipped inside the Mossad, and they, that is to say the Mossad, dropped him. I'd hate to think that, but desperate times, and so on. Or someone dropped the hint that he killed Sacci, and one of Sacci's friends, who would be on the opposite side of the street, so to speak, set him up and killed him as revenge. A fitting application of the Code of Hammurabi for them. There is a third possibility, but we'll hold on that for now."

"I think you're fishing here, Ike, so please get on with it."

"Don't play dumb with me, Charlie. Wainwright was one of yours. So what happened? Someone leaked it that Wainwright was Sacci's killer? You don't want that someone, or any of the other likely suspects, peripheral players, or spear carriers on a plane and out of the country inside an hour. And that third possibility, the one you'd rather didn't exist but that you must be considering anyway, stinks. You want me to have these guys because you need to know what happened to Wainwright and they can lead you to the answer."

Chapter Forty

The phone rang three times. Louis thought he would be transferred to voice mail. On the fourth Lorraine answered.

"Hold on a minute. I'm driving and there isn't an easy place to pull off close by." Louis listened to traffic noise and Lorraine's muttering. Finally the engine noise subsided. "What is it, Louis?"

"I need to ask you a question. When you picked up the Virgin of Tenderness in Egypt, did you notice anything odd about it?"

"Odd, what do you mean, odd? Nothing except we got a fabulous price and transporting it out of the country seemed, I don't know, expedited. Why? What's this all about?"

"There is something not right about this whole business. We need to talk."

"Louis I am on a pull-off on I-81. Trucks are whipping by me at a zillion miles an hour and nearly knocking the car over. Why do you want to talk about the icon now? I give up. It's too much. You keep and sell it. I am done with this whole rotten business."

"Don't hang up, this is important. Just bear with me. It didn't strike you as unusual, the bargain price, the greased wheels in customs? No, I suppose it wouldn't. But that's not what I meant. Tell me about the icon itself. Did you notice if there was an imperfection on its surface, on the Virgin's eye, for example?"

"Damn, there goes another one. I'm going to get myself killed sitting out here like this. On the eye? Which eye? I don't remember any, no. But I don't think I would have noticed it in any event. You called me about seeing it in the catalog, and what a great buy it would be if we could get it. I went to Cairo to see it and then Franco said…I bought it and took it to Italy, end of story."

"Right, I know that part. Another question, and please don't be angry at me for asking, but when did Sacci show up, relative to the purchase, I mean."

"I don't see what…if you're trying to stir up something here—"

"Lorraine, I promise you, I'm not. What's done is done. I'm not happy about that, but there it is. Listen, am I correct in thinking that Sacci appeared about the time you arrived in Cairo, seemed to be an insider, so to speak, facilitated the sale, and then returned to Italy with you? That's what you told the police, right?" Louis waited for a response and receiving none, pressed on. "Okay, I'll assume that's yes. Lorraine, there is something fishy about this whole business...wait, hear me out. You told the sheriff that you brought the icon into this country but that Sacci came a week afterwards. What happened then?"

"Then?"

"Yes, did your relationship with him seem to change after he arrived?"

"I don't see where this is going, Louis. Now I must get back on the road."

"Please, Lorraine, answer the question. I am not trying to...to imply anything, but I think the icon was tampered with, and I think Sacci knew all about it. See, by the time he'd arrived in the country, the icon was gone. I'd taken it. He was supposed to deliver it to someone after he landed, and I guess he got desperate. He needed to produce it or the thing on it, or he was in trouble with some one, and he couldn't. Then somehow, don't ask me how, he found out that it was with me here, and he came to Picketsville to fetch it. Only I think he must have picked up some other people who came with him and..."

"And what? You mean those other people killed him? But why?"

"Because they wanted what was glued on the Virgin's eye. Because he was supposed to deliver to a party once it arrived in the country and couldn't. They were not his friends, or if they were, they must have figured they were done with him and didn't want to leave any, I don't know, traces behind, maybe these others wanted it for themselves. That's why I asked about any change. There was that delay of a week or so, don't you see?"

"There was a problem with his visa and they held his baggage for a week. Yes, I already told you—"

"I want to know about him and the icon."

"What about them?"

"When he'd cleared customs, or whatever his problem was, it came time to produce the icon for the people he was supposed to be escorting it into the country for—"

"You can't possibly know that."

"Okay, I'm guessing, you understand, but anyway, when he came for it, like I said, I'd already taken it away and he didn't know where right away. You said he told you he was going to New York but he came here. Now do you see it?"

"I don't understand what...You keep saying there was something on the icon. What was it?"

"I think it was a microchip or microdot, a spy thing, with secrets embedded in it. I don't know what kind, but something important, probably. You know secret plans maybe, or a list of names. Remember, the police said his name, his real name was Farouk Zaki and he was born near the Gaza. Right?"

"You trying to tell me he didn't…He was using me to…that he's a terrorist? Louis that's an awful thing to say."

"I know, for your sake I'm sorry, but it's the only explanation for everything that's happened to us. And I thought you…"

"I'd what?"

"I thought you might want to help me get the people who killed him."

"Get the people who…? You and me? You can't be serious. You are. How? No, this is crazy. All the security courses we took emphasized do not confront criminals or, indeed, even a potential lawbreaker, whatever the circumstance might be. You must remember that."

He did. He didn't care. Enough was enough. "They will come back tonight to steal the icon; I'm sure of it. The police are counting on it. Come back here. We will be waiting for them in the house. They won't expect us to be there because they will have seen me leave already. Before we turn them over to the police, we will have a chat, maybe. Maybe more."

"You still have your guns?"

"I do."

"This is insane."

"These people ruined my life, yours, too. Destroyed us. I don't want them to get away with it."

"But the police, the FBI, whoever does those things. Won't they catch them?'

"They don't care about you or me, Lorraine. They will find them and then all kinds of international negotiating and cover-ups will take place. Spies aren't real people with real names. Mark my words, they will disappear into some super-secret black hole, and you and I will be out in the cold with nothing, no explanation, no justice, nothing."

"You think?"

"Yes."

"I'll…have to think about it."

"Come back to think about it then. We can do this together."

"This is crazy, but okay, I'll come back, but only to think about it."

"Park in the next block over and wait for me. I have to leave the house so the police and the thieves will see me go. We'll sneak back through the hedge at the rear of the house and wait with the lights off."

"I may live to regret this but, okay, I'm on my way."

◇◇◇

Ruth was not going to be happy, but Ike had the itch. Something was going down this evening, and he needed to be there. There were too many players in the game.

"I have to go into town. I'm sorry. Something came up."

"You've been talking to Charlie again, haven't you?"

"I have."

"You're going to play hero again."

"Not tonight. I need to nip something in the bud. We have a very unhappy CIA, a soon to be very unhappy FBI, I'm guessing, and a possible international incident about to burst into full flower, you could say, right here in 'River City.'"

"And so, as I said, you're going to play hero."

"Nope, I'm going to play sheriff and nab me a murderer or two, then I'm going to play hero."

"If I wear my badge and hat, can I come too?"

"No."

"I let you come to my faculty meetings. How much more lethal can what you're doing be than that?"

"You have a point, but no. There's dodging verbal barbs and there's dodging bullets. Not that I expect to have to dodge either tonight, but these are bad guys with no place to run. I'll be back before midnight. Stay here and keep your badge warm."

"Jacob is angry. We stole the wrong icon. He wants us to go back to that man's house and search again and not come out until we have it."

"What if the man is there?"

"You still have your gun, don't you?"

"Of course."

"So?"

"Killing another person in this town is not so wise, you think, after Zaki, I mean. Serak said Avi Kolb is dead too. He was shot."

"So, he's dead. What is that to us?"

"Nothing, except maybe knowing who did it would be nice. We could be next."

"Would be nice? What is this with you? You know who did it. Friends of Zaki."

"You think? It wasn't one of our people?"

"Just get ready."

Chapter Forty-one

Ike stopped at a Walmart on the highway outside of town and purchased a disposable cell phone. He pulled over to the end of the parking lot next to a mammoth RV and called Shmuel Gold.

"שלום?"

"Yes, hello, I need to speak to Shmuel, please."

"Is asleep. Sorry, call back later,"

"Tell him it's Isaac Schwartz from the United States. Tell him it's urgent. Tell him it's about the icon and the things we discussed earlier. Tell him it's important."

"Wait a minute." Ike could hear raised voices in the background. Shmuel came on the phone.

"So, you weren't fooled. I told them you wouldn't be. So, what is so urgent I need to hear from you in the middle of the night?" Ike heard the distinctive sound of a match being struck and then Shmuel sucking on his pipe stem. He remembered the Turkish blend Shmuel favored and reflexively cleared his throat.

"A man going by the name of Avi Kolb was gunned down in Washington a few days ago. You remember? We had a chat about him with your friend from the Mossad, or was it SHABAK. It doesn't matter. I need to know if one of your people did it."

"Isaac, Isaac, you are on the phone to Shmuel. How can I answer such a question?"

"It's an untraceable phone operating on a bandwidth not assigned to me or the police. If someone is monitoring my calls it will take them several minutes to find me, assuming they were looking. Talk to me."

Shmuel cleared his throat. "My friend, if I don't know what happened, I can't tell you any-thing. As far as I know, this Avi Kolb was not terminated by any of our people."

"Would you know if he was?"

"I would know in the way you know these things when certain people talk, you understand. No one says this or that, but you know. So, not one of ours."

"My old colleagues over in Langley, Virginia, will come after your people if they did, and that would not be good for our countries, now would it? That's why I asked. Heads up either way."

"Isaac, I can only say this. This man who called himself Avi Kolb was not one of ours, but he pretended to be to some contractors we engaged, you see, but that is all."

"Contractors hired to intercept an icon with damaging information about the *USS Liberty* on a microchip, before the intended recipients could get their hands on it. I figured that part out. I don't know why yet, but that will come. What I can't figure is why did you think you had to go covert over here? Why not tip the FBI or the CIA and let them pick up the chip? It's in no one's interest for those documents to surface."

"They were fakes."

"So, you say. I don't know, and at the remove of nearly fifty years, I don't care. But now one of our agents is dead, two of your guys, hired muscle or not, are being sought for a murder, and there will be hell to pay if we can't defuse this thing. Shmuel, talk to me. I'm running out of safe minutes on this phone."

"Okay, but we never talked, yes? Our boys did not shoot the Kolb person. The word is that it was done by Jihadists—Shiites, Iranians, Jihadists anyway, but I am not convinced of that, yes? What would be the point? They are in your country in deep cover. The last thing they need is for someone looking for them, at least not for the killing of one person, CIA man or not. A thousand CIA men, maybe, they would do, but not one, I don't think.

They are crazy but not that crazy, not on US territory. You look for someone else."

"If not your people and not Jihadists, that only leaves one choice and I don't like it."

"It is an unfortunate business we play at, Isaac. We both know that. If you need some Arab names to check with, it will take longer than we have right now, and I'm not sure I could get them anyway."

"I don't need names; the CIA does. They will get them if they want them. I only want to find those contractors of yours and put them out of business. Do your people understand what this little intervention has produced?"

"It looked like a risk we should take. In retrospect…? I think you should be more interested in where the documents are going, don't you? Why are they still after it? There are copies, I think, and there is always tomorrow. Patient men would wait, wouldn't they?"

"Or they've been turned."

"An interesting thought, Isaac. It had not occurred to me."

"You might pass it along to the folks back in Jerusalem. And now you will go after them and the originals?"

"Of course."

"Even if they are, as you say, fakes?"

"Isaac…"

"Very well, I'm for the men who killed the messenger. You won't try to protect them?"

"We contracted this business out for a reason."

The line clicked off. Ike pried open the back of the phone and removed its memory chip. Then he stepped out of his car, positioned the phone under the back wheel and, to the wonderment of the owner of the RV who'd that instant stepped out for air, drove over it three times. He retrieved the wreckage and carried it to a nearby trash receptacle and dropped it in. The chip he would toss into some newly-laid wet cement on a sidewalk repair job a block from his office.

"We thought we picked up some phone chatter from near the area you wanted us to monitor, Mr. Garland."

Charlie banged his fist on the desk top in frustration. "What did you hear?"

"Not much. One man, we assume it is your person of interest said, 'I'm for the men who killed the messenger. You won't try to protect them?' And the other voice, we think it was an overseas call, said, 'We contracted this business out for a reason.'"

"That's it? Where overseas?"

"Best guess, Israel."

"Crap. That tears it. We're going to have to

move in. My friend, the sheriff, is playing loose cannon again."

Twilight. Frank Sutherlin and Amos Pettigrew eased their unmarked car, headlights out, down the street toward Dakis' house. They watched and carefully noted the time he left to go to the movie in Roanoke. They'd been told that was his plan. So, he was out of the way. Once he'd cleared out, they repositioned the car to give them a clearer view of both the rear and front of the house. The thieves could come from any direction. Best guess would be through the back door, although they knew Dakis had left the phony icon in the front of the house in plain sight and an easy access for a grab and run. Further down the block a second cruiser lurked in the shadows, ready to move in as soon as they had contact. Nothing to do now but wait.

"What's that?" Amos pointed down the street.

Frank had been checking the settings on his radio, looked up. "Where?"

"I could swear I saw a vehicle with its head-lights off, turn the corner and park. There...over there."

Frank could barely make out the outlines of a large SUV parked fifty yards further down the street. "That must be them." He called the second cruiser. "We have company. Get ready."

At that moment a third car turned the corner, and with its lights on drove slowly down the street toward them. As it passed the parked SUV, Frank noted that there didn't seem to be anyone in the front seat.

"Down," he rasped to Amos and the two men scrunched low in the seats. When the car passed they straightened. "Where is it?"

"Turned the corner. Must be a neighbor."

"Or a new wrinkle. Keep your eye on that SUV. I need to talk to Ike."

Chapter Forty-two

Through her rear view mirror Lorraine saw Louis exit his car, glance up and down the street, and approach her car along the sidewalk. She lit a cigarette and coughed. She hadn't smoked in three years, but she'd found a pack of Franco's Melachrinos in the glove box and lit one up. The acrid smoke forced her to lower her window. Louis opened the door and slipped into the passenger seat.

"When did you start smoking again?" He rolled down the other window to let the smoke out. "What is that? It smells like you're smoking rope."

"Just now. I found these in the car. They were…left in here and I thought one might calm me." She stubbed out the cigarette and turned to face him. "What are we doing, Louis? This is lunacy. We should call the police." She reached for her cell phone.

"There's no need. By now they will have staked out the house. If I'm right, they will wait for the people who tried to steal the icon to try again. That is, they will wait until they come out of the house with it."

A car turned the corner in front of them, pulled to the curb, and turned off its headlights.

"Who's that?"

"I don't know, Lorraine, I barely know my neighbors next door, much less the ones on this block."

"I don't like this. We could be in real trouble. Suppose they have guns?"

Louis pulled the .25 caliber pistol from his jacket pocket. "Suppose they do. So do we, and we will have the drop on them."

"You said the police have staked out the house. How will we get in without being seen? Won't they, like, think we're the ones breaking in?"

"That's the good part. There's a stairwell to the basement on the north side that is almost completely hidden. You have to know it's there. The hedge down the side of the house comes within a few feet of it. We will stay on the other side of the hedge out of sight up to the point where the stairs are, push through real fast, drop into the stairwell, and go in through the basement. I worked the door free this afternoon and oiled the hinges. The police will be watching the back and front. They'll never see us. Then we wait for the bastards to arrive."

It was a longish speech but Louis spoke so rapidly and with such passion that Lorraine could only nod her agreement.

"You're sure this will work? I'm scared, Louis. No, this is crazy."

"If we want to get the people who killed your...friend, then we have to."

"My friend? You mean Franco, or whoever he was. My God, I didn't even know him well enough to know his name. I didn't know him at all. What was I thinking?" She stared straight ahead, unblinking. "But what's in it for you, Louis?"

A good question. Why was he doing this? He must have an answer. Was he angry and frustrated? Did he think forcing her to face these men would make it right again? But still, he must have his doubts. She was right. It was crazy. He didn't care.

"Because I want to do something about the people who ruined my life. That icon and its secret are at the heart of this charade and I want my... my pound of flesh."

"Okay, I'll buy that as long as you remember that Shylock never got it."

"What? Shylock never got what?"

"His pound of flesh. It's from the *Merchant of Venice,* don't you remember? Shylock loans the money to the guy and if he doesn't pay, Shylock gets a pound of flesh. Then Portia...*the quality of mercy*…never mind. I'm going to hate myself in the morning, but if we're going to do this thing we need to do it now."

"There were cars parked on the street when we drove by. They could be cops."

"Of course there are cops. So what? You didn't think they were going to let this go, did you? So, you have your gun with the noise suppressor. I have mine. We have a shotgun. What kind of hick police department will stand up to that?"

"They'll be watching the back and front."

"Yes, they will but there is another way in. Yesterday I went through the neighborhood in a water-meter reader's uniform. There's a stairwell on the side of the house very close to that hedge. All we have to do is slide along that hedge, you know, keep in the shadows, and go into the basement and up the stairs. We grab the icon and leave the same way. The cops will still be there in the morning wondering what happened."

"Did someone get out of the car down the block?"

"I didn't see. No problem. We wait five minutes and then we go."

"Frank, I swear someone got out of the SUV down

the street a moment before that car drove by with its headlights on. I wish we had those night vision goggles. I feel like I'm blind."

"Stay calm, Amos. Where'd he go?"

"Not sure. When we ducked down, the headlights knocked out my night vision. Down the block? Maybe across the street."

"Okay, no panic...Ike?" Frank had raised his boss on the phone. "We have a problem." Frank paused. "Okay, there's an SUV down the street that looks too big to be our anonymous burglars. Amos thinks someone got out and crossed the street to the house."

"I didn't say that. I said they might have done."

Frank waved Amos off with his hand "Okay, we'll hold until you get here. The other car with two more deputies is standing by."

The man in question had, indeed, slipped across the street behind the car when he thought he could do so unseen. Now he was positioned in the shadows of a Japanese cherry tree, which he guessed was close to blooming, not that he cared, on the southern edge of the back yard.

"In position, sir," he said and lowered his night vision goggles over his eyes. He'd only used them once before, in training down on the farm as a new

CIA recruit. It wasn't that long ago, but tonight here in the dark and on a mission that didn't quite make sense, it seemed years. They were heavier than he remembered. "Nothing to report."

"Hang on, they will come, they have to. Remember, we extricate them before the locals can react."

"Roger that."

"Lorraine, not so much noise. You sound like a cow in a cornfield."

"Oh, that's nice. And you jabbering, what's that, crows in the cornfield?"

"I'm whispering. I didn't mean you look like a…oh, never mind, shhhh…"

The two figures pushed through the hedge and dropped quickly into the stairwell. As Louis had promised, the door opened noiselessly on oiled hinges. Once inside he twisted on a small maglite and shined it up the stairs.

"This way." He stepped gingerly on the first step which creaked. He didn't remember the creaking when he'd come down earlier.

Lorraine hesitated at the foot of the stairs. "Shouldn't we lock the door behind us?"

"Better not. We will have to use this as our escape route."

"You think? I'm not sure. Suppose they sneak up on us?"

"Nobody else knows about this stairwell."

"You can't be sure." Lorraine retreated back down the steps. "I'm locking the door." She slid the bolt into the receiver, gave the door a tug, and climbed back up the stairs.

Louis cracked the landing door. "See, we're off the little corridor that leads from the living room area to the kitchen. There's the icon. I put it out where anybody could see it easily and left a night light on to make it even easier to see."

"Not much light."

"It's enough. All we do now is wait. The second they come through the door to take it, we nail them."

"Nail? Louis, you're sounding like an action hero in a bad movie. How do you expect to nail them?"

"Shhh…"

Chapter Forty-three

Her caller ID read E. ST. C. Ruth wondered what her mother, the would-be author and reimagined Eden Saint Claire, wanted.

"Mother? How is your visit going with the Schwartzes?"

"Not so hot, Honey. Dolly Frankenfeld fell into a spell of the vapors after lunch and said she had to pack up and go home to Richmond. I don't think she took to me. I wonder why?"

"You didn't, maybe, pay too much attention to Abe? I don't know you anymore, Mother, but if you were on him the way you moved in on my faculty men, Dolly's difficulties are easily explainable."

"Nonsense, Abe is old enough to be your father. Older, in fact. And, of course, he will be; in-law that is, anyway. And I don't 'come on.' I am merely a people person and interested in what they have to say. I mean, if I'm going to write a book—"

"All right. So what happened?"

"Nothing happened. I went out there with them and first thing they showed me around the farm. Did you know they had cows? Lovely brown eyes, they had. I said so to Abe. And then we had lunch on the terrace. It's a very nice old farm house. Picturesque."

"I know. I've been there. That can't have been all. You didn't, by any chance, accidently fall into Abe's arms. Batting your eyelashes, did you?"

"No, of course not. I slipped and fell and it *was* an accident."

"And Dolly? How'd she take the *accident?*"

"Dolly? I'm sure I don't know. Abe is very strong for a man his age. Did you know that?"

"No idea. Don't need to know. I have the son to keep corralled, remember? So, then what happened?"

"Well, as I was saying, we had lunch, Dolly felt ill, and that was that. Abe was very gentlemanly. He drove me back to your house before he and Dolly took off for Richmond, although I'd bet by the time he got back to that old farm of his, Dolly'd recovered."

"You can't know that."

"No, I can't. I'm just saying… Well, how's your weekend going up in the mountains? Maybe if you gave me directions, I could join you."

"I'll be home tomorrow evening. Trying to find this place on your own the first time is not recommended, particularly after dark. Besides, Ike was called back to town. Some sort of urgent business."

"Well, maybe when his urgent business is completed, he could drive me out."

"Um, no, I don't think so. He'll be late. Listen, you settle in and I'll see you first thing tomorrow evening. Help yourself to whatever you find in the kitchen."

"I already did. Lots of canapés and things left over from your party. You know the shrimp won't keep."

"You go for it. Eat up the leftovers and get a good night's sleep."

"I think I'll step out and take a walk."

"That might not be such a good idea either. You're new to the area and could get lost in the dark."

"Don't be silly. I have a very fine sense of direction. I never get lost. I will see you tomorrow. Monday, let's go shopping."

"Monday, I have work. We'll see."

Ruth hung up, paused, and called Campus Security.

"Claude, my mother might be wandering around the campus tonight. Do me a favor and keep an eye on her, will you? Be discreet, you know, but keep her in sight."

"Mr. Garland, the director said you were in charge

and that we should tell you what's going on at the house. We are pulling up to the street corner now. Before we turn, I thought I'd better check in. We may have a problem."

"And what would that be?"

"Well, my understanding was we were to go to this place and make sure the men who would likely break into the house were taken into custody by us."

"Yes, that's exactly right."

"And we were to be diplomatic with the local police because we didn't have jurisdiction."

"Correct."

"Sir, the intel we're getting is there is another group already on station, one of ours that is and already on the scene. Should we coordinate with them?"

"Whoa. Absolutely not. Ah, splendid I was right. No, stay back. Slip out and keep the area under surveillance. We are moving to plan B."

"Plan B? Sir, I am not aware of any—"

"I'll be there in five. Keep out of sight and monitor their com frequency. Listen to what they're saying. Under no circumstances short of gun fire are you to make your presence felt until I get there. That's plan B."

"Yes sir."

"Tony, two men are coming into the yard. They're

hugging the hedge and deep in the shadows. I think they're headed to the back door."

"Keep them in sight. Once they're in, we move."

"Yes sir. Keeping them in sight. They're almost to the back porch...okay, they're there. They should be on it in a second."

"Are they?"

"I don't know how, but I've lost them, sir."

"Lost them? How lost them? Are they at the back door or not?"

"They never climbed onto the porch, I don't think. Do you suppose they're headed for the front door?"

"Don't be an idiot. They're going in a window. Get over there and see."

"Moving."

"Frank, someone darted across the back yard. He moved from that cherry tree and ran to the corner of the house."

Frank keyed his radio. "Elroy, who's with you?"

"Billy."

"Billy, what are you doing out here? You're supposed to be home knitting booties or something."

"Need the comp time big brother. Besides I don't knit."

"Okay, the two of you head for the back yard. Stay on the other side of the hedge until you can punch through and see both sides of the house. Our guys are on the move. So far only one. Don't know what that means. Ike you getting all this?"

"Got it, sit tight and wait. I'm three minutes away. I want those guys intact. We'll wait until they come out."

Lorraine grabbed Louis' arm. "What was that?"

"What was what?"

"Shhh, I heard something that sounded like breaking glass. Wait, isn't that the basement door bolt being slid back? They're coming up the stairs. What do we do now?"

"Quick, into the kitchen. If they come this way, we'll be behind them. As soon as they reach for the icon we'll get them."

"Are you sure? I'm scared. Supposed they have guns."

Louis pushed her into the corridor and back into the kitchen. They crouched down behind the table, wedged in between it, the trash compacter, and the fridge. Lorraine nearly jumped out of her skin when the latter kicked on.

"Shhhh…they're on the steps."

Chapter Forty-four

"Ruth, what's Ike's number?"

"Mother, why do you need his number? I told you he's answering an emergency. He won't want a call right now. What can I do?"

"Nothing, you're out at that cabin place and hours away. This is my emergency. I need a policeman."

"What's wrong? Did you trip and fall? Are you lost?"

"No, of course not. I'm fine. I mean, no, I didn't fall and I'm not lost." She didn't sound so sure about the last bit.

"What, then?"

"I'm pretty sure I'm being followed. I swear every time I turn a corner, a man ducks back into the shadows. I need Ike to call a policeman to come out here and arrest the man."

"That would be Claude."

"Excuse me, that would be who?"

"I asked Security to keep an eye on you. You were walking around in the dark in a strange place, and I asked Claude to—"

"Tail me? Ruth, I am a grown woman and I do not need someone to serve as my duenna, thank you. How do I know this is Claude, as you say, and not some mugger?"

"Call him."

"What? Call to the man? What do I say?"

"How about, 'Claude, is that you?'"

Ruth listened as her mother lowered the phone and cleared her throat. "Claude…what's his name. Claude who?"

"Brigstock."

"Mr. Brigstock, Claude Brigstock. This is President Harris' mother speaking. Is that you?"

Ruth started to comment on her mother's mixed pronoun usage and thought better of it. She heard what must have been Claude's reply.

"Well, you're right. Mr. Brigstock has identified himself. Oh my, he's in uniform, too. How nice."

"Claude will see you home."

"I'm not finished taking my walk. Mr. Brigstock will accompany me."

"Where are you?"

"I have no idea. Mr. Brigstock, where are we?" There was a brief pause. Ruth waited until Eden handed the phone to Claude.

"On Faculty Row, Miz President, down toward the end of the street."

"Well, be careful."

Ruth clicked off and dialed Ike. "Hey, I know you are in the middle of saving the nation from imminent destruction, but this is a heads-up. My mother, accompanied by a security guard, is wandering around the campus in the dark. Where are you?"

"Wandering around the campus in the dark. Where is your mother?"

"Claude said they were on Faculty Row."

"Oh, hell. Call them back and tell them to get out of there, now."

"What's going on?"

"Never mind, just do it."

Wow, Ike had never sounded that hot before. Ruth called Security with instructions to send a car out to extricate her mother and Claude from whatever was happening. This is not what campuses were supposed to be about. Not out in the sticks anyway.

The man inched his way up to the back porch and up the steps. "I'm on the porch and looking around the corner where the two guys disappeared. There's no sign of them."

"They didn't come out front. Check and

see if there's a window they might have climbed through."

"Roger that…No, no window. Well, there's a window but it's like, ten feet off the ground, one of those skinny ones that usually have stained glass in them."

"You must have missed them climbing up onto the porch. Stand by the back door. When I give the signal you come in and cover it."

"Okay, wait, I hear voices. They must be in. I'm standing by."

"When they turn the corner and move toward the living room, Lorraine, you slam the basement door and lock it so they can't get away. I'll yell freeze and then we'll have them."

"Louis, this is crazy, I'm telling you. They are probably armed to the teeth and will shoot you as soon as look at you. I say we sit tight and let the cops do their thing."

"Too late for that now."

Two figures slipped into the corridor, paused, and moved toward the icon, which was leaning against the wall in the living room.

Louis stood and stepped quietly toward the two men. When Lorraine was in position, he jerked the slide back on his little automatic to chamber a round.

"Freeze," he yelled.

Lorraine kicked the door shut and fumbled with the key.

The three men left in the SUV tumbled out, raced across the street and crashed through the front door.

"Hands up. Federal agents, freeze," their apparent leader barked. "Hands up. Drop your weapons, all of you!"

"The door is locked. The woman locked the door."

"Oh, my God, do as they say, Louis."

"Everybody, stay where you are. You heard me, federal agents. Nobody move. Jesus, how many of you are there?"

"They're federal agents, Louis, put down the gun."

"We don't know that."

"But they said—"

"The bitch locked the door."

"Another one is right behind us, Louis. For God's sake drop your gun before they kill us." Louis Dakis dropped his weapon and raised his hands in the air.

"Give me the key, you stupid bitch."

"I know you. You were with that other man who asked about the icon. This is one of the men who came to the store, Louis, asking about the Virgin of Tenderness. What happened to your friend?"

"Dead. Not my friend. Now give me the key."

Lorraine tossed the key into the living room. It fell at the feet of one of the men claiming to be federal agents who scooped it up.

"I ought to…"

"You'll do nothing." The lead fed shouted and stared at the Dakises. "Who the hell are you two and what are you doing here?"

"I'm Louis Dakis and this is my wife. We live here. That is, I live here. She doesn't We're separated and so she doesn't—"

"Shut up."

"—live here, yes sir."

"Shit, now what are we supposed to do with these two."

"We'll see. We should be able to extract the other two and then…one move toward that shotgun, hot shot, and you're dead…and then figure a way to clear this without having to worry about Mr. and Mrs. Idiot, here. I don't want to shoot them, but these two others might do it for me."

"Shoot them, Tony? I don't understand."

"Let me think."

You see that? It looks like a raid, for God's sake. Billy, you and Elwood cover the back. No one leaves."

"It's Elroy, Frank, not Elwood."

"Listen, I want you to get your rear end over there and shut up…Ike, the place is full of people. I'm moving the car to block theirs, and we'll hold them for you."

"Easy does it, Frank. Just hold them in place."

"Mr. Garland, they, the other team that is, moved into the house. Who are they?"

"Okay, move around the corner and wait for me. You'll find out who they are soon enough."

Chapter Forty-five

Frank wheeled the cruiser around so that it sat blocking the street. He turned the headlights and spot light full on. The front yard lit up like noon. When he'd done that, Billy and Elroy turned on the halogen lamps they carried and illuminated the rear as well. Frank cranked up the loud speaker.

"This is the Picketsville sheriff's office. You, in there, all of you, drop your weapons and come out with your hands on your head."

"We're federal agents. You stand down."

Ike drove up and parked parallel to Frank, adding still more light to the scene. He stepped over and relieved Frank of the mike, motioning him to join the two men in the rear.

"You heard the man. Weapons down, hands on your head, now."

"I said, we're federal agents and you should stand down."

"So you say. If you are, drop your IDs by the

door as you come out, but I want your weapons on the floor, hands on your head. Last call before we assume you are a threat and start shooting."

"You idiot. Can't you hear? We're the federal government and—"

"And you have no jurisdiction here, if you are the federal agency I think you are. Out!"

Another SUV pulled up next to his car. Charlie Garland stepped out.

"Everything under control here, Ike?"

"What took you so long? I was beginning to think these bozos were yours."

"No, they are someone else's bozos. Mine are around the corner waiting for me to call them in. These guys were recruited for this operation under the mistaken notion they were on an authorized raid, I think. Most of them have no idea why they're here. Why don't you fire your weapon or something?"

"No need, they'll be out in a moment." Ike keyed the microphone on. "I'm running out of patience, people…Who are they, Charlie, I mean besides rogue agents? Do they have a name?"

"As I said, most of them have no idea why they've been dragged down here. They think they're on an intervention of some sort. This night is not going to look good in their personnel file, I can tell you. But the important thing is that one of them

is trying, unsuccessfully as it turns out, to cover his
ass. We'll see when he comes out."

"Tony, what the hell? They won't budge. What do
we do now? Those are local cops out there."

"Come on, Lorraine. We're leaving. Put your
hands up in the air like the man outside said, and
let's get out of here."

"You two stay put." The leader inched to the
window. "We have a hostage situation here. You
need to pull back."

"Tony, this is crazy. We have to get out, show
them our ID and sort this out. We're off the farm
and we don't have backup of any sort."

"Shut up. You, what's your name? Keep your
eyes on these two guys. If they move, shoot." Tony
swung his Glock around and aimed it at the two men.
The taller of the two studied the face behind the gun.

"You're the man," he said. "You are the contact
Serak told us about. He said you would cover—"

"I said, shut up."

A youngish and very anxious member of the
federal group whose name, he'd told Tony repeatedly, was Saunders, pointed to the two men by the
door, "Bullshit, this whole deal stinks. We're out
of here. You two, you first. Mr. and Mrs. Whoever
the hell you are, you're next."

Lorraine and Louis moved to the door behind the two men.

"Why did you kill Franco?" she asked the one closest to her.

"Lorraine, for God's sake, don't start."

The man shrugged. The second said, "Was an accident. Avi Kolb wanted information from him about that stupid icon and he wouldn't talk. He jumped like a rabbit, like he wanted to run. Bang. Reflex. He was a bad man, lady. He deserved to die."

"He was not a bad man."

"You don't know. You were stupid. He was a Jihadist. All you Americans are stupid when it comes to what the Jihadists mean to do to you. He wanted to hurt your country and mine as well. He was a bad man."

"No, he was an art importer, he was…" Lorraine voice trailed off as the enormity of what had happened to her finally crystallized. Franco Sacci *was* Farouk Zaki, as she'd been told. He *had* used her to enter the country and it was all about that damned icon. Nothing more. She wanted to cry but was too scared.

"Out the door, Lorraine, before these people, whoever they are, panic and we get caught in the middle." Louis shoved her out the door and followed her before anyone could stop them. The two men, Sacci's killers, stepped through next.

"Well, well, Mr. and Mrs. Dakis. You are not good at following directions." Ike said through the loudspeaker.

"Who are they?" Charlie asked.

"He is the man with the icon you so admired, and surely you recognize his wife. You visited her, did you not?"

"Is there anything you don't know about this case?"

"You leave a wide path when you walk through the weeds, Charlie, but in this case, a good guess. What I don't know is why the Dakises were in the house. They could have been killed."

"Probably would have been if the others hadn't arrived. And these two coming out now are your contracted operatives, I assume."

"I think they must be. Dakises, over here. Now, you two, on the ground face down."

The men dropped to the ground and lay face down in the grass. "We have diplomatic immunity," one shouted.

"I don't think so. Besides, you are in my juris-diction now. I don't see any flags on your bumper, no special license plates. How is that?"

Ike turned to Charlie. "These are my murder suspects. I am going to arrest them and put them in jail. If you have other plans for them, you will have to go through channels. Now, why *are* you here?"

"There are more people in there. I am interested in confirming who they are."

"You don't know?"

"I do, but I must be absolutely sure. I have back-up around the corner if we need it, by the way. Do we?"

"Let's see how desperate your people in there are."

Eden Saint Claire stepped out of the shadows and tapped Ike on the shoulder.

"My goodness, this is exciting. Are those people desperate criminals?"

"Sorry, Sheriff," Claude said. "I tried to take her home but she wouldn't go."

"It's okay, Claude...Ms. Saint Claire, let me introduce you to Charles Garland. You two have a lot in common. He specializes in fiction, too. Charlie, this is Ruth's mother, Eden Saint Claire."

"Really? Is that correct, Mr. Garland, you write fiction?"

"Your future son-in-law has a low sense of humor, Ms. Saint Claire. I am in the public relations business."

"Oh, then you do write fiction."

Ike returned to his microphone. "Okay, that leaves the rest of you. Out now with your hands on your heads. And please don't tell me you are federal agents again. I have a real one out here and he says you aren't. The back door is covered. You will come out now or we will come in and get you. You do not want that to happen."

Chapter Forty-six

Charlie spoke into his hand-held, and a second black SUV rounded the corner and pulled up next to Charlie's car.

"The US Calvary," he said and motioned the occupants to step out. Two men and two women walked over and drew their weapons. Amos zip-tied the two on the ground, who kept muttering about diplomatic immunity and needing to call the embassy. The Dakises huddled behind Frank's cruiser, his arm around her shoulder. Nothing happened in the house, but Ike could hear what he took to be an argument in progress. Finally one man exited. He held his ID wallet in his hand and dropped it on the porch. A moment later a second and third followed.

"On the ground, please, thank you. Charlie, I take it these are yours. Maybe you can have these nice people," he gestured vaguely in the direction of the men and women off to the side, "pat them

down and cuff them. One more to go, it appears…
Come out, come out, whoever you are." Ike keyed
off the mike. "Charlie, I take it this is your ultimate
target. Perhaps you'd like to talk him out."

"In a second, Ike. He's all alone in there. I'd
like to give him a chance to do the decent thing."
Charlie waved his newly arrived group into place

"You think he'll shoot himself?"

"I would, were I in his shoes. Save us all a lot
of time, paperwork, and embarrassment."

"Cold, Charlie, very cold. Now, as for my
two, I will put them into the system. Perhaps I
can make a case and have them sent away, perhaps
not. I certainly don't want them to spoil my fun
by checking out prematurely. By the way, where is
the FBI? I would have thought…" Charlie stared
straight ahead. "Oh, okay, we'll talk later."

Eden Saint Claire had removed her cell phone
from her purse and was busily snapping pictures.
One of Charlie's female agents—Charlie's Angels?
No, too much, Charlie might not appreciate it
under the circumstances, and Ike was certain the
woman would not. She approached Eden and
snatched her phone from her hand.

"Ma'am, you cannot photograph this
operation."

"Who says I can't? I am a very good friend
of the sheriff here, my daughter is the president

of this university, and I have First Amendment rights. Ike, tell this young woman who I am. She took my phone."

"Ms. Saint Claire," Charlie said, "This is one of those instances you read about but would not wish to believe, where the government lays its heavy hand on you, deprives you of one or more of your constitutional rights, and doesn't even apologize. I will have this woman, Special Agent Pushkin, delete your pictures and hold the phone until we leave. Then she will return it and perhaps even apologize for the inconvenience. I'm not too sure about that, however. Sensitivity training is not a big part of our indoctrination routine anymore. So, if she does or doesn't will depend on her mood at the moment and whether her mother taught her any manners." Agent Pushkin scowled at Charlie and deleted Eden's photos and shut down the phone.

"Mr. Garland…may I call you Charlie? Yes? Charlie, that was a most elegant speech. You must be very good at what you do, I think."

"Thank you. Now, for your sake, please step back. The man in the house is desperate. He may do something irrational. Perhaps induce a CAS, and that might involve some gun fire."

"CAS? What's that?"

"C.A.S., Ms. Saint Claire: cop-assisted-suicide."

"If I call you Charlie, you must call me Eden.

Fine, a suicide assisted by police? How would that work? You assist them? How?"

"No, we don't. Not in the sense you mean. No, a desperate criminal with nothing to lose, might come through the door and shoot at somebody, or nobody, just shoot. All these people here are trained to return fire. One shot from the bad guy and a half-dozen people will empty their clips into him. Cop-assisted suicide. Now please step back behind the vehicle."

"Is that Lorraine Dakis? Lorraine, is that you? It's me, Eden. What are you doing down here? Isn't this exciting?"

"Paula? Wait, you're not Paula any more. My goodness, what have you done? You look so different."

"It's the new me. New name, new body, new life. I am Eden Saint Claire, writer and traveler."

"Excuse me," Ike moved toward the two women. "You know each other?"

"Oh yes. We met in Washington many times back before…well before. I bought a few little things from Lorraine. Oh, and here is Louis. You're here too. How nice."

"It's a long story, Paula. Sorry, Eden. Some other time. I think we should do as these men tell us. The people who were in that house are dangerous. This is beyond exciting."

The three moved back behind the larger of the SUVs. Ike was aware of the steady buzz of conversation between them but kept his eyes on the front door.

"Running out of time out here. You have no hostages, no back door, no chance to escape. Come on out and let's get this over with. Your colleagues are here ready to take you back where you belong."

The front door banged open and a lone figure wearing a stereotypical black suit, white shirt, and red tie, stepped out onto the porch.

"Hands up. Please."

"Don't be ridiculous," the man said and slouched down the steps toward the group. "I am a federal agent and these are my people. They work for me. You are within an ace of having a whole lot of bad shit handed to you."

Ike cocked his revolver and leveled it. "I'd hate to put down one of Uncle Sam's brightest and best, well, not so bright and certainly not best, but I will if I must. If I'm in a heap of trouble, as you say, dropping you can't make it any worse. But my friend here who has taken your people into custody would not be happy, I think."

"I'd do as he says." Charlie added. "I have no control over this man. He has a reputation for shooting first, asking questions after. He's a sheriff, after all."

"Who are you?" The man asked.

"Don't you recognize me, Tony? Tsk, tsk, and all this time I thought you were a professional."

"Garland?"

"Bingo. On the ground, or I will shoot you myself if the sheriff doesn't, you son of a bitch."

Chapter Forty-seven

"Who *is* that, Charlie?"

"You remember Tony Fugarelli?"

"Ah, the absent Fugarelli. The agent with a head cold who couldn't make your party on the Eastern Shore last fall, that Tony Fugarelli?"

"It was your party more than it was mine. But yes, that Fugarelli."

"You're too modest."

"A necessary character trait in my line of business, you could say. You do know what I do?"

Ike did not reply, but he knew.

"Well, we had one of those situations that required my attention, and then you had this robbery/murder thing and the job of finding out the who, you could say, seemed a little clearer. There, for a moment, I thought you were going to blow it for me, by the way."

"How clearer?"

"The icon was the clue, of course. Someone

was after it, and the likelihood was it would be the Arabs, but we had a man on it, so that meant the Mossad as well. Zaki was supposed to get the icon, turn it over to his contact and disappear into the woodwork. But he was intercepted by the Israelis, and things got complicated, but it did narrow the scope a bit."

"Okay, but why is Fugarelli here? I expected you, and frankly, I thought they, that is, he *was* with you. Then when you showed up with the troops, I wasn't so sure."

"Yes, well, let me put these three on an express bus to Langley, and then we'll talk. I won't bother with the two Bozos on the ground, I guess. I may want to interrogate them later; that is if Fugarelli doesn't fold his cards and fess up. They belong to you. You may hear from an embassy about them, however."

"Not likely. I told you, Shmuel Gold said they were contract players. Volunteers almost, fanatics for the cause and all that. I promise you the embassy will not know their names, although they may supply an expensive lawyer to spring them. Now, I need to have a heart-to-heart with the Dakises about following instructions. They could have been killed."

"I'd let that bit slide, if I were you. They certainly should not have been there, but they saved your bad guys and your bust, Ike."

"How's that?"

"Fugarelli had too much on his plate, I guess. I am almost positive he intended to stage a fire-fight to take out your two, and he would have, except the couple popped up. Desperate as he was, four killings, maybe five, must have seemed over the top, even for him. So, he hesitated, and because he hesitated, the door closed. So you might want to thank them."

"You will sort all this out for me later, I hope."

"Are you sure you want me to?"

"No."

"Of course you don't. Where shall we have our coffee and debriefing? Your place or mine?"

The Crossroads Diner stayed open all night. Whether this was a good thing or not was debated by the townsfolk. The plusses of having a place to eat twenty-four seven meant that insomniacs, students on their way back to Charlottesville, Lexington, or Blacksburg, swing shift workers, and those with inverted circadian rhythms had a place to grab a cup of coffee and something to eat late at night on their way in, out, or wherever. The downside was that the morning regulars were convinced they were served the old burnt coffee that had been sitting in the urn since midnight.

Charlie and Ike shared a booth in the back and avoided the coffee in front of them.

"Okay, I need a fill-in, Charlie. Fugarelli was one of yours. Who…who what? Stepped off the reservation? How?"

"You were in the business long enough to know how it works. Some days the bad guys are there, some days they're somewhere else. Today's ally can be tomorrow's enemy. Iran was our friend, and then the Shah went away. Now they are our enemies. Venezuela? Who knows? We spy on them; they spy on us. Some of them are good at it; some are bad."

"Fugarelli was a double?"

"Not exactly. Here's a hypothetical. You are in the business, let's say, and a friendly nation approaches you. 'Agent Schwartz,' they say, 'would you do us a favor and tell us thus-and-so about what you're up to in our country?' They go on to remind you that they can probably get the information by simply going through diplomatic channels but… You see?"

"A friendly nation asks that of me?"

"Friendly, yes. And probably offers you a small recompense for your trouble. "

"Fugarelli was selling intel to a friendly nation, and your boss didn't like it."

"A fine line, you know. They are referred to as

'white moles.' Don't ask me why *white*. Something to do with stereotypical hats, I guess. Okay, so, again hypothetically, if I tell the Brits some things, have I done any real harm? Probably not. But, if I sell to China or, God forbid, North Korea…well you see how it works. Where do you draw the line?"

"You draw it right up tight. Double agents are double agents no matter whose pocket they've crawled into."

"My thoughts exactly. The problem with that is so many people, when they hear that one of ours is going away for a long time in a federal penitentiary for helping their favorite favored nation, so to speak, get all mushy about that. This is particularly true with the people who sell to Israel. Somehow, the behavior seems less treasonous when they're involved."

"Ah, that's the connection. Fugarelli was feeding the Israelis with intel, and these two guys who bumped off Zaki/Sacci were his, in a way."

"Only in a way, but yes. Using the Agency's resources, he helped them locate Zaki and the probable location of the microchip. I can place him in the Dakis' store before all this went down."

"Then the idiots, who now know the location, do their patriotic duty and shoot Zaki, and Fugarelli now has a murder on his hands that can be traced back to him if I catch them."

"We don't think the shooting was intended, but yes. And he knows enough about you to assume you may very well succeed."

"You could say so. But that's not all, I don't think, Charlie. There has to be more."

"What has to be more?"

"Tommy Wainwright is more. Did Fugarelli out Wainwright to somebody? Is that why Wainwright, as Avi Kolb, disappeared so suddenly, and then he ends up with a bullet in his head in Rock Creek Park? Fugarelli set him up?"

"Maybe, or he was afraid Wainwright was too close. And you know this how? Oh, yes, Samantha Ryder and her magic computer. You know that will end forthwith. You must steel yourself to returning to a small-town sheriff's office after today."

"How come?"

"This afternoon my people ferreted out Ms. Ryder at her boyfriend's apartment. Ike, did you think we couldn't find her? She has a cell phone. You called her. We had her on the map shortly after. Anyway, our friends from the attorney general's office gave her a choice, one she couldn't refuse."

"Do I want to hear this? If you guys mess with Sam, you will have me on you like white on rice."

"Tut. You needn't get excited. I know what you could do if you put your mind to it. It would go hard on you and yours in the end, but I have no doubt you'd do it. You are wonderfully loyal, Ike. I wish I could persuade you to come back in."

"Ask me again in November. No, forget I said that. It will never happen. So, what have you done with Sam?"

"As I said, we made her an offer. She can fight us and be prosecuted for hacking into not only the CIA, but the FBI as well, and if her logger is correct, numerous other governmental and foreign concerns, all of which are federal offenses...or she can accept our offer to become staff at the NSA where her talents will be both legal and appreciated by a grateful nation. I had a similar situation once, and..."

Ike waited for the end of the sentence. It did not come. "You want to tell me about it?"

"No, I'd rather not, someday maybe. So moving on to your deputy, it will put her into closer proximity to Karl Hedrick, who, I might add, thought the deal a very good one. I take it he was concerned with the path of corruption down which you were leading the poor girl."

Ike sipped his coffee and made a face. "It had to happen sooner or later, I guess. I once hoped to recruit Karl here, but rural sheriffs' departments do not have the cachet of the Federal Bureau of Investigation."

"Not if you are bootstrapping your way into a profession."

"No, I suppose not. Sooner or later, she was going to bolt. So, at least this way she moves upward and onward. Thank you for that, Charlie. I will want some notice from Sam. We need to have a party for her, at least. You say Karl is happy with this?"

"Ecstatic, if I hear aright."

"So, back to Fugarelli. I know what I know, as you surmised, because of Sam and her poking into your dirty laundry. She found out that Wainwright was assigned to Mossad. She didn't know what that meant, but I did. You guys sent him in to unearth the double. He got close to this bizarre icon caper, because that's where the trail led him. Then, Fugarelli feels the heat and outs him to whom?… the Israelis or the Arabs—which, I wondered—but instead of coming in, Wainwright takes a stab at closing the business out and is shot. I'm guessing your boy Fugarelli realized that the two guys must have let it out that Kolb—that is, Wainwright— killed Zaki in the hopes the forces on the other side of this idiotic equation would kill him. Very Mideastern, desert justice and all that. Shmuel disagreed with that, by the way."

"How? He thinks what? Surely he's not willing to admit his people did it."

"No, his exact words were 'The word is that it was done by Jihadists, but I am not so sure. What would be the point? They are in your country. They do not need anyone looking for them, at least not for killing one person, CIA man or not. A thousand, maybe, but not one. I don't think.' So, as much as I hate to contemplate it, I think Fugarelli must have panicked as did Tommy Wainwright, figuring everyone would blame the boys in the burnooses."

Charlie sat grim-faced, staring at his coffee. "It's possible, you know, probable, in fact. We'll find out when we get him back on the farm. I hate to think so, but he must have done it."

"Who else could it have been? The only others with a motive, a weak one at that, would be our friends in the Mossad. But they knew that we knew that they knew, etcetera. There was no real need. But Fugarelli had the only compelling motive I'm thinking. For anyone else in the field, Tommy was small potatoes. But, as you told me, he was ready to retire. If he's caught passing secrets, no matter how benign, he swaps his pension for a prison jump suit. He's on his way to the slammer for forever and a day."

"It isn't something we like to contemplate. It happens, as you know from back when…back then."

"I do. They were not heady days for me, looking back. So, you have a double who may be, and in my view is, directly responsible for having one of yours killed. You will concede indirectly, certainly. You can't have that. You have to haul him in and given the choices on the table, you're right, it would have been better if he'd blown out his brains right then and there."

"It would have, indeed. Is that it? Are you done with me?"

"Not quite. I owe you an apology for messing up your plans to get the fake information out. Any idea where it was headed?"

"No apology necessary. As soon as we confirmed what you were up to, we moved to Plan B. We will have our own messenger deliver the chip in its revised form, of course, to the parties Zaki was engaged with. I will want that icon of yours, by the way, so we have something to deliver."

"It's yours with my blessing. To whom or what will it be delivered, an embedded terrorist cell?"

"Yes and no. Politics, as we all know, makes for strange bedfellows. These guys were working with some folks from one of those the Liberty Tree groups, maybe even a little right of them; we're not sure. The latter are ignorant of who the former might be and think they will have documents that will increase the current level of societal distrust and eventually lead to what they have been calling the final chapter of the American Revolution, wherein the righteous

'Right' will reestablish a country and a code that never existed in the first place. Thus, they both have the same thing in common, but with radically different ideas of what constitutes righteousness."

"This is all very baroque, Charlie. If it weren't so dangerous, it would make a very funny operetta. Rudolph Friml could have a field day with this."

"Franz Lehar would be your man, I think."

"Or Peter Ustinov. A darker version of *Romanoff and Juliet*."

"Possibly, but I don't think so. Anyway, it is the great irony of our times that groups or individuals who hate or fear each other passionately will frequently espouse identical goals, in this case, violence in order to take down the government of the United States. Domestic terrorists and the imported variety are sisters under the skin. The whole business is peculiarly paradoxical."

"I would say it's more along the lines of oxymoronic."

"I'm not sure of the oxy part, but it is certainly moronic. Timothy McVeigh, it would seem, lives on wearing a keffiyeh."

"Right. One last question, Charlie, and then I'm off. How did you manage to keep the FBI away? This is their turf. I can't believe they rolled over for you."

"A trade-off, Ike. We explained to them our

need to haul in our double, and they agreed to let us have the day if we gave them Plan B. So, at long last the era of interagency cooperation has arrived. They will take it from here. It's just as well. They have better contacts in that murky area of Americana than we do. They will deliver the phony icon and its bogus documents to the local terrorist cell who, in turn, will slip it to a group composed of our homegrown variety. You can imagine what they will do with it. I expect you will see the documents reported in hysterical detail on cable news in a day or two. And then, of course, the forgeries will be exposed, and all hell will break loose in what we laughingly refer to as the responsible media."

Ike snorted. His coffee was cold, and he was tired. He stood and slipped on his jacket. "We live in interesting times, as the Chinese might say. Time to say goodnight, Charlie. I am tired. Ruth waits with a candle burning in the window, I hope, and on the morrow there is her mother to contend with, extended family to sort out, bad guys to put away, and Essie Sutherlin's impending calving. I need peace and quiet and sleep."

Ike gave Charlie a desultory wave and walked out into the night, fatigued but alert and entertaining quirky and, some might add unworthy, thoughts of plum sauce, sheriff's badges, and Smoky the Bear hats.

To receive a free catalog of Poisoned Pen Press titles, please contact us in one of the following ways:

Phone: 1-800-421-3976
Facsimile: 1-480-949-1707
Email: info@poisonedpenpress.com
Website: www.poisonedpenpress.com

Poisoned Pen Press
6962 E. First Ave. Ste. 103
Scottsdale, AZ 85251

LaVergne, TN USA
11 June 2010
185796LV00001B/39/P